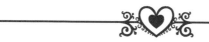

Billionaire Unclaimed

THE BILLIONAIRE'S OBSESSION
Chase

J. S. SCOTT

Billionaire Unclaimed

Copyright © 2022 by J. S. Scott

Cover Photo by Wander Aguiar Photography
Proof Editing by Virginia Tesi Carey

ISBN: 9798364824028 (Print)
ISBN: 9781951102746 (E-Book)

Contents

Prologue

Savannah

Several Months Earlier...

"I don't think I ever really thanked you for everything you did for Torie after she was kidnapped," Chase Durand said to me as we sat in the kitchen of a very extravagant Las Vegas suite.

It was the venue where his sister Torie's wedding reception had been held earlier.

I wasn't sure exactly how Chase and I had ended up alone, sharing a much-too- cozy espresso moment at the kitchen table after all of the other wedding guests were gone.

Maybe...it was because I loved a really good latte, and Chase was fond of espresso?

Okay...maybe not.

Yeah, that explanation would work for why *Chase* was still here after every single guest had left.

Me?

If I was being completely honest, I knew I'd finally been unable to resist spending a little more time with Chase Durand, even though I absolutely knew that giving in to that impulse was dangerous.

And incredibly stupid.

Chase had always treated me like a second little sister, no different than he treated my best friend, Torie.

Unfortunately, I couldn't quite look at him as an honorary big brother anymore, and that scared the shit out of me.

This encounter was a little too intimate now that we were adults.

I knew I should be leaving this place like I was evacuating for some sort of dire emergency. I'd avoided spending time alone in Chase's company for the last decade because I was attracted to him. I was always afraid someone would notice that my thoughts about him were far from brotherly.

I'd be totally mortified if Torie found out that I secretly drooled over her older brother. I'd be even more horrified if Chase discovered how I really felt about him.

Of course, he'd never know. It's not like I wore my heart on my sleeve. I hid that information like it was a matter of national security.

I was an investigative journalist. I knew exactly how to bury my emotions so deeply that no one could ever see them. If I didn't, I'd completely lose my mind in my line of work.

I have to compartmentalize and just pretend that this is no more than a conversation between old family friends.

Which was exactly what was happening. Well, for Chase, anyway.

Irritated with myself for being so flustered over being alone with him, I answered, "Torie is my best friend. I'd do anything for her. I always wished I could have done more. I think Cooper Montgomery is the best thing that ever happened to her. They seemed so happy to be getting married today. He's helped her through a few of her lingering issues from her kidnapping that I never even knew about."

I chose my words carefully. There were things that Chase didn't know, and possibly never would, about Torie's kidnapping. There were incidents that Torie hadn't wanted to reveal to her two older brothers because they already foolishly blamed themselves for what had happened to her.

Chase shot me a doubtful expression as he replied, "Don't belittle the importance of you being there for her when she really needed you, Vanna," he insisted. "You put your own career on hold to help her through her recovery."

"Maybe I needed some time off, too," I suggested, uncomfortable with being thanked for something that had been necessary and not at all an inconvenience at the time.

I loved Torie like a sister. There was nowhere else I'd wanted to be when she was hurting that badly.

Frankly, that time off I'd spent with Torie *had* benefited me as well. I'd never realized how emotionally exhausted I was from chasing story after story for so many years. Every one of those assignments had been soul sucking because I didn't exactly report on uplifting international events.

He lifted an eyebrow as he asked gruffly, "Did you need time off?"

I squirmed in my seat as he waited patiently for my answer.

His beautiful gray eyes studied me like he was interested in nothing else *except* my answer.

Shit! I'd always felt like Chase could see right through me and into the dark pit of emotions I didn't want to acknowledge. That was one of the things that made him so dangerous, yet so damn alluring. He had the ability to make a person feel like they were the most important person in the world to him simply because he really…listened.

Most likely, it was a trait that he'd learned to use to his advantage as a billionaire business mogul, but for me, it was incredibly unnerving and captivating at the same time.

He made me want to spill my guts to him, but I knew I wouldn't.

Being vulnerable to anyone was a lot more scary than my need to discuss my feelings.

Besides, once I opened that floodgate, it would probably never close again. I hadn't worked this hard for over a decade to stifle those emotions only to lose control of them now.

Especially not with…*him.*

Because he thought of himself as my honorary big brother, he'd probably wring me dry until I told him *everything.* Chase would try to "fix" anything that was wrong in my life, just like he'd done when Torie and I were kids. Unfortunately, I was all grown up and so was Chase. A Band-Aid or a piece of my favorite candy wasn't going to fix what was wrong with me anymore.

I nodded slowly, knowing I had to be intentionally vague. "I was tired. It was good for both of us to spend time together."

He sat back in his chair and continued to study me as he answered, "I very much doubt you mean that since you spent a hell of a lot of that time in the hospital with her. That's not exactly some kind of relaxing vacay, Vanna."

I nearly sighed as I ogled the gorgeous man across from me, convinced no man could make a tuxedo look as good as Chase Durand could.

He was gorgeous, from his mesmerizing gray eyes to the attractive mixed shades of brown hair on his head.

This man was familiar, but also an enigma to me. How he managed to be both down-to-earth *and* incredibly sophisticated had never quite jived in my mind.

It was probably much better if I *didn't* think about how damn fit and muscular his body was, or how far he towered over me with his almost intimidating height. I was a little taller than average for a female, but Chase actually made me feel diminutive when we were standing side by side.

I couldn't say that he hadn't become harder and slightly more cynical from his years spent in special forces, but strangely, it made him all the more fascinating. How many guys who were born wealthy like Chase ended up in special forces?

He and his older brother, Wyatt, never talked much about their years in the military, nor did either of them brag like some guys would about being special forces. According to Torie, they were pretty close-lipped and blew off most of the questions she'd asked about those years.

The way they avoided that subject always made me wonder if they kept quiet because of the secrecy of their missions, or because they were so traumatic they didn't want to think about them anymore.

❧ ❦ ❧

"I didn't mind," I said softly, really meaning those words.

My best friend had been shattered physically and emotionally after she'd been kidnapped and left for dead in the Amazon. All I'd really wanted was to be there for her. Truthfully, I'd been pretty damn grateful she hadn't died. I'd been thankful that it was still possible to spend time with her, wherever that might be.

"Now *that* I definitely believe since you and Torie have always been so close," Chase replied. "And you're right about Cooper. He is good for her, and vice versa. The two of them are almost ridiculously...in love."

I smiled at him, amused by the way he'd spat out those last two words. It seemed almost normal for the two of us to have this kind of conversation, even though we never did.

During our infrequent meetings after we'd become adults, we usually antagonized the crap out of each other and debated just about everything.

For me, it had always been safer to stay friendly adversaries.

"You don't believe in love?" I asked, the words slipping out of my mouth before I could check them.

I'd always dreaded the day when I'd discover that Chase was seriously involved with someone, even though I knew I *shouldn't* feel that way.

He'd had girlfriends, probably more than I could count, especially during his high school and college years.

I knew from Torie that he'd had a few fleeting relationships while he was in the military as well.

Chase had his dad's natural ability to be completely charming when he wanted to be. Torie's father had been a charismatic, extremely lovable Frenchman. It was easy to see that his youngest son had some of the same characteristics.

Strangely, I didn't think there had been anyone special since Chase had gotten out of the military to join his older brother, Wyatt, as a co-CEO of Durand Industries.

If there was, Torie had never told me about the woman in Chase's life, which was entirely possible since I definitely didn't ask. The only thing my best friend had made very clear was her displeasure about not having any nieces and nephews to adore. Well, and her two brothers' lack of interest in getting married someday.

But that didn't mean that there *wasn't* a female in Chase's life. How could there not be? I'd actually been surprised when he'd shown up solo for his sister's wedding.

Come to think of it, there hadn't been a woman beside him throughout the period when Torie was recovering, either, which was...odd.

For a bachelor as eligible as Chase, it did seem bizarre that I'd never seen him with a woman since the end of his military career.

Then again, we could go a year or more without running into each other sometimes.

It had been well over a year since I'd seen him prior to today.

It wasn't like I didn't *want* Chase to be happy. I just hadn't wanted to *watch* that happen...up close and personal.

Dammit! Why couldn't I just get over this ridiculous infatuation with my best friend's brother? It's not like it would *ever* go anywhere. It hadn't in the last decade, and I was quickly approaching my mid-thirties. Having a mad, decade-long crush on a guy that was completely unrequited at my age was nonsensical.

And I was a realist, through and through. An investigative journalist who saw raw truth and the worst of humanitarian crises around the world on a regular basis.

There was no such thing as fairy tales for me.

Yes, I'd had relationships over the last decade. Several of them. I'd even managed to forget about how ridiculously attracted I was to Chase while I was involved with someone else.

Then, I'd run into him again, and those silly emotions would rush back like they'd never left.

I couldn't even say precisely why I felt this way.

It wasn't just the fact that Chase was attractive. I worked in the entertainment and news field. I saw drop-dead gorgeous men every single day, but none of them made me feel like I was a moony teenager experiencing my first major crush.

There was so much more than just his gorgeous face and body that drew me to Chase Durand. Maybe that's why I'd never quite figured out exactly how to shake those feelings off.

He grinned at me, and my damn heart actually skittered in reaction. I had to remind myself once again that Chase and I would never have anything other than a sibling like relationship.

"I definitely believe in love for Torie," he explained. "No one deserves a happily ever after more than she does. What about you? I heard you were dating some A- list celebrity a while ago. Why isn't he here today?"

I swallowed hard, trying not to remember how hurt and humiliated I'd been after that particular relationship had ended so publicly. Obviously, Chase paid no attention to the gossip rags or he would know exactly why Bradley wasn't here.

"We broke up a while ago," I said hastily, not really wanting to discuss my short-lived love affair with the famous actor. "We both had to travel a lot. It didn't work out."

He frowned. "I have a hard time believing that you gave up that easily if you really cared about him, Vanna."

Damn! Chase obviously wasn't going to let things drop until he got some kind of explanation. "He had no idea how to have a monogamous relationship, especially when I was away so much," I confessed. "He couldn't keep his dick in his pants when I wasn't around."

"That's too bad," Chase said empathetically. "Although I have no idea why he'd want anyone else when he had you."

I assessed his sympathetic gaze as I answered drily, "Apparently, women were interchangeable for him. I guess he didn't mind when I was out of the country because there was always another woman nearby. Lots of them actually."

Honestly, I'd probably never been Bradley Warner's type. But I'd thought that I'd finally found a guy who didn't mind if I preferred spending more time traipsing around the world in mud boots and dirty jeans than attending swanky parties.

Obviously, I'd been completely wrong.

Whatever brief interest he'd had in a woman like me had faded just as quickly as it had manifested.

"Then he definitely didn't deserve you," Chase grumbled.

I tried to keep my tone light as I replied, "No worries. I don't think my career is really conducive to a serious relationship anyway. My job takes over my life most of the time."

"You need somebody who treats you a hell of a lot better," Chase replied. "Don't settle for anything less, Savannah."

Disconcerted that I was actually discussing my love life with Chase Durand, I stood and took my mug to the sink. "I suppose I should get going back to my own room," I said uncomfortably.

"Hey," Chase said as he stood and moved toward me. "I didn't mean to make you run off. Did that bastard really hurt you, Vanna?"

He stopped much too close to me as I answered, "Not really. We were only exclusive for less than a year. He was a big movie star. I do special reports on a small cable news channel."

"Bullshit!" Chase said in a graveled voice. "*Deadline America* isn't some small, insignificant television program. You're famous because your work is incredible."

I was surprised as I turned to him and saw the genuine expression on his face. "You've actually seen my specials?" I asked.

I was far from famous. I was simply a recognizable face for people who were into global current events and watched cable news. My show had amassed a decent following over the years, but I wasn't *that* familiar to the general population. Being the dumped girl-friend of Bradley Warner had probably given me more notoriety than *Deadline America*.

He let out an exasperated breath as he pierced me with those beautiful gray eyes. "Of course I've seen them. What you do is riveting, even though it's a little unnerving to see you in some of those locations. If that bastard didn't love you for the intelligent, compassionate woman you are, he didn't fucking deserve you."

"He wasn't the right guy," I confessed softly. "I doubt any man will ever adore me the way Cooper loves Torie. Or the way any of the Montgomery brothers worship the women they love."

I'd met Cooper Montgomery's two older brothers, Hudson and Jax, at the reception. Maybe I didn't know them well, but it was obvious that they were both wholeheartedly committed to the women in their lives.

Chase grinned. "The Montgomerys are definitely intense, but I can't say that I'm *not* happy that Cooper Montgomery ended up falling in love with my little sister. He'd die before he'd let anything or anyone hurt her."

I smiled back at him. "I doubt he'll ever be a cheater. I don't think he sees any other woman but Torie."

Maybe I *should* be cynical after my own experience with a cheater, but I wasn't. Not when I looked at Torie and Cooper together. It was obvious they had something special that I'd certainly never experienced in my own love life. But just because I'd never encountered it, that didn't mean a love like that didn't exist.

"Good thing for him that he doesn't see any woman but my little sister," Chase answered gruffly. "I doubt Wyatt and I could have stomached giving her away to a guy who wasn't completely devoted to her. Torie has suffered enough."

I immediately wanted to remind him that it was Torie's choice who she married. I also wanted to point out the fact that he and Wyatt hadn't *literally* given her away. However, for once in my life, I didn't want to argue with Chase.

I knew what he meant when he said that Torie had suffered enough. I'd personally watched what she'd gone through, and seeing her with Cooper now made me want to weep with happiness.

And I very rarely cried over anything, especially not over something that made me...happy.

I'd seen the agonized looks on both of the Durand brothers' faces when Torie was critically injured and fighting for her life after her kidnapping. I couldn't blame them for feeling somewhat protective, really. I felt that way myself sometimes.

There had always been so much love between the Durand siblings that it was almost palpable.

Sure, the three of them razzed each other constantly, but what close siblings didn't tease each other?

Wyatt and Chase had always been Torie's protectors for as long as I could remember. If they felt even more protective after what had happened to her, who was I to criticize?

My guess was that Chase *had* become even more protective of his sister after her near-death experience in the Amazon.

While I had no blood siblings myself, I completely understood Wyatt and Chase's fear right after and beyond Torie's kidnapping. I'd been completely out of my mind with worry about her, too. She was more like a sister to me than a best friend.

"She's happy now," I reminded him softly as I viewed the concerned look on his face.

Chase released a long breath and ran a hand over his face like he was trying to make those horrific memories disappear. "She is," he agreed. "I think I was so damn upset by what those bastards had done to her that it's hard to remember it's over sometimes and that she is a grown woman who is perfectly capable of running her own life."

I knew that. I also knew he and Wyatt blamed themselves for not watching out for their younger sister now that both of their parents were gone, which was completely absurd. Torie was my age and a thoroughly independent female. There was no possible way Chase and Wyatt could have predicted what had happened to Torie in the Amazon. She was supposed to be on a vacation, and unless Chase and Wyatt were psychics, there had been absolutely no reason for concern.

"She looked so beautiful and so incredibly happy today, Chase. It's over," I said firmly, hating the way he still seemed to blame himself for the freak incident. "Let the past be the past. Torie's definitely not wallowing in anything except her present bliss."

It was past time for the Durand brothers to stop blaming themselves for Torie's nightmare experience.

She was well, healthy, and ecstatic with her new husband.

The tension slowly faded from his expression as he answered, "You're right. It is over. It's just not so easy to forget, I guess."

I nodded. "I know. But she's fine and starting a whole new exciting chapter of her life, Chase."

A shiver ran down my spine as he eyed me from head to toe. "What about you, Vanna?" he asked. "Where are you headed next? Are you coming home for a while?"

I laughed, hoping to lighten the mood. "Since I'm currently homeless after selling my mom's house, I'm going to spend a few days here in Vegas before I move on to my next assignment. I'll buy myself a condo or rent something in San Diego, eventually. I haven't had enough time there yet to seriously look."

It had been ten years since my mother had died in a bush plane accident while collecting samples for scientific research in Alaska. It had always been just the two of us, and I'd been devastated when I'd lost her so unexpectedly. We'd been really close, so it had taken me an entire decade to let go of the home I'd grown up in after Mom had died. Even though the place had never really worked for my globetrotting lifestyle.

"It's not like you have a lack of places to stay in San Diego," Chase answered. "Cooper has a ridiculously huge place on the water in La Jolla."

I snorted. "Do you really think I'd play the third wheel with my best friend when she just got married?"

His expression was earnest as he told me, "I have a pretty large place myself, not far from Cooper and Torie. Certainly you know you're always welcome there, Vanna."

I licked my lips and swallowed hard, trying not to release the nervous cough that was caught in my throat.

Seriously? Does he honestly think I'd stay with...him?

As I thought about his offer, I realized he probably *did* think the suggestion was no big deal because he was supposed to be like a brother to me, right?

Oh, God, that is never going to happen.

If I accidentally saw this man naked, I'd never be able to walk away like an embarrassed houseguest and promptly forget it had ever happened.

Just being alone with him and within touching distance was way too much of a temptation right now.

"What are you doing tomorrow?" he asked casually. "I could easily extend my stay for a day or two. Maybe we could spend the day together. We could do a show or dinner tomorrow night, too."

I shook my head reflexively. I probably couldn't spend more time in Chase's company without revealing the way my feelings had changed over the years. "Can't," I said nervously. "I have a spa appointment and a spot with my name on it at the pool."

I didn't. I was totally lying. But spending a day and an evening with a man I was attracted to who saw me as a second little sister would be absolutely tortuous.

Chase shrugged as he studied me carefully. "Dinner after that?" he insisted.

I shook my head harder. "I have other plans. I'm sorry."

The room was completely silent as he looked at me like he was trying to figure out if I was telling him the truth.

And truly, I really felt guilty because I wasn't being honest with him.

Chase and I had known each other since I was a kid. Long before I'd developed this stupid infatuation with him, he *had* been like the big brother I'd never had.

My heart skipped several beats and I took a deep, anxious breath before I said, "I better get going, Chase. It was nice seeing you again, but I've taken up enough of your time. You're a busy billionaire CEO. I'm sure you have better things to do than sitting here talking to your sister's best friend."

I sounded nervous and I knew it, but there was nothing I could do about the stupid attraction I had to Chase Durand every time I saw him again. It just got worse every single year.

I could have sat here all evening shooting the breeze with *Wyatt*. He still felt like an honorary brother to me.

Just the thought of doing the same with Chase made me...panicky.

I walked to the table to get my purse, feeling Chase's stare drilling into me as he said in a low, mesmerizing tone, "I'm not so sure there *is* anything else I'd rather be doing than spending some time with you, Savannah. It's been way too long since we've had a chance to catch up."

Holy shit!

I knew he didn't mean for that smooth baritone of his to be seductive, but it tempted me in a way nothing else possibly could.

Get it together, Savannah! He's not into you that way!

I let out an agitated breath and turned to face him with my purse in hand.

Forcing myself not to flee like an idiot, I smiled at him. "You say that in such a charming way that I almost believe you," I teased as I moved forward and forced myself to give him a sisterly hug.

I tried not to breathe in his unique, enticingly masculine scent, but failed miserably.

I closed my eyes, fighting the instinct to bury my entire face into his neck.

Crap! He felt so damn good, smelled so incredibly amazing that I could barely keep myself from moaning with pleasure.

I sunk my teeth into my lower lip as he wrapped a strong arm around my waist to return the embrace.

When I finally realized I was lingering just a little bit too long, my eyes popped open again, and I hastily ripped myself away from his gloriously muscular body.

The action was almost painful, but I either had to separate myself from Chase or embarrass myself with my best friend's older brother.

"Take care, Chase," I said, forcing my voice to be casual as I headed toward the exit to the suite.

"Savannah?" he questioned hoarsely as I started to leave the kitchen.

I turned because I couldn't stop myself from getting one more look at the one man I wanted but could never have. "Yes?"

I held my breath as I saw the intensity and conflict in his eyes.

Chase looked like he wanted to say something, but wasn't quite sure what he wanted to express.

Our eyes locked and my heart leapt as his irises shifted to a dark gray, almost like he might be...attracted to me.

He wasn't. I knew that. It was simply a trick of the light in the room, but a woman could have a few seconds of fantasy, right?

In that moment, I wanted to tell him how I really felt.

I wanted to tell him that I'd love to spend the day with him tomorrow—and all night, too, if that's what he wanted.

Anything to assuage the nagging ache this man left inside me.

He took a deep breath, and my brief period of insanity left me as he finally said in a husky voice, "Be careful out there, Vanna."

Disappointment flooded my being.

But really, what had I expected him to say? While I considered myself attractive enough, I wasn't exactly the gorgeous supermodel type Chase usually dated when he was younger.

I had curves, dirty blonde hair rather than platinum, and my eyes were a nondescript hazel. There was nothing about my appearance that would inspire lust or even mild interest from a guy like Chase Durand.

I spent most of my time trudging around the planet in some wildly undesirable places, which was far from glamorous.

He's not attracted to you, Savannah. Get real.

"I will," I muttered as I turned my back and fled toward the door as fast as I could go without looking entirely eager to escape.

As I left the beautiful hotel suite, I vowed to myself I'd never come that mortifyingly close to revealing how I felt about Chase Durand ever again.

My friendship with Torie meant everything to me, and I wasn't about to let some ridiculous leftover crush come between me and my best friend.

I'd avoided being alone with Chase for years.

I could easily do it for as long as necessary in the future.

Chapter 1

Chase

The Present...

"What in the fuck do you mean?" I asked Marshall as he briefed us on a possible rescue situation in the large mission room at Last Hope headquarters. "How in the hell can Savannah Anderson be missing?"

Seven sets of eyes were trained on the leader of Last Hope as we waited for Marshall to explain.

It nearly killed me to see the anguish on my little sister Torie's face. Savannah had been Torie's best friend since childhood, and the two of them were still incredibly close.

I looked at my older brother, Wyatt, who was sitting next to me, and I recognized his troubled expression, which probably mirrored my own.

Hudson Montgomery was also present, along with his brothers, Jax and Cooper.

Jax's wife, Harlow, who was a volunteer weather specialist at Last Hope, was looking at Marshall expectantly as well.

Marshall had sent out an emergency rescue code to get our asses gathered here at Last Hope headquarters as soon as possible, so I knew whatever he had to say *couldn't* be good.

"I meant exactly what I just said," Marshall said irritably from his position at the head of the large meeting table. "She went missing a week ago while she was on an assignment in Bajo Chiquito. No one is calling it a kidnapping. The authorities in Panama say it's likely she wandered away and got lost. The village is surrounded by jungle. However, all attempts to search for her have come up empty."

I watched as Marshall slid a large envelope to each one of us. I grabbed mine with very little interest, already knowing what was inside. It would contain a detailed background check on Savannah and any intel Marshall had on the case. It was normal procedure when our volunteer rescue operation was considering some kind of rescue.

At the moment, I had more pressing things to consider than information on paper, especially since I'd known Savannah since she was a child. I didn't need her fucking bio. I had to know what was really going on.

Christ! I knew by the way Marshall had carefully chosen his words that there was still a lot that he *hadn't* told us.

"That area is pretty remote," Hudson said in a thoughtful voice. "What was she doing there in that area of Panama?"

The Darien Gap was a treacherous and highly dangerous route that connected North and South America. It was used mainly by migrants to escape intolerable circumstances in other countries. Not only did that area present extreme physical challenges when crossing, but the very real possibility of kidnappings and attacks from criminal gangs who made their home in the Darien jungle as well.

"She was doing a special report for *Deadline America* on the humanitarian crisis there from the elevated number of people crossing through the Darien Gap right now. The amount of children coming through that hellish sixty mile stretch of the jungle is particularly alarming," Marshall explained.

"She was supposed to return to San Diego almost a week ago to look for a new place," Torie said in a nervous tone. "After trying to reach her for days after she didn't show, I finally asked Marshall to help me. It's not like Vanna to just change her plans and not let me know. I knew something was wrong."

"I found it hard to believe that an experienced journalist like Savannah had just wandered into the jungle," Marshall commented thoughtfully. "After checking with some of my sources and talking to her frantic producer, I know she didn't."

Marshall's *sources* were legendary. He had people who could provide some intel and resources in almost every nook and cranny on the planet—probably on both sides of the law. But none of us had ever doubted the accuracy of his information. The guy had a perfect track record.

Hudson Montgomery folded his arms across his chest as he said, "Just tell us what happened, Marshall. It's pretty clear that you know where she is. If she was kidnapped, where in the hell are the ransom demands?"

"That's the problem," Marshall answered. "There haven't been any. The government, both in Panama and the United States, is still treating this as a missing persons case."

"But *you* apparently have the truth," Jax said wryly.

"As close as I can get to it, anyway," Marshall replied stoically. "My sources say that she was kidnapped by a rebel Colombian criminal gang. They initially thought she'd bring a good price in the human trafficking market because she's an American television personality. The idiots didn't realize they'd have a hard time trafficking her because her face *is* recognizable. Nobody wants to be caught with an American woman, much less one who has a higher profile."

Fuck! It wasn't like I didn't understand just how much drug and human trafficking went on in the remote Darien jungle, but... "I thought the Colombian gangs avoided crossing into Panama because they didn't want to risk capture by the Senafront," I said aloud, wondering why the criminals hadn't been concerned about Panama's border patrol police.

Marshall nodded. "Normally, they don't come very far into Panama for just that reason. Migrants going through the Darien

Gap are generally safe once they get into Panama and reach Bajo Chiquito. This apparently isn't a very organized crime ring. Just a few rogues who broke away from a larger group. They don't really control any territory in Colombia, so they had to get a lot bolder and make a move in Panama to make money."

"It's insane for them to move that far into Panama to kidnap someone. This shit usually only happens while immigrants are passing through the Darien Gap," Jax pointed out.

Marshall lifted a brow. "Exactly. I'm sure the crew of *Deadline America* rightly thought they were relatively safe filming from that area," he agreed. "So that tells you what kind of lunatics we'll be dealing with here."

Wyatt grunted his agreement before he asked, "You have a location?"

"Yes, but it's a remote area of Colombia in the Darien," Marshall warned.

I wasn't about to question the need for us to go in.

It could take both governments way too much time to abandon the missing person theory, and Savannah didn't have that kind of time.

We were already almost a week behind the kidnapping.

Even though I didn't doubt that Marshall had a good location *now*, that could change at any time if these assholes found a taker for Savannah.

My gut ached with the thought of how much could have happened to her already. There had been days now that we hadn't even been aware that she'd been kidnapped.

I really liked Savannah. Always had. She'd just been starting high school when I'd left for college, but we'd bumped into each other occasionally over the years because she and Torie were close.

I tried my damndest not to think about how much I'd noticed just how grown up she'd become *very recently*. When I'd last seen her at Cooper and Torie's wedding several months ago, the woman she'd become had been almost impossible for me to ignore.

"It's not like we aren't used to doing a rescue in harsh locations," I reminded Marshall. "I'm in. We're going to need a helicopter to get closer to that location. I'm your damn pilot."

As a previous 160th SOAR Night Stalker aviator, I was one of the few helicopter pilots involved in Last Hope. I also knew I was the best and the most capable of getting in and out of tight situations safely.

Marshall shot me a dubious look. "You don't have to do this personally, Chase. We could use—"

"Not happening," I interrupted hoarsely. "I'm going. I've known Savannah since she was a kid, Marshall. This is something I *need* to do personally."

I wasn't going to let anyone else go after my sister's best friend.

Okay, so I wasn't about to admit to anyone that something inside me was gnawing at my gut to go after Savannah myself, but those instincts were there. It wasn't something I could just ignore.

"I'm going, too," Wyatt said in a tone that probably *no one* was going to argue with.

Marshall rolled his eyes and let out a sigh of resignation. "What happened to all of you no longer running missions yourselves?"

"That was before some bastards decided to fuck with somebody we know and care about," I answered angrily, still trying to get my emotions in check.

"I get that," Hudson commented. "I've been through that myself. I'm not about to object."

I nodded my head, grateful that Hudson understood my position.

I was also glad that Wyatt had volunteered. I needed his steadiness and skills on this particular operation.

"Do I need to ask if you two need any backup?" Marshall questioned drily.

"I'm in if they do," Cooper said firmly.

"Me, too," Hudson grumbled.

"And me," Jax volunteered.

Wyatt and I shook our heads at the same time. While I appreciated the fact that they were all willing to put their asses on the line, Wyatt and I could be more covert if we were alone. I'd briefly considered Jax's help because he had more medical training than the rest of us, but I knew Wyatt could handle just about anything that came up until we could get Vanna to a hospital.

"Probably better that way," Marshall agreed. "This operation needs to be as quiet as possible since neither government is ready to admit that she was even taken."

"Even though she's my best friend, I've never told Vanna about Last Hope since we operate in absolute secrecy," Torie said quietly from her seat beside me. "She won't exactly be expecting you two to show up. I want you to go because I trust you both to bring Vanna back safely. But I also don't want you to get hurt."

A lump formed in my throat as I saw the torn look in Torie's eyes.

Hell, I was glad she trusted Wyatt and I to bring Savannah back home. I just wished I had the same faith that we could bring her back unharmed. Considering who the enemy was this time, I wasn't sure what kind of shape Vanna would be in when she was rescued.

I also had to at least consider the fact that she could be dead in the jungle by now. Especially if she became more trouble than she was worth to these assholes. Their goal had been a quick sale and on to the next.

My gut wrenched at the thought of anyone hurting Savannah, but I couldn't give in to those thoughts right now. I wouldn't be able to focus.

I grinned at my little sister to reassure her as I said, "Haven't died yet, and plenty of people have wanted to kill me."

Torie slugged me in the arm as she answered, "Stop that cocky bullshit. You and Wyatt might be tough, but you're not completely untouchable. You're human, too."

Didn't I know that? I'd come closer to dying and death than I wanted to admit to my little sister.

"We'll be fine, Torie," Wyatt said firmly before he looked at Marshall. "What else do we know?"

Marshall frowned. "I spoke with Savannah's producer, Jennifer, earlier. She said that she raised the alarm almost immediately after Savannah failed to return from an outdoor shower area before it got dark. When the film crew started to look for her, all they found was Savannah's dirty clothes scattered on the ground at the base of the steps outside. Sounds like she dropped them when she was taken."

"Why is the government so damn set on believing she wandered off?" Jax asked. "Like you said, Savannah is no newbie when it comes to surviving in dangerous locations. I've met her. She's extremely intelligent. It's not really feasible that she just wandered away into the jungle and left her clothing on the ground."

Marshall shrugged. "Probably because kidnappings don't normally happen in that area. It's the only possibility they want to accept right now."

"She's savvier than that," Torie said, her voice quivering with emotion. "Vanna is pragmatic and rational. I knew from the very beginning that she'd never do something to put herself in that kind of position. We have to find her. I *know* what she's probably going through right now."

I watched as Cooper scooted his chair closer to Torie and wrapped a protective arm around her. "We'll find her, sweetheart," he reassured my little sister.

Watching Torie's distress made me want to tear the head off every one of Savannah's kidnappers. Not only was my sibling concerned for her best friend, but the circumstances were bound to bring back horrific memories for Torie of her own kidnapping.

I was also pissed off because Savannah had always been like a second sister to me.

Well, until *recently*. Until the day Cooper and Torie had gotten married. For me, something had changed that day.

It wasn't like I'd never realized how attractive Savannah Anderson was, but it wasn't just my dick prompting me that day to stay longer in Vegas to spend some time with her. Whatever had encouraged me to act so out of character that day had been strong enough to make me override my common sense.

Had I really thought that she'd ever see me as anything other than her best friend's brother?

Hell, I had no idea why I'd been so damn disappointed when she'd blown me off like I was a pain in her ass. But I hadn't stopped thinking about that swift rejection since the day it had happened.

Fuck! I really needed to stop trying to figure out why Savannah had left that day like her gorgeous ass was on fire.

Obviously, she hadn't wanted to spend another minute in my company.

Did it really matter *why* she felt that way?

I'd definitely gotten the message. Unfortunately, her lack of enthusiasm to hang out with me hadn't changed my desire to be with *her*.

I'd still thought about her since Cooper and Torie's wedding. *Every. Single. Fucking. Day.*

I stood up, so agitated that I couldn't sit on my ass any longer. "Can you line up a small helicopter for us in Panama?" I asked Marshall. "I'll need something I can put down in a tight space. Wyatt and I need to get moving."

It was a long plane flight to Central America, and I didn't want to wait any longer to get started.

Every moment we wasted put Savannah more at risk, and the urge to get to her was killing me.

Whether she wanted to see my face or not, I *was* going to rescue Savannah Anderson.

After I knew she was safe, I'd keep myself so occupied that I wouldn't have time to think about the fact that she was the first woman I'd wanted to spend time with for a very long time.

Chapter 2

Chase

"A re you sure you don't need a translator?" Torie asked anxiously as she watched me assemble two backpacks for me and Wyatt in the equipment room. "I know you speak French like a native, but I doubt you can hold a conversation in Spanish."

I shot her a no-way-in-hell-are-you-going-with-us look before I went back to packing. I was *not* taking my little sister into a hellhole, even if Savannah *was* like a sister to her.

And it wasn't just Wyatt and me who would object this time.

"Not happening," I said firmly. "Cooper would cut my balls off."

She shot me a sad smile. "I know I'd never be able to keep up with you two, but the waiting is going to make me crazy. Vanna is tough as nails. I know that. But I'm terrified that she won't come back, Chase."

A chill shot down my spine after Torie mentioned the possibility I couldn't allow myself to think about right now. "She's coming back," I rumbled, not sure if I was trying to convince Torie or myself that my statement was the truth.

Failure wasn't an option.

B. A. Scott

Savannah Anderson *was* alive, and we *were* bringing her home. Period. There was no other possible outcome.

"You're worried, too," she said softly. "I can tell."

"I'm...concerned," I mumbled. "Savannah was like a little sister to me when we were younger."

"And now?" she asked.

Fuck! How did I answer that question, and when exactly had Savannah stopped being an honorary sibling to me?

Honestly, I'd been thinking about that a lot lately. It had probably happened before she'd blown me off at Torie and Cooper's wedding, but I'd had enough sense to ignore that possibly before then.

There was something about the injured look in Savannah's beautiful eyes when she talked about her failed relationship that had sent me reeling that day.

The fact that some bastard had cheated on her was more than I could take, evidently.

Knowing that Savannah was alone and vulnerable had kicked in a whole different kind of protective instinct for me.

At some point, I'd decided that she definitely deserved better, and I'd ridiculously come to the conclusion that she'd be much better off dating a guy who would never hurt her. Someone like...me.

She'd been out the door before I'd finally wised up and realized what a dumb idea that had been.

So yeah, maybe that irresistible attraction *had* been there before Torie's wedding, but I'd just been smart enough to disregard it before that day.

I'd watched every story she'd done for *Deadline America* with a mixture of horror and admiration over the years.

I'd always wanted to protect Savannah, even when she was a kid, so it was hard to decipher exactly when the concern about her safety had become less... brotherly.

Not that I'd ever mentioned my concerns to her, or anyone else for that matter.

She was, after all, a grown ass woman, and going into dangerous situations was part of her job.

28

As I watched her specials on television, I'd also known she could take care of herself, and that she had more common sense than the average person.

But that didn't stop me from wishing she wouldn't put herself in harm's way so damn often.

"I still care about her well-being, Torie," I finally answered as I added some first aid items to our backpacks.

Torie frowned. "I think you care about more than that. I saw the way you looked at her at my wedding, Chase. Maybe I was a little slow to notice, but I think you're attracted to her."

Fuck! Had I really been *that* obvious? "I'm not," I lied without hesitation. "And even if I was, Vanna doesn't feel that way about me. We're friends, Torie. She's brilliant and I enjoy a lively debate every time we meet up. That's all we are."

"I'm not so sure about that," Torie mused. "It seemed to me that *she* was looking at you the same way you were looking at her."

"She wasn't," I said flatly as I crammed more supplies into the bags. Hell, I might as well nip this in the bud. I knew my little sister, and she'd hound me to death if she thought her best friend really liked me. "Savannah and I stayed after all the guests were gone. I told her I'd like to hang out with her the next day. She turned me down flat."

"She did?" Torie asked in a confused tone. "That's weird. Maybe she's just hesitant after what Bradley did to her."

Torie's comment immediately sparked my interest. "What did that bastard do?"

From my sister's tone, I could tell the situation wasn't as straightforward as Vanna had portrayed.

She let out an exasperated breath. "Don't you ever watch the entertainment news? Videos of him and another woman—when he was still supposed to be with Vanna—were everywhere, and he made it very clear that it was sexual. He very publicly humiliated the crap out of Vanna. The paparazzi hounded her for months to get her to comment on how she felt when the asshole dumped her. She was really hurt, even though she tried to act like it was no big deal. Vanna hasn't dated anyone since then, and it happened almost two years ago."

Shit! Where had I been when *that* had happened? Then again, I wasn't big on following the entertainment news, and Wyatt and I had spent a lot of time in France the last several years. "I didn't know," I confessed. "You told me that she was dating an A-lister. I didn't realize it had ended that long ago. She told me that he cheated, but she acted like it was no big deal to her. I kind of suspected that wasn't true."

I'd probably avoided hearing anything about her relationship. Even then, it *had* nagged at me that she might be serious about another guy. I probably just hadn't wanted to admit it. Even to myself.

Knowing what I knew now, I should have paid attention. Just the thought of some bastard hurting *and* humiliating Vanna made my gut roll.

"When has Vanna ever admitted that she was anything other than fine?" Torie asked with a sigh. "I can see through that rhinoceros hide she wears to protect herself, but I doubt many people do."

"She has to be tough to do what she does," I reminded Torie.

"I know," she answered. "But I think we both know that's not the real Vanna. She has a soft heart underneath all that thick skin. I'm scared for her, Chase. I know what it's like to be held hostage with very little hope of living through that situation. She must be terrified."

"Torie," I said carefully, worried that she might not be prepared to see the Vanna we might end up bringing back to her. I knew I sure as hell wasn't, and I'd seen a lot of things I hoped my little sister would never even have to know about. "You do realize that Vanna might not be the same when she comes back, right?"

I'd dealt with way too many hostages. People were rarely the same after being held prisoner.

"It doesn't matter," she answered stubbornly. "She took care of me even though my experience changed me pretty profoundly. I was always the same Torie to her. Vanna helped me keep my sanity. I'll do the same for her."

"Your situations might be different," I cautioned.

"Or they could be extremely similar," she countered. "I was held captive by a criminal gang who had no respect for life, too, Chase."

"But you weren't—"

"Sexually assaulted?" she interrupted breathlessly, sounding slightly panicked. "I was, Chase. I know this isn't a good time to talk about this, but I have to. I never wanted you and Wyatt to know because you already ridiculously blamed yourselves for a kidnapping you never could have prevented. I know exactly what it's like to feel that kind of hopelessness and helplessness. I never should have lied to you and Wyatt, but I wanted you to stop feeling guilty, and I wasn't ready to discuss it, especially with my two older brothers. Now, it doesn't really matter. I've gotten through all that, and I'm happier than I've ever been in my entire life. I just want you to know that I *would* understand if that happened to Vanna."

My body tensed as I turned to look at her. I wanted to be angry, but I knew that I had no right to be. What happened to her were her secrets to share with whoever the fuck she wanted. I also realized that even when she'd been so damn broken, her thoughts were all about saving Wyatt and me some extra grief. "Does Coop know?" I asked huskily.

She nodded. "Yes, of course. He and Vanna are the only ones who know that it happened."

I swallowed hard. "You know Wyatt and I would have understood."

"I know that, too," she replied softly. "I just wasn't ready to tell either one of you. I want you to know now because it just doesn't matter anymore. I'll tell Wyatt the truth, too, before the two of you leave. I need both of you to know that whatever happened to Vanna, I can deal with it because I've been through it. Those bastards who kidnapped me don't deserve to linger in a single one of my thoughts anymore. I have Cooper now, and I'd much prefer to think about my amazing husband."

I opened my arms and Torie threw herself into them without hesitation.

I held her so tightly that it probably wasn't comfortable for her, but she didn't complain. "Jesus! I'm so damn sorry, Torie," I muttered against her hair.

She hugged me hard as she said, "I'm okay, Chase. I swear. They can never touch me again, physically or emotionally. Please don't blame Cooper or Vanna for not telling you. I asked them not to say anything."

"Hell, I can't be pissed at either of them if that's what you wanted. You have a right to your privacy. I definitely can't be mad at Cooper for trying to protect the woman he loves," I told her.

Truthfully, I was glad that Coop was loyal as hell to Torie.

I just hated the fact that she'd suffered even worse than we'd thought.

Did I have a right to be mad because she didn't tell her male siblings everything, especially something so personal?

Hell, no. It wasn't like I didn't have things I didn't want to talk about, either.

"I've healed, Chase. I have an amazing life that I could have never even dreamed of a year ago. I've moved on. I hope you and Wyatt have, too."

I let Torie go as she wiggled out of my hold.

Vanna had told me to put what happened to Torie in the past where it belonged, and she was right.

"I guess we'll have to," I admitted, still not quite sure how to turn off my big brother protective instincts toward my little sister. Most likely, they'd never go away, but she had Cooper now, and I did trust him to watch Torie's back.

"You *do* have to," she insisted. "Cooper worries about me enough for both you and Wyatt, unfortunately. The last thing I need is another person fussing over my well-being."

I grinned at her. Not so long ago, it would have been really hard for me to imagine Cooper Montgomery losing his shit over anything, especially a female. "His genius logic and reasoning ability do seem to go out the window when it comes to you," I agreed.

She folded her arms over her chest as she said, "It does. Completely. If I didn't love him the same way, his drive to keep me protected might drive me totally insane. But I do and it doesn't, even though I'm more than able to take care of myself."

"Then what can I do to be a better big brother now that you do have Cooper?" I asked hoarsely.

She whacked my arm before she said, "You and Wyatt have always been the best brothers I could ever hope to have. I love you both so much. Just keep loving me and supporting me like you always have. I'll never be too old or too grown up to need that."

Hell, Torie was one of the strongest women I'd ever known. She'd globetrotted around the world for years as a translator for the UN before her kidnapping. Maybe Wyatt and I had been a little overbearing since that kidnapping incident because our dad wasn't around anymore. But it was obvious that she didn't need us to act like a protective parent anymore. Maybe she never had.

I lifted my hands jokingly in surrender. "I'll do my best, but if Cooper ever screws up—"

"He won't," she said confidently. "Now get moving and bring my best friend back to me. As long as she's still alive, I can handle whatever hell she's been through. I just need to see her face again, Chase."

"Me, too," I confessed without really stopping to think about my words.

Torie snorted. "Then stop trying to convince me that this mission is *only* about rescuing a childhood friend. I know you, Chase."

I ignored her assumption because I thought it was best to just let *that* subject drop. "You'll stand by here in case we do need a translator?"

"You know I will, and that we'll all be monitoring the entire operation," she answered. "Vanna speaks some Spanish, so she's not going to be totally ignorant about what's happening."

I lifted a brow. "Is there anything else we should know?"

Torie nodded slowly. "Even if she doesn't show it, she's not completely unbreakable. Every sad story she reports on eats a little piece of her soul because she's got more compassion and empathy for people who are suffering than she cares to admit. I know you two joked around and debated with each other a lot when you've met up in the past, but there's so much more to Vanna than you see on the surface."

I knew that. Savannah had been much less guarded as a child. "If we can rescue her, I'll be careful not to hurt her," I promised Torie. "Please be safe. Both of you," she said in a pleading tone.

I hefted both of the packs onto one shoulder and kissed Torie on the forehead before I said, "There's no way in hell that Wyatt and I are going to let some idiots get the jump on either one of us."

She shot me a skeptical look. "I'm sure that's what Cooper thought when he took me back to the Amazon, and look what happened there. None of you are invincible and bad things happen sometimes."

"Not this time," I answered gruffly. There was too much at stake to fuck up this particular rescue.

I needed to bring Savannah Anderson home where she belonged.

Where she was safe.

Where she didn't need to be afraid.

Where no one could hurt her.

I'd never have a single moment of peace until I did.

Chapter 3

Savannah

I desperately wanted a drink of water, but I couldn't even open my eyes, much less get out of bed to get one.

Pain exploded from my face and then through my entire body, most noticeably my left shoulder and my ribs.

And I was hot. So damn hot and thirsty.

Where am I?

For some reason, I wasn't capable of reasoning out what was happening to me, or why the surface beneath me was so damn hard.

I'm definitely not in a bed.

Why can't I open my eyes?

Why is my mind so damn foggy?

I could vaguely recall starting to wake up this way before, but then…nothing.

Shit! I had to get my eyes open. I needed to see what was going on.

I tried to focus, and then felt utterly helpless because I failed to lift my eyelids.

Don't give up. Keep trying.

I stopped concentrating on getting my eyes open for a moment and just…listened.

The chorus of insects was unmistakable, along with the occasional cry of a bird I didn't recognize.

Jungle sounds.

How was it possible that I was still in the jungle?

The last thing I remembered was talking to my producer about our schedule, and the fact that we were leaving Panama the next morning.

What had happened *after* that?

Dammit! The more I tried to remember, the less clear those events seemed.

Little snippets of what I assumed were memories flashed through my mind, and I didn't know if they were true or imagined.

Had I really headed to the outdoor shower after I'd chatted with Jen?

My body tensed as I remembered a moment of panic like I'd never experienced before in my entire life.

I hadn't been able to breathe.

Had I really been attacked from behind?

Shit! Why couldn't I remember?

None of this made sense.

Maybe I was hallucinating.

Maybe none of that had happened.

Maybe I was dreaming.

If so, I was having one hell of a hard time waking myself up.

My body started to shiver even though I felt like I was about to spontaneously combust from the heat.

I tried to wrap my arms around my body, but my hands barely moved.

Shit! Why wouldn't my hands move?

And why was the pain so horrendous every time I tried?

Fear, pain, and frustration took over as I failed to even put my arms in motion.

Shit! Shit! Shit!

Somehow, I had to make sense of what was happening to me.

Instinct was telling me that my life probably depended on my ability to shake off whatever was hampering my movements.

I had to cool off.

I had to get water.

I had to fight whatever was causing my pain and lack of mobility.

Most of all, I *had* to clear my head so I could figure out exactly what to do.

I was almost certain that I *wasn't* dreaming.

I was in trouble.

I could *sense* that this situation was real, and it was that same gut instinct that had saved my ass several times over the years.

The haziness in my brain started to clear just slightly. Enough for me to realize I was, in fact, still in the jungle.

My discussion with Jen, my producer, *had* actually happened.

We'd been scheduled to leave Panama the following day.

But something had happened.

I was either injured or sick—or both—in the Darien jungle.

I couldn't remember exactly what had happened after I'd talked with Jen, but I knew we had never departed from Central America.

I *was* still in the Darien jungle.

I had to get up. I needed to find my crew and let them know that something was definitely wrong with me.

I *had* to use this moment of clarity to move my ass.

Get up, Savannah! Get the hell up!

I couldn't get my eyes open. My arms weren't working. Maybe if I could sit up, that would help.

I was laying on my back, so I tried to bend my knees a little to help me sit up. I ignored the horrific pain it caused when I started to rock my body to get into a sitting position.

I was so weak that I could hardly move, but I tried to power through it.

Before I could completely rock myself into a sitting position, I was suddenly slammed onto my back again by a powerful blow to my ribs.

"Stupid bitch!" an evil sounding male voice exclaimed in heavily accented English. "I think you want to die."

An icy sensation ran down my spine as I realized that I recognized that grating baritone.

This bastard was the reason I hurt everywhere.

It was probably a good thing that I was too weak and my mouth was too dry to speak.

My recall ability suddenly went into overdrive, and it sent a jolt of terror through me.

Trying to fight, trying to escape, hadn't gotten me anywhere. Every time I had resisted, I'd gotten pummeled.

I remembered now, even though my brain wasn't totally clear.

I couldn't move my hands because I was tightly bound.

More than likely, I couldn't open my eyes because they were swollen shut.

I'd fought my kidnappers hard, but I'd lost that battle and every additional one I'd engaged in since then.

Panic filled my being as I recognized the fact that I no longer knew how long I'd been held captive in the middle of the jungle.

I'd repeated this cycle of forgetting and then remembering some of what had happened to me so many times that I'd lost count.

After the first time, my memories had gotten more and more confused.

It was taking me longer and longer to remember that I was being held hostage by four assholes who saw me only as a possible payday.

My condition was rapidly deteriorating.

Would I even wake up the next time?

Terror flooded through me as I heard my jailer rummaging through his belongings.

Please, not again! Not again!

My body was beaten and broken, but I at least wanted to keep my brain intact.

I choked back a sob of anger and helplessness as I felt the needle go into my arm.

The drugs this criminal gang possessed were potent, and I knew I only had a few moments before I'd sink into the darkness, wondering if I was ever going to wake up again.

Judging by my confusion with each awakening, I was fairly certain they were upping the dose with every injection, hoping to keep me quiet for a longer period of time.

I knew my fight to stay conscious was fruitless, but I tried to struggle against the effects of the drugs anyway.

Someone must have noticed that I'm missing.

My crew must be looking for me.

My death wasn't a *total* certainty as long as rescue was possible, right?

I tried to not to panic and hang onto that tiny thread of hope as I tumbled into the big black hole that instantly swallowed me whole—again.

Chapter 4

Chase

"You doing okay?" Wyatt asked quietly from his seat in a recliner as we made our way to Panama in my private jet.

My brother and I had discussed the confession that Torie had made at headquarters right after we'd boarded, but we'd been fairly quiet for the last few hours.

My eyes flew to his face as I listened to the quiet rumble of the jet engine bringing us closer and closer to our destination. We'd both been going through the paperwork that Marshall had given us on Savannah. "Yeah. Why do you ask?"

Wyatt shrugged. "I haven't seen you bouncing your leg around like that for years. Are you nervous?"

I opened my mouth to deny that I was anxious, but suddenly realized that I *had* reverted to a nervous habit that I'd broken a long time ago.

My leg was jumpy, like I was more than impatient to arrive at the airport in Central America.

Shit! I had nixed that annoying and telling habit years ago—right after I'd joined the 160th. Showing any sign of emotion during an operation was dangerous.

I immediately stopped the jerky motion.

"Sorry," I mumbled as I noticed the concern in Wyatt's gaze. "I'm not nervous about the mission in general, even though we haven't done one ourselves in a long time. I'll have your back. I just want to get Vanna the hell out of there."

My older brother's expression was grim as he answered, "Never once did I worry about the mission or your abilities. I'm asking as your older brother if you're jittery about Savannah. To be honest, I'm worried about her, too. It's going to kill Torie if we can't bring her back alive. And I've always liked Savannah. I didn't spend as much time with her as you have in the past, but she's a good person, and a damn good journalist. She doesn't deserve this."

I let out a heavy sigh. Wyatt and I had always been close. Yeah, we argued and he could be a sarcastic, cynical asshole at times, but I never doubted that he gave a shit about his family and people he cared about. He was usually all business when he was on a mission, but this one was obviously a little different because he knew and cared about Savannah, and she meant everything to Torie.

I may have spent more years with Savannah when she was younger, before I was off to college, but that didn't mean he didn't consider her family. She was Torie's best friend and a woman who had been at our little sister's side during the worst experience of her life. That was good enough for Wyatt to feel protective of Savannah.

"She's more than a good person," I admitted. "She's fucking amazing, Wyatt. Just the thought of her being in pain or being in trouble doesn't sit well with me."

He nodded. "I figured," he said simply.

"What does that mean?" I asked as I shot him a confused look.

"She's more to you than just Torie's best friend," Wyatt replied, his tone annoyingly confident.

"She's not," I said hurriedly. "I mean, she shouldn't be. Fuck! She can't be. The fact is, she *is* Torie's best friend. She sees me as an honorary big brother, Wyatt. She always has."

He lifted a brow. "Maybe I don't say much, but do you really think anyone missed the way you two looked at each other at Torie's wedding? Maybe you two were engaged in a debate, as usual. But your eyes were saying something else completely."

"Christ!" I spat out in disgust. "Does everyone think they saw something that doesn't exist?"

First Torie, and now Wyatt?

"Oh, it was there," he corrected. "I think it was you who didn't see it. I doubt *everyone* noticed. Just the people who know you. It's been a long time since you've looked at a woman like you wished that the two of you were alone and naked."

"She's attractive," I muttered. "I noticed it at Torie's wedding. End of story."

"And?" Wyatt prompted.

"She's intelligent," I added reluctantly. "She's always been fun to argue with in a friendly debate sort of way."

Wyatt didn't speak. He just shot me an expectant look.

Shit! I hated the way that my older brother could make me talk without saying a word. "Okay, dammit!" I said gruffly. "I wish we were there already. I hate the thought of anyone hurting Vanna. Yes, I lost my mind momentarily when the two of us where alone together after Torie's wedding. I asked her out. She turned me down flat. That was the end of it. But that doesn't mean I don't still consider her a...family friend."

"Bullshit," Wyatt grumbled.

I glared at him. "What does that mean?"

I was getting sick and tired of asking him that question.

"A guy doesn't just stop being attracted to a woman because she turns him down. And if I'm not mistaken, that interest went both ways," Wyatt answered.

I suddenly hated the way Wyatt could appear disinterested, but really noticed every fucking detail of his surroundings.

"It didn't go both ways. Take my word on that," I answered irritably. "Just drop it, Wyatt. She's an important rescue because she means so much to Torie."

Fuck knew that Savannah had made it crystal clear that she couldn't wait to leave *after* I'd asked her out that day.

It was obvious that I'd made her uncomfortable.

She'd probably known that my dick was hard and it had sent her running for the door.

"I still think you're full of shit," Wyatt drawled. "But if you don't want to talk about it, I'll let it go…for now. We need to stay focused on the rescue part of this situation right now."

Hell, I didn't want to talk about this whole thing later, either.

"It was nothing anyway," I said hoarsely. "Just a very brief period of temporary insanity. I'm over it."

"When was the last time you had one of those?"

I thought about Wyatt's question before I hedged, "None of them come to mind right now."

"Exactly," he replied quietly. "Now, let's focus on this operation."

I sent him an irritated glance before I looked back at the file we were both studying.

It wasn't like Wyatt had any reason to be giving advice on relationships. I couldn't remember the last time he'd gone out on a date or shown any real interest in anyone other than family or friends.

For the most part, we were both workaholics who had been trying to prove that we'd been worthy of inheriting our father's massive empire.

Last Hope took up whatever time we had available outside of Durand Industries.

Now that we'd finally relocated most of our headquarters back to San Diego from Paris, we'd probably have more spare time. I just wasn't sure if either one of us would have the inclination to spend less time on business.

After all, I had a very good reason to avoid relationships, which was something I'd temporarily forgotten about when I'd followed that impulse to ask Savannah out.

Wyatt, however, really didn't. Or if he did, I certainly didn't know about it. He was just adamant about maintaining his status as one of the most eligible bachelors in the world. Not that I thought he *wanted* that title. Mostly, he just wanted to be left alone.

"There's nothing major here that I don't already know," I said as I put the papers back in order.

"I never knew that she was dating Bradley Warner," Wyatt mused. "The bastard made her public life miserable, and her face even more recognizable, unfortunately. Maybe that's why she's just not ready to try going out with another high profile guy. Can't say that I blame her."

"I knew she was dating an A-lister. I just didn't know who it was until I read the paperwork," I informed him, hoping he'd go in another direction. The last thing I wanted to think about was Savannah's sex life.

Warner was a total prick, an action movie star who probably looked good on screen, but had shit for brains and zero motivation to help anyone but himself in real life.

"It wouldn't make sense for the kidnappers to kill her," Wyatt said thoughtfully as he shuffled through the papers. "They're supposedly trying to form their own criminal gang. They need funds."

"What happens if the heat gets to be too much for them and they can't sell her?" I asked. "She's high profile, and her captors are idiots. Who's to say that they won't want to kill her if they can't find a private buyer?"

My gut reacted negatively to the thought of finding Savannah dead, but I fought against even considering that option.

While it was also a possibility that she'd be sold off and moved before we could reach her, I tried not to think about that, either.

No matter where they took her, I'd fucking find her.

"Doubtful," Wyatt answered. "I doubt they're feeling much heat in the Colombian portion of the Darien jungle. Not to mention the fact that she's their only prize at the moment. Drugs are plentiful there, but they need connections to sell them. Hell, if they had any of those connections already, she'd be gone to who-knows-where by now. In some ways, I guess we're lucky she was kidnapped by morons."

I nodded. Wyatt was right. If an experienced gang had taken Savannah, they would have trafficked her fairly easily with their connections, even though she had a recognizable face. "On the other hand, I doubt the ones with experience would have taken her captive in the first place," I grumbled.

Smart and established criminal gangs wouldn't have risked it. They controlled large territories and they had plenty of possible victims since a barrage of migrants crossed through the Darien Gap every year.

"True," Wyatt agreed. "Regardless, we're getting her back."

I turned my head to see a determined look on my older brother's face. "You feel up to this?" I asked him. "It's been a while."

He shot me an irritated glance. "Are you trying to say I'm too old for this? I spent years leading a team of elite Delta Force members on highly classified operations a hell of a lot more difficult than this one."

Okay, was Wyatt getting a little defensive about the fact that he was going to be forty on his next birthday or what?

Shit! He didn't need to get touchy about that. I was only a few years behind him.

It wasn't like I doubted his experience or his skills. My brother had balls of steel, and he was also fitter than most guys half his age.

"Hell, no," I told him. "That's not what I'm saying, but it has been a few years since we've personally done a rescue."

Like the Montgomery brothers, Wyatt and I tried to keep a low profile with our involvement in Last Hope since our faces were recognizable.

Secrecy was an important advantage for us, and we knew it.

"I'm always ready," he snapped. "What about you?"

I grinned at him as I quoted the motto of the 160th SOAR. "Night Stalkers never quit."

In a more serious tone, I added, "You know I trust you more than anyone to watch my six."

Wyatt nodded sharply. "Same. I couldn't sit back and watch you take this on without me being there. I know the importance of keeping a low profile, but I also get why you volunteered. This one is personal."

"I couldn't sit in Last Hope headquarters running this mission while someone else was out there looking for Savannah," I confessed.

"You're not," Wyatt reassured me. "We'll find her, Chase, and we'll bring her home."

A lump began to form in my throat as I answered tightly, "We have to."

"I know," my brother shot back.

Thankfully, he didn't pursue my admission.

Instead, he pulled out the map and started to study it. "You should be able to land your bird in a small clearing that's fairly close to Savannah's location," he said in a no-nonsense voice. "From there, we'll do a short boat paddle to get to a good location to penetrate the jungle. Marshall will have a local guide waiting to keep an eye on the helicopter."

I already knew that "short boat paddle" was actually a fairly long stretch of river.

I'd already memorized the entire route and our plans by heart, but I didn't mind going over the details. It kept me from thinking about anything else. "I don't think Marshall missed a single detail," I told Wyatt.

We'd planned the operation time so the entire mission would happen under the cover of darkness, which wasn't a problem for me. I'd spent most of my military career flying night and twilight missions.

"Does Marshall ever miss any details?" Wyatt asked drily. "I'm pretty sure the guy never sleeps."

I chuckled. "Everyone involved in Last Hope is really anal. We have to be. But Marshall is one of those guys who excels at thinking about every single thing that could go wrong and having a plan in place for every possibility."

"Which is why he's so respected and the guys coming out of special ops are willing to put their asses on the line in the civilian world," my brother pointed out.

"True," I agreed. "There wouldn't be a Last Hope without Marshall. Sometimes I do wonder why he chose to dedicate his civilian life to this volunteer organization, though."

"I don't think he was ready to retire," Wyatt mused. "He needed a purpose. I get that, but the man could definitely use some time off occasionally." He started to put the map away as he added, "I think we're ready. We need to try to get some sleep before we land. We've got a few hours."

He was right. We needed to be as rested as possible.

I stood to make my way back to my bed.

"Chase?" my brother said roughly.

"Yeah?"

"Make sure you actually sleep," Wyatt demanded. "There's nothing we can do until we get to Panama."

I nodded.

I'd sleep because I had to, but I highly doubted I'd be dreaming about anything or anyone else but Savannah.

Chapter 5

Savannah

"Vanna? Talk to me, sweetheart! Come on!"
I heard the voice urgently calling to me in a hoarse whisper against my ear, but I *couldn't* quite wake up. Why was I even being asked to do that?

"Savannah! Fuck! Talk to me, dammit!"

The voice that had sounded so far away got a little bit closer.

As some of my senses started to awaken, I noticed something I hadn't felt for what seemed like forever: a slight breeze on my face.

I suddenly became aware that someone had a gentle hand on me, apparently trying to shake me awake.

Definitely not one of my captors since this touch is painless.

"I gave her some Narcan before we got in the boat because she was so heavily drugged that she was barely breathing," a different voice remarked in a harsher whisper. "But I doubt she was only getting opiates. It won't reverse some of the other drugs."

Through my brain fog, I began to wonder if someone was trying to…help me.

At least two people, actually.

Both were male, but were these two guys friend or foe?

As my mind cleared a little more, I also noted that the second voice had mentioned...a boat?

Shit! Was I dreaming?

I listened, trying to shake my confusion enough to figure out what was going on.

We were definitely in the water. I could feel the sway of being in motion on the river.

A moment of panic seized me, but I shoved it back down.

Where were they taking me?

"She's breathing, but her pulse is racing, and her whole body is shaking. Come on, Savannah. Talk to me. Argue with me if you want. I'll even let you win this debate," the first voice cajoled in a calmer tone as he lightly shook me again.

"I think she might be septic from her injuries," voice number two replied. "I didn't have much time to get a good look, but some of Savannah's wounds look severely infected."

Okay, they were using *my name.* That was...different.

Maybe I should have been terrified that I was being taken away from my previous location, but for some reason, I wasn't anymore.

I finally recognized the fact that I was being cradled carefully on someone's lap, a firm but gentle arm securely around my waist.

"Savannah," the voice sounded again right next to my ear. "Torie's worried about you. I want to be able to tell her that you're going to be okay. Talk to me. Even if you just tell me to go to hell. I need to know that your brain is functioning."

My entire being was shocked into paying very close attention.

Dear God, I recognized *this* voice now.

Chase?

The possibility of Chase Durand being here in the Darien jungle was less than zero, but I couldn't shake the instinct that it *was* him holding me, begging me to wake up.

I willed my eyes to open, and they finally obeyed, but I couldn't see anything except darkness. Everything was pitch black.

"So thirsty," I managed to say in a voice that didn't sound at all like my own.

My throat felt like sandpaper, and it was a relief when the person holding onto me offered me a drink.

Instinct took over and I drank, even though I couldn't see a damn thing.

"Go slow," the voice said, his tone sounding relieved that I'd finally opened my eyes.

I took another sip. And then another. I drank slowly until I was eventually satisfied.

"Please tell me that you're here to take me back home," I choked out.

"We're here to protect you and take you home," the slightly amused voice replied obediently.

Wait? Wasn't that what they said in the movies when the Marines were sent in to rescue someone?

I shook my head, hoping it would shake away the confusion.

It didn't.

"Military?" I questioned.

"Not exactly, but we used to be if that makes you feel any better."

"Chase?" I blurted out his name without thinking. "Is that you?"

"It's me, sweetheart. Wyatt is currently rowing us to safety," he told me quietly. "It's over, Vanna. You're safe."

I was still disoriented, but the relief that flooded over my body was very, very real.

I tried to hold back a sob, but the gentle hand stroking my hair made me lose that battle.

I buried my face against Chase's shoulder, trying to be quiet because I wasn't certain we were completely out of danger. I tried to keep my voice low as I asked, "How is this even possible? Where are we? How did you get here? Why are you here? How did you rescue me? And how can you see anything? It's pitch dark out here."

"That's a whole lot of questions at one time. Relax, Vanna," he directed. "I'll answer all your questions eventually. How are you feeling?"

"I think I'm sick, Chase," I murmured, unable to stop my body from shivering uncontrollably. "I know I was heavily drugged, and I'm not sure where I'm injured because my entire body hurts."

"I know, sweetheart. We're getting you to a good hospital as quickly as possible. Once we get to the helicopter, Wyatt can look at your injuries while I'm hauling ass to get you to the hospital. You're hurt, dehydrated, undernourished, and probably septic from infection. I'm not going to lie to you."

Strangely, it was actually comforting that he was being completely honest. "Thank you. It helps to know the truth. I've been so drugged that I'm not actually sure how long I've been here."

"It's been a week now," he answered. "It took a while for us to realize you were kidnapped because no one saw or heard anything. The government thought you just wandered off and got lost. There were endless search parties that turned up nothing. Torie sounded the alarm when you didn't get back to San Diego on time. She knew something was wrong."

"How did you find me?" I questioned, my brain still muddled.

"Now that's a longer story," he said gently. "Let's focus on simpler things right now."

"God, I feel so dazed," I groaned. "I'm still not sure that I'm not hallucinating."

"It's the drugs and the infection," he replied. "Wyatt and I are here, and we're getting you home. You'll have to trust me. I want to orient you, but I don't want to overwhelm you right now. You can get all the complicated answers later. I just want you to know you're safe, Vanna."

Safe?

Honestly, I hadn't experienced anything except fear and pain since the moment I'd realized that I was being kidnapped.

"I was so scared, Chase," I admitted softly, my heart acknowledging what my brain couldn't at the moment.

Chase was here.

He was real.

He and Wyatt *were* actually rescuing me.

As ludicrous as this all might seem, it was truly happening.

"I tried to escape," I explained. "I was beaten for every attempt. I knew they were going to traffic me. I guess it just became easier for them to keep me unconscious. That's when I started losing track of time."

Chase rocked my body slowly. "You were brave, Vanna, and you'd have to be crazy *not* to be scared shitless. Especially since you realized what their intentions were. Did they sexually assault you? We have to know so we can treat you for that when we get to the hospital."

I shook my head slowly. "I don't think so. If they did, I don't remember it. But I've been so out of it—"

"It's okay," Chase said in a husky tone. "We'll get you checked over for that anyway. Don't get frustrated because you don't remember things. You were drugged. Wyatt gave you Narcan to reverse the opiates, but I'm sure you were sedated, too, which is why you still can't think clearly."

"I want to remember," I told him. "I just...can't."

So much of the whole experience was still a big blank spot in my head.

I'd been held captive for an entire week, but all I could recall was the first day or so.

"It's okay, Vanna. Let's just get you well right now," Chase replied in a steady, comforting voice.

I let out a small sigh. Like I had a choice? It was highly unlikely that my head would suddenly clear. "I guess I'll have to focus on that," I told him. "I'm definitely not up to debating you right now."

This Chase was new to me. This man who was holding me, gently reassuring me, and making me feel safe was a part of him I hadn't seen since I was child. He'd patched me up several times when I was a kid, but I'd probably forgotten exactly how kind and reassuring he could be.

But this time we were all grown up, and it was undeniably.... different.

"Damn," he said in a teasing tone. "With you in this condition, I might have a chance of winning a debate."

"You always win anyway," I protested weakly.

"My father was a Parisian," he grumbled. "I had plenty of practice. And you got your point across often enough."

I tried to smile, but it was painful. I remembered how much Torie's father had loved a lively debate.

"We're here," Wyatt said in a firm, no-nonsense tone. "Let's get this bird moving."

I felt the bump of the boat connecting with land and grimaced. *Shit!* I hurt everywhere.

"This is going to be painful, Vanna. I have to move you to the helicopter. I'm sorry," Chase said, his voice radiating with remorse.

"I can't see anything, Chase. Is someone here to fly us out of here?" I asked, disoriented because I couldn't see anything but darkness.

I assumed that Chase and Wyatt were wearing some kind of night vision goggles since they appeared to have no problem navigating in the dark.

"Yeah," he answered in a joking tone. "Me. You ready to put your life in my hands, sweetheart?"

It suddenly dawned on me that Chase was piloting me out of here *himself.*

I held back a cry as he shifted me in his arms. "Not frightened at all," I answered honestly as I panted through the pain. "According to Torie, you used to be one of the best helicopter pilots on the planet."

"Still am," he shot back as he stood. "Hang tight, Vanna. This is the really unpleasant part."

I let out a whimper of pain I couldn't stifle as he started to move. Everything hurt so much that I felt the darkness closing in. I fought it. I was finally somewhat aware of what was going on. I didn't want to lose that awareness now.

"Christ! I'm sorry, Vanna, but I have to get you off this damn boat. I think your shoulder is dislocated, and I know this is going to hurt like hell," Chase rasped against my ear.

When he hopped off the boat, the agony of my injuries became too much to handle, and I decisively lost my battle not to fall into unconsciousness.

Chapter 6

Chase

Two weeks later, I felt like I'd been dragged through hell and back again.

Savannah had recovered at the best medical center in Panama City, but the road to that improvement had been way too precarious for me.

When I'd finally seen her condition in the light of day, I'd wanted to kill all four of the bastards who had abused her.

Now, I still wanted to kill them, but my mind was slightly calmer since she'd made it through the rough patches. It also helped that the four assholes responsible for her kidnapping had all been apprehended, pled guilty and had been put in prison already.

I knew I'd never forget the cry of anguish that had left her mouth the moment I'd jumped down from the boat to get her on the helicopter. Or the helpless whimpers of agony after that.

The flight to Panama City had seemed like the longest I'd ever flown, even though it was relatively short. Vanna had lost consciousness and had stayed out cold for the entire duration of the flight, which had been a blessing for her.

In hindsight, it was a damn miracle that Vanna had even had the strength to speak while she was on that boat.

They'd fixed her dislocated shoulder and it was out of a sling. Her fractured ribs were healing. A plastic surgeon had done his best to repair the deep wounds on her face. The doctors had gotten her pain under control soon after we'd arrived, and after so many IV antibiotics that I'd lost track of them, she was finally clear of the infection that had invaded her entire body.

So why did I *still* feel so hypervigilant even though her condition was improving and I was taking her home to finish her recovery?

Hell, truth was that she still *looked* fucking fragile as she sat on the bed in my bedroom on board my private jet.

She hadn't regained all the weight she'd lost, and the repaired lacerations on her face looked painful and angry against her pale skin.

She was smiling at me as she put me in check on the chessboard, but her beautiful hazel eyes were still slightly haunted.

Not that she really talked about her fears much, and the woman had been braver than an injured soldier twice her size during her recovery, but I could sense that the uneasiness was still there.

It was going to take time. I knew that. Hopefully, she'd feel more secure once we were back in the States.

"Check," she said as she finished her move.

I lifted a brow from my cross-legged position on the other side of the board. "Do you really think I can't get out of this one?"

I could absolutely get myself out of check, but hell, I had to give Vanna credit that she could play so well while she was still recovering from her injuries.

The sigh that she released from her lips went straight through me as she answered wistfully, "I'm sure you can, but it's fun to watch you do it."

"Evil woman," I muttered as I figured out which move to make.

Savannah was a worthy opponent, and I was sure she could win as many games as she lost judging by her skill in her current condition.

"Thank you for staying with me until I was better," she said as she watched me make my move. "You missed the holidays with your family, Chase."

I shrugged. "It's not a big deal. Torie would have been even more miserable if you'd been here alone. She was chomping at the bit to get to Panama."

Not that I would have left Vanna, even if Torie had shown up.

My little sister had come down with a bad case of the flu, which had kept her in California. She and Savannah had spoken by phone, and Vanna had assured Torie that she'd see her soon to keep my little sister from getting on Cooper's jet.

Wyatt had stayed several days to make sure that Vanna was out of danger. He'd returned to the States to handle a few things at Durand that had to be completed by the beginning of the year.

"It *is* a big deal," she argued. "I don't know what I would have done without you."

I wasn't sure how to answer.

Like I would have been anywhere else?

I'd been apprehensive even though I was right here by her side.

I would have been completely wrecked if I was far away.

I wasn't sure how it had happened, but I was totally obsessed with protecting her until she was well again.

To me, the way I felt made sense.

She was my little sister's best friend, and I'd treated Vanna like a sister when she was a kid.

Yeah, maybe those old protective instincts toward Vanna had resurfaced with a vengeance, but wasn't it natural considering the circumstances?

I couldn't have left her even if I wanted to, and I couldn't fucking imagine not wanting to be here for her.

Maybe, during a happier time, I had a brief moment when I'd wanted to get her naked.

That had been a very bad idea and totally unrealistic, especially when I already knew that kind of intimacy wasn't in the cards for me anymore.

I had no idea what I'd been thinking the day of Torie's wedding in Vegas. I wasn't a guy any woman wanted in her bed next to her anymore.

I wasn't sure how I'd forgotten that for a single second.

The only thing I could ever be to Vanna was a friend and protector.

Neither one of *those* roles were undoable for me. In fact, I was pretty much adamant that I was the perfect man for that job.

Vanna was vulnerable, and she needed both a protector and a friend right now.

"Checkmate," I informed her as I finally made my move.

Her brow wrinkled as she viewed the board. "Dammit, Chase! I thought I had you. Why didn't I see that one coming?"

Well, let's see…maybe because she had nearly died a short time ago and was still recovering?

Nah…Vanna would never cut herself a break for that.

"That's the whole idea, right?" I teased. "You're not supposed to see it coming."

"I suppose," she said, sounding disgruntled as she leaned back against the headboard.

I fought off the urge to laugh.

Oh yeah, that was another thing. She *really* didn't like to lose. I couldn't call her a sore loser. She just expected perfection from herself at all times.

"You look tired," I told her as I put the chess set away. "That's enough chess games for now."

"I'm tired all the time," she said mournfully. "And before you suggest it, I don't need a nap. All I've done is sleep. I think it's time you explained exactly why and how you and Wyatt came to my rescue. You told me you'd explain later. I'm better. Tell me."

She wasn't exactly *better* since she was just discharged from the hospital.

Vanna had asked me the same questions several times over the last few days because she was more oriented, and I'd brushed them off. All I'd wanted her to concentrate on was healing. Now that she was perfectly coherent, those inquiries were coming more and more often.

Judging by the stubborn look on her face, I wasn't going to get away with not explaining any longer.

Besides, she was a Last Hope rescue. She'd have to know sooner or later.

"Like I said, it's kind of a long story," I warned her as I dropped the box with the chess set onto the side table.

She folded her arms across her chest. "Well, you're in luck because it seems I have nothing but time right now. It's a long flight and I'm not taking a nap right now, so spill it."

I grinned because I loved her sassiness. It was a sure sign that she was feeling better.

I completely understood now what Torie had said about Vanna's rhino hide exterior. Even when she was vulnerable, she tried to hide those emotions. Sometimes she'd succeeded. Sometimes…not, especially in the early days of her rehabilitation, but holy fuck the woman was resilient. I couldn't help but marvel over the way she'd handled her recovery.

I scooted my body back against the headboard so we were sitting side by side before I started to explain. "Before I tell you exactly what happened, I have to emphasize how important it is that none of this information ever gets to anyone on the outside."

She hesitated before she asked, "What information?"

I let out a heavy breath. I hadn't needed to describe Last Hope to anyone who didn't know about it for a long time. "You were freed by a civilian volunteer rescue organization known as Last Hope. Not keeping that information to yourself could be detrimental to our volunteers and contacts all over the globe."

"I'm not sure I completely understand," she said, sounding confused.

I wasn't surprised since I wasn't exactly clarifying things all that well. "It's complicated."

"I'm listening," she said calmly.

"Last Hope is a nongovernment organization that's successfully been rescuing kidnapped victims for years now. Marshall, the leader of the group, was former special operations. He retired after an injury that forced him into that retirement way earlier than he wanted. If the government doesn't want to touch a hostage situation, Last

Hope is usually willing to step up to the plate. Every volunteer who actually carries out our missions is previous special forces."

I turned my head to look at her face. I could see the wheels turning as she tried to process what I was telling her.

"Exactly how large is this organization?" she asked.

"Worldwide," I informed her. "It didn't start out that way, but it's grown in size over the years."

"You and Wyatt are both involved?" she queried.

"Yes," I confirmed. "Both of us, along with the Montgomery brothers, help to finance and plan the operations."

As she turned her head to look at me, I could see surprise and astonishment in her gaze as she asked, "Hudson, Jax, and Cooper are involved, too?"

I nodded. "They signed up a little before we did. Wyatt jumped on board right after he was discharged, and then I volunteered when I got out after he told me about it. We're the only organization left that has the scale and size to do almost any rescue without government involvement. But our continued existence relies on secrecy."

She shook her head slightly, like she was still letting the information sink in. "How did Last Hope end up coming to my rescue? How often do you and Wyatt have to trudge through jungles to bring hostages home? God, do you know how incredible all of this sounds? I know you're telling me the truth, but it all seems so unbelievable. How many filthy rich men are willing to step into dangerous hostage situations?"

I grinned. "Just the ones who had already done it many times in the military, and the five of us don't usually carry out missions ourselves anymore. In fact, we all decided not to because our faces are recognizable, and we have plenty of volunteers who are willing to work in the field. We mostly do strategic planning and backup from headquarters."

"You came and rescued *me*," she pointed out.

I shrugged. "It was personal, and we needed a helicopter pilot who could fly at night and move into a very tight space. Do you really think we were going to leave your fate to someone else, Savannah?

Wyatt and I have known you for most of your life. In your case, Torie was worried when you didn't get back to San Diego on your target date, so she went to Marshall. We stepped in because you were considered a missing person, and neither government was ready to come off that stance. Last Hope knew differently, but Marshall's sources aren't necessarily people the government would see as credible. None of us have any issues with his information. Marshall has never been wrong or let us down when we needed something. Unfortunately, we were certain that you couldn't wait for the governments to figure everything out on their own. So we moved as soon as Marshall had a good location on you. We all decided the operation would be more covert if it was just me and Wyatt, but everyone cared about your safety, Vanna, especially Torie, but Cooper and his brothers volunteered their services, too."

I saw her swallow hard before she said, "I had no idea about any of this, so I'm still in shock. So Torie knows?"

"She does now, but she didn't until recently," I told her. "After recovering from her kidnapping, she decided to investigate some rumors she'd heard about Last Hope while she was working for the FBI. When she finally tracked down Marshall, she volunteered her services as a translator. Soon after that, she discovered that Wyatt and I had been part of Last Hope for years."

"Torie is a volunteer, too? How is that possible if your volunteers need to be previous special forces?"

"Recent policy change," I explained. "No one except ex-special forces can run field missions, but Marshall decided to start relaxing that rule when it came to special services. Jax's wife, Harlow, was a weather specialist in the military. She was the first exception. Torie's skills as a translator are valuable, so Marshall signed her up, too."

"Wait," she mumbled. "I thought Harlow said she and Jax were getting married on Valentine's Day when I met her at Torie's wedding."

I smirked. "You're right, that *was* the plan. But Jax got impatient and they ran away to Vegas instead. Since Harlow wasn't all that thrilled about a bigger wedding, I'd say she encouraged the whole thing."

The event had been so spontaneous that the immediate family and friends had barely gotten there on time for the wedding. Wyatt and I had cut it close, and we had private jets at our disposal.

"What about Hudson and Taylor?" she asked curiously.

"Oh, they had their wedding as planned in October," I shared. "A lot has happened since Torie's wedding."

"I guess," she said wistfully. "I went out of the country several times after Torie got married. We were going to catch up as soon as I got back to San Diego. Is Taylor part of this organization as well?"

"As of right now, no," I told her. "Taylor is just finishing her doctorate and working as a geologist for Montgomery Mining full-time. She's already told Hudson that she wants to be an advisor as soon as her doctoral studies are completed."

"An advisor?" she questioned. "Is that a volunteer?"

"Not exactly. She couldn't mention it before, but Taylor was a Last Hope rescue. She and Harlow were in the same hostage situation while they were working out in the field in Lania for Montgomery Mining," I explained. "Sometimes previous captives want to be involved in Last Hope after they recover. Who knows more about how to get through that recovery process than a previous hostage? We have some great advisors who are volunteers, but some are previous rescues, too. The trauma of being kidnapped extends way beyond physical recovery. Essentially, those advisors are there for aftercare. We also have some professionals, like counselors and physicians who know about Last Hope but keep our secret."

She was silent for a moment before she spoke again. "Are you telling me that you have an entire network set up to care for all of a victim's needs?"

"Yes," I said simply. "That network gets more complete every year. That's one of the biggest reasons we've been able to fly under the radar. We can't force anyone into treatment they don't want, but we haven't had anyone betray our existence yet."

"So, does the government know about Last Hope? You said Torie heard about it from the FBI."

"*Officially,* they don't know we exist. But yeah, they know. I think Marshall was so well respected when he was a special forces commander that nobody in the government wants to pull the plug on this operation. We try not to step on their toes when it's something they're willing to handle. In return, they pretend they've never heard of us. In all honesty, we're pretty sure we get unofficial tip-offs from them sometimes when there's nothing they can do, but we can't prove it."

She rubbed her temples distractedly as she said, "God, this is all so crazy. Taylor and Harlow never mentioned their kidnapping for obvious reasons. Even though I'm an investigative journalist involved in foreign affairs, I never heard a peep about the organization."

"We like to keep it that way," I replied honestly. "None of us are in it for the recognition or notoriety. We think what we do is important. We fill in a gap that needs to be filled. Hopefully, no one will ever hear about what happened to you, either. We went with a cover story since you'd already been reported as a missing person, and the authorities had apprehended and imprisoned your captors."

"I'll do whatever you want," she answered immediately. "I wouldn't ever want to jeopardize the existence of Last Hope. They saved my life. You and Wyatt saved my life. Torie did, too, since she's the one who took my disappearance to Marshall. You were right. The government wheels were turning too slowly. I would have died out there in the jungle before they even realized I was kidnapped. God, it's possible they never would have figured it out."

"I promised you I'd be truthful with you," I said carefully. "Time wasn't on your side, and we knew it. If you hadn't gotten treatment…"

Fuck! I didn't even want to think about what could have happened if she'd remained a prisoner for even a few more days.

"I would have died of sepsis," she finished softly. "Do you think I don't know that? I knew I was slowly dying, Chase. Most of my hopes of getting rescued were already gone. I owe Last Hope, you, Torie, and Wyatt more than I can ever possibly repay."

"Seeing you get well again is payment enough," I said gruffly.

She sighed. "You know I'll cooperate with anything I need to do to help Last Hope. Will you need to find me an advisor to guide me through this?"

"Nope. You already have one," I informed her.

"Torie?" she queried.

"She's too new in the organization to handle that duty," I said hoarsely. "The best person for that job would be...me."

Chapter 7

Savannah

I nearly choked on my tongue when he told me that he was going to act as my advisor. "You've already done enough for me, Chase. You've spent the last two weeks rescuing and taking care of me already. Between Durand Industries and Last Hope, you must be insanely busy."

After all that had happened, all I wanted to do was stay close to the man who had saved my life.

Even if I *did* hate being dependent on anyone else except myself, I had been scared, I had needed someone to lean on, and I had nearly died.

Chase had been there every time I'd woken in the hospital terrified and vulnerable, but clinging to him like a lifeline now that I knew I was going to recover wasn't exactly fair to him.

He had a life.

Yes, he was my best friend's brother and I'd known him for most of my life, but we weren't exactly...friends.

"I'm not turning your well-being over to someone else, Vanna," he said huskily. "It's too important. You're stuck with me, whether you like it or not. I'm taking some time off from Durand with Wyatt's blessing. I can work from home while you recover. Torie will be close by, too. She and Cooper are within walking distance of my place."

Wait! He couldn't possibly think I'd put him out by staying at his home, could he?

"I can't stay with you, Chase," I said adamantly.

"Why not?" he asked, his expression perplexed. "You haven't found a place of your own yet in San Diego. Where else are you going to stay? Someone needs to be available if you need help, and Torie's at her job with the university during the day."

"I'll find something," I said, trying to put my foot down with this stubborn man.

I wasn't the type of woman who ever counted on someone else. Ever. And Chase had already done so much for me.

"Not right now," he insisted. "Jesus Christ, Savannah! You're in no condition to be looking for a new home. Be reasonable."

My immediate plan had been to get a decent hotel room until I could find something a little more permanent. It would be small and easy to get around. Okay, so that probably wasn't a possibility he wanted to hear about right now.

"I—I'll think of a solution," I sputtered. "I'll get something temporary until—"

"Not happening," he interrupted. "You're a friend and I've got a big place."

"How are you going to explain my presence to whoever you're dating?" I questioned, feeling desperate for a good excuse, but dreading his answer just the same.

"I don't have to since I'm not seeing *anyone*," he said stubbornly. "You did mention that you didn't want to intrude on the newlyweds. I know Torie would take a leave of absence from her job at the university, but that's not necessary since I'm willing and available."

I didn't even want to acknowledge the ridiculous amount of relief I felt after his answer.

Shit! Now what could I say?

He was right. Really, I had nowhere else to go at the moment. Before the kidnapping, I'd been planning to get back to San Diego perfectly healthy and finally find a new place as soon as possible.

Getting kidnapped, injured, and sick had screwed up those plans completely.

I was so weak right now I could barely get out of bed to pee, much less go traipsing around San Diego trying to find a new home.

I was sensible. I did need time to recover. I just didn't want to be a burden to Chase after all he'd done for me.

Honestly, our relationship had changed. I really couldn't say he *wasn't* a friend anymore. Not after all he'd gone through with me during the last few weeks.

Unfortunately, the friendship was pretty one-sided at this point. Really, what had I done to help *him*?

"I'll try not to be too much trouble," I conceded reluctantly. "As soon as I'm well enough, I'll start looking for my own place. I should have done that a long time ago."

I startled when Chase gently wrapped his larger hand around mine. "You'll never be an inconvenience, Vanna. I'd be honored to be a friend and advisor to you. You didn't ask for this. You were just trying to do your job. It never should have happened."

I savored the warmth of physical contact as I let out an anxious breath. Chase had become my support, both physically and mentally. I had no idea how to break that habit, and I wasn't sure I wanted to right now. "Oh, God, my crew."

Jen, my producer, was probably worried to death, along with the rest of the small crew I'd had with me in Bajo Chiquito.

"Your producer was frantic," Chase confirmed. "Everyone who works close to you at *Deadline America* was relieved to find out that you were going to be okay. Marshall didn't tell them much. Just that you got lost, and had been kidnapped in the jungle. He also said that you'd later been found by hikers after you'd escaped your kidnappers and that you'd been sent to Panama City to recover. That's the cover story. We'll work out the details of how you got lost later."

"I'm not sure that Jen will completely buy the fact that I got lost," I told him skeptically. "She's been my producer for years. We follow a lot of safety protocols that don't include being stupid enough to wander away from our base station after dark."

He squeezed my hand as he said, "You'd be surprised at how creative Marshall can be when it comes to making up believable cover stories. He'll twist it until it suits your personality. Trust me."

"You're right," I agreed. "That's probably the least of my worries."

"No worries," Chase insisted. "We *will* work everything out. We've gotten very good at covering our asses on the details."

"I have a job to do, Chase," I said regretfully. "I have to do narration in the studio to fill in gaps for this special report about the Darien Gap before it's finished. I was done with all my interviews, and we were actually getting ready to leave for the States the following day, but it's not ready to air yet."

"That can wait until you're healthy," Chase grumbled. "Relax, Vanna. Are you worried about money? If you are, I can—"

"No!" I said hastily. "It's not the money. I'm fine financially."

I'd made good money over the years, and I'd just sold my mother's house not long ago. Cable news didn't pay me like I was an A-list movie star, but I had more than enough money in the bank to sustain me for now.

"Then what are you worried about?" Chase inquired gently.

Tears began to roll down my cheeks as I whimpered, "I don't know. This whole experience just feels overwhelming right now. I'm anxious about everything, and that's not like me."

I felt weak, raw, and vulnerable.

I felt completely unable to bury my emotions when I was around Chase, and *that* was terrifying for me.

He let go of my hand and wrapped a strong arm around my waist. "It's totally normal for you to feel that way," he informed me huskily. "You've been through hell, sweetheart, emotionally and physically."

God, I really loved it when he called me by some of his sweet pet names, even though I knew it was just a friendship comfort thing.

I really was pathetic.

I let out a long, anxious breath, leaned my head against his shoulder and savored the feel of his warm, strong body as he cradled me against him.

For now, I'd allow myself to take comfort in Chase's friendship and confidence that things would be all right and that I'd get through this. I didn't have the strength to do anything else.

If he wanted to be my friend and my advisor, I'd accept that because I needed that more than I needed to obsess about my attraction to him. Besides, sex was the last thing on my mind at the moment.

"Talk to me, Vanna," Chase encouraged as he stroked my hair.

"I remember so little about what happened, Chase. I can recall what happened the day of the kidnapping, and how I was taken right after I came out of the shower area. It was so warm that day, and I spent more time in the shower than I should have. But it was right next to our sleeping quarters, so I didn't have to walk more than a few steps to get to the stairs that led up to the small building we were occupying. Everything happened so fast. Night was falling and they came up behind me. One of them slapped a hand over my mouth before I could scream for help. Another one punched me until I was so dazed I couldn't even think. I had no choice but to start walking into the jungle with them. It was more like they were carrying me than me actually walking when we left Bajo Chiquito."

"How did your feet get so torn up?" he asked.

I cringed. My feet were a mess, although they were much better than they had been.

"Once I realized exactly what was happening, I tried to escape several times. I knew if I didn't, I was going to die or be trafficked until I *wished* I was dead. I wasn't sure I cared if they shot me. So they took my boots. I had to walk through the jungle without them. It was daylight before we got to their makeshift camp," I explained, the terror I'd felt rushing back to me. "When they tried to tie me up before tossing me into a tent, I tried to make my escape again, boots or no boots. I knew it was my last chance. It didn't take them long to catch me and yank my arms together to finish tying me up. That's when my shoulder got dislocated. They beat me until I lost consciousness. When I came to after that, they started to drug me. I'd wake up occasionally, but the moment they knew I was conscious, they'd kick me around and drug me again. Other than those brief moments when I woke up so thirsty I was ready to beg for water, everything else is a blank. They gave me just enough water to stay alive, and I started losing track of time. By the time you and Wyatt came, I was so confused that I wasn't sure if you were there to help me or to finish me off."

"It's not unusual for you to think that," he replied as I cuddled closer to his warmth. "Captives are often kept as weak and confused as possible so they don't resist."

"Will I ever remember more?" I asked apprehensively. "I hate not knowing what happened. It's like I lost an entire week of my life. I don't even know if they sexually assaulted me. The doctor said he saw no evidence that it happened, but he wasn't one hundred percent certain. They gave me preventative drugs and I'm still on antibiotics, but it will be a few months before they can definitively rule out HIV or hepatitis from a possible assault or dirty needles."

"I don't know if you'll remember anything else. Because of the large amount of drugs they gave you, it's possible that you won't," he said frankly. "And it's unlikely that you were sexually assaulted by those assholes if it wasn't evident. The way they treated you was brutal."

I was quiet as I let his words sink in.

"Thank you for being honest," I finally answered.

Ugly or not, I could count on Chase to be truthful. He'd been that way since day one, which was a huge relief to me because I preferred brutal honesty to bullshit right now.

"I told you I wouldn't lie to you," he reminded me. "Sometimes not knowing is scarier than getting the truth."

Exactly!

"Honestly," I said, my voice cracking with emotion. "I've never been so terrified. I've stepped into some of the most dangerous situations on the planet, but this is the first time I had no idea what to do."

It wasn't easy for me to admit that, but I knew Chase wasn't going to judge.

"Which is exactly why you need an advisor," he interjected. "It won't be this way forever, Vanna. It will just take a while to get back on your feet again. You're intelligent and entirely capable of taking care of yourself, but it's difficult to reason things out alone after you've been through something like this. That's why Last Hope has support services available long after a rescue is healed physically."

I had to admit that I was still having a hard time wrapping my head around a private rescue organization as sophisticated as Last Hope.

Or the fact that five filthy rich billionaires chose to dedicate most of their spare time to running that rescue organization.

Then again, maybe I shouldn't be all that surprised.

I didn't know the Montgomerys well, but the Durand family had never been pretentious or selfish. They'd always chosen love, duty, and family over money.

There had been absolutely no reason for Chase and Wyatt to go into the military. They'd always known that they would take over Durand Industries someday.

They'd gone simply because they wanted to serve their country.

Torie's father had been uneasy about his sons' safety, but he'd also never stopped talking about how proud he was of both of them.

"I think I'm pretty lucky to have you as my advisor," I said sincerely.

This side of Chase was utterly unfamiliar to me, but it was one I really wanted to get to know, attraction or no attraction.

For years, I'd tried to keep things superficial and light between the two of us.

I'd avoided getting to really know the man he'd become after we'd both grown up.

Now, I regretted not allowing myself to get any closer to a guy who was obviously worth knowing, even if it was difficult because I was attracted to him.

Maybe that's what happened when you got within a hair's breadth of dying. I knew I was probably going to start rethinking a lot of choices I'd made.

"You might say you're lucky to have me as an advisor *now*, but you may think I'm a pain in your ass in the future," he warned jokingly. "I'll be checking in with you a lot."

I yawned against his shoulder, suddenly feeling completely exhausted.

Chase slid off the headboard until his head was on the pillow, gently taking me down with him until my head was on his chest. "Sleep, Vanna," he rumbled. "Rest is your number one priority right now. Do you need something for pain?"

I shook my head as I closed my eyes. "No. Not right now."

I almost purred like a contented cat as Chase stroked a hand over my hair.

I'd much rather savor being this close to Chase without dulling my brain with pain medications.

Chapter 8

Savannah

"I still look really horrible," I told Torie two weeks later as we both viewed my recent haircut in the bathroom mirror. I ran my hand through what hair I had left with a sigh. "I do feel better though. Thank you for finding someone to cut my hair."

The angry looking lacerations on my face would eventually fade, but they'd always be visible. Chase had gotten me the best doctor available to try to repair those facial wounds in Panama, but they'd been days old and awkward cuts.

Torie had found a stylist to come cut my hair today because it was a mess. It had still been matted and tangled, even though I'd tried everything to fix it.

I'd finally given up and just asked the beautician to cut it right beneath my jawline in a shorter bob.

"It's adorable," Torie said with a smile. "It suits you. It's very sassy."

I rolled my eyes. I was glad I looked that way, but I didn't exactly feel like my old self again. "It's healthy," I emphasized. "And there's not a thing I can do about these scars." I traced one of those marks from the top of my cheek to where it ended beneath my chin.

Torie took my hand and led me into my bedroom at Chase's place. She sat and pulled me down beside her on the bed as she said, "I know how you feel. I remember feeling like my wounds would never heal. But they will, Vanna. You look so much better than you did two weeks ago."

I tried very hard not to whine too much since Torie had been through much worse, but I really did still feel horrible.

I snorted. "I've definitely gained some weight back. More than I need to, really. You never told me that your brother could cook."

Torie snickered. "Mom *made* both of them cook, clean, and do laundry as teenagers. She used to say there was nothing less attractive than a man who couldn't take care of himself. Honestly, I think Chase might be a better cook than I am. He actually enjoyed it. Wyatt cooks simply because he really likes to eat."

"He makes the most amazing crepes," I told her.

"*That* he learned from my father," Torie shared. "I don't think Dad ever met a crepe he didn't love, savory or sweet."

"I've had plenty of both, and the size of my ass is going to start showing it pretty soon," I informed her wistfully.

Torie frowned. "You're still lighter than you were before the kidnapping."

"Not for long if your brother keeps making those crepes," I joked. "When I told him that I couldn't possibly eat another crepe, he moved on to chicken stew and quiche. Honestly, everything he cooks is delicious, but I probably need a few salad nights. We're going to start sharing cooking duties. It's not like I'm working, and I'd really like to do something useful to help him."

"Those were also my dad's recipes," Torie confided. "He did love his French dishes, and so did we. Mom was more into American comfort food, which we definitely didn't mind, either."

"I remember," I told her fondly.

As wealthy as the Durand family was, they'd never had a cook. They made preparing an evening meal a family affair, and I'd been lucky enough to be included many times.

"You should just let him cook," Torie insisted. "Aren't you still doing physical therapy on your shoulder?"

I nodded. "I'll be done pretty soon. I have to baby it a little, but it's fine. Really. I need something to do to keep me busy."

The more idle I was, the more time I had to think, and none of those thoughts were positive at the moment.

"Please don't try to tell me you aren't working," Torie cautioned. "I saw you on your computer when I got here earlier."

I shrugged. "I'm just working on some of the voiceover narration text I need to do on the Darien Gap special."

"Do you ever stop working?" Torie asked in an exasperated tone.

"Not very often," I admitted. "But I love being a journalist, so it's not all work for me."

"You need to rest, Vanna, and that includes giving your mind a break. You need something to occupy your brain outside of work for a while," she advised. "That story is really important, but also very depressing."

"My counselor said the same thing," I said. "But I'm not sure she completely understands that work has *always* been the main thing on my mind. I've had to work really hard to get to where I am in my career."

"You're already successful, Vanna," Torie reminded me. "You can take some time off. Don't you ever get tired of spending your entire life working?"

I was silent for a moment before I finally answered truthfully, "I used to thrive on it, but I'm not so sure I always do anymore. I think I'm a little burned out. This particular story was heartbreaking. What those children had been through just getting to Bajo Chiquito was horrific. Some of them had lost their parents or siblings during the crossing, and some of the females were sexually assaulted. And they were just kids, Torie."

She took my hand. "You mostly cover humanitarian crises, Vanna. Anyone would be burned out from a decade of making those kinds of stories their life's work with nothing else pleasant in between."

I nodded because I knew Torie understood. "There's no joy in my life anymore, Torie. Right before I left for Panama, I tried to remember the last time I'd done something fun and failed miserably.

I know I'm doing something important by telling these stories, but my job has also eaten part of my soul because every one of those stories is about human misery. Living out of a suitcase all the time gets exhausting, too."

At one time, that travel and thirst for a story had motivated me. Lately, I was beginning to dread starting a new assignment right after the last one was finished.

She squeezed my hand. "You don't need anyone's permission to rest right now, Vanna, and I'm not talking about sleeping. I know you're tired of doing that. I know how traumatic it is to be kidnapped. Take that piece of your soul back. Make use of Chase's pool that he never uses. Watch a marathon of movies in his theater room. Take a glass of wine and watch the sunset. It really is okay to do…nothing important. You don't have to be saving the world every moment that you're awake. Save your sanity instead. If you don't take a break, I guarantee that job will eat the rest of your soul. No matter how strong you are, the trauma of what happened to you will catch up with you if you don't deal with it."

"You know I don't remember that much," I said weakly, knowing she was right.

"What you do remember is bad enough," Torie said, her expression troubled. "I also know how difficult it can be to wait a few months to make sure you're clear of STDs, hepatitis, and HIV."

"But they don't think—"

"Don't bullshit me, Vanna. We've been like sisters for way too long. You're thinking about that, no matter what the doctors said."

I nodded. "I can't help it. Even though I know the chances are small that I was sexually assaulted, there's also the needle situation because I was drugged so much. I know that seems crazy—"

"It doesn't," Torie assured me. "It's normal after what happened. I know you remember me whining about it."

I did, but her situation had been different. She'd known that she had been raped more than once.

She'd also been much worse off than me with her physical injuries. It had taken her a long time to heal both emotionally and physically.

"Your injuries were so horrible," I said in a tone full of remorse for all that Torie had suffered.

"That doesn't make what happened to you any less frightening or horrible. It also doesn't mean you don't need time to heal," she scolded. "I recognize post-traumatic stress when I see it, and you nearly jump out of your skin every time I enter a room behind you."

I closed my eyes and released a breath. I should have known that Torie would notice anything that was different about my behavior. It wasn't that I didn't *want* to share with her. She was my best friend. I just didn't want my experience to trigger memories of her own kidnapping.

She was so happy now.

I wanted her to stay that way.

"I was attacked from behind," I admitted as I opened my eyes again. "My therapist said it will take a while for those knee-jerk reactions to go away."

"Please don't be afraid to talk to me, Vanna," Torie said softly. "It took a long time, but I'm finally over my own experience. Helping you, listening to you isn't going to cause me to have flashbacks. You were there for me. I want to be here for you. Everyone processes trauma differently, but for women especially, a lot of our experiences are the same. I jumped at every little sound I didn't recognize, or every male voice that didn't belong to my brothers. Has everything been okay here with Chase? I know you've known him forever, but staying with him could be a little different."

I knew she was asking if the fact that I was staying with a man actually bothered me.

I shook my head. "He's been amazing, Torie. I don't think I could ever be afraid of him. Recognizing his voice in the darkness when he rescued me was the best thing I'd ever heard. I just feel more than a little guilty that I'm taking up space in his house. We were never exactly...friends. We were more like...friendly adversaries who loved to debate everything."

"And now?" she asked quietly.

"He's very generously offered his friendship and more," I said honestly. "It took a while for me to realize what a big commitment it was for him to offer himself up as my advisor."

"Oh, it is huge," Torie said with a sly smile. "Jax Montgomery was Harlow's advisor, and look where *they* are now."

I snorted. "They're married. That is definitely *not* going to happen. But being a Last Hope advisor is a responsibility that not every person would want to take on. Either that, or your brother takes the job very seriously. He makes sure I'm okay, no matter what I'm doing. He checks in with me emotionally about a gazillion times a day right now. You know me. I'm not exactly used to something like that, but I have to admit that it's comforting. And he worries about every single injury I have. He arranged for me to have *everything* I needed here. He even made sure that I got my suitcases and other things from my producer. He's even slugged through my storage space. The man cooks like a professional chef just so he can tempt me to eat. All that, and in his spare time, he runs one of the most profitable corporations on the planet and volunteers his time to a private rescue organization. He's disgustingly perfect."

Torie lifted a brow. "He's my brother, so I *know* he isn't a saint. He can be a bossy pest when he wants to be. So can Wyatt for that matter."

I laughed. "I know that side of him a little, but you know it a lot better since you're his little sister."

"But I also know that he's an amazing guy," she confessed. "I wish he could find a woman who could appreciate that."

My eyes scrutinized Torie's plaintive expression. "He said he's not seeing anyone. It sounds like it's been a while."

She shrugged. "No interest on his side. Something happened to Chase right before he got out of the military. I know he was injured, but that's about all I know. I was unreachable when it happened because I was doing a remote hiking trip without cell service. It took a while for me to even find out that he was injured, and he doesn't talk about it. Either that, or he can't talk about it because it was something top secret. He seems fine physically. He had a few casual dates after he joined Wyatt at Durand Industries, but it's like he just...gave up. I have no idea why because he's always loved women. All women of any age. One of his college girlfriends used to say he could charm the meanest woman in any room. I think she was right, but I haven't really seen that playful part of him in a long time."

I frowned, not liking the thought of Chase getting hurt. "Maybe he got dumped or some woman played him?" I suggested.

Even as I said those words, I couldn't imagine *any* female dropping Chase Durand for another guy. She'd have to be blind, a complete idiot, or both.

"I suppose it could happen," Torie agreed. "But I find it hard to believe a woman could find a better catch. He's filthy rich, well-educated, he used to know how to have fun, and I suppose some women would think he's hot. Ew...it's hard for me to think of my brother that way."

I snickered. "Take my word for it, as a woman who *isn't* his sister, he's ridiculously hot." I let out a small cough once I realized what I'd just said. "Well, he would be to other women. Aesthetically speaking, I mean."

Torie zoomed in on my mistake immediately. "You think he's attractive?"

"I might not be interested, but I'm not blind," I said hastily.

"What if I said that he thinks you're attractive, too," she fished, sounding slightly hesitant.

My eyes widened. "I'd say you were completely out of your mind. Chase wants to be my friend and advisor. That's all. God, what kind of crazy man would take a look at me right now and be anything except repulsed? I look like something the cat dragged in after playing with it for days."

"Attraction is more than just physical," Torie pointed out.

I held a hand up. "Stop! Chase and I are friends. We are not attracted to each other that way, Torie."

Okay, maybe I did secretly lust after Chase Durand, but it wasn't something I was about to share with Torie. She'd hound me with hints about a possible relationship with her brother forever.

She made no bones about the fact that she wanted Chase and Wyatt to find a good woman.

Her trying to hook the two of us up would be embarrassing considering that Chase Durand would never look at me that way.

He was protective, caring, and considerate about getting me everything I needed right now. Chase listened to me with the concern of a friend who didn't want to see me in pain.

He did not, however, look at me like he wanted to get me naked. Not now, or any time previously, for as long as I'd known him.

"Okay," she agreed amiably. "I'll try not to say that I told you so someday."

"Thanks a lot," I muttered, dismissing her warning.

"You do enjoy his company though, right?" she persisted.

Really, how could I not like Chase Durand? Especially after everything he was doing for me. "Every minute we spend together," I said honestly. "There's something about Chase that makes me feel... safe. As an advisor, he's made me feel so comfortable that I can tell him almost anything about my kidnapping and know that he won't judge. You know that's big for me. I'm usually not all that trusting."

Torie nodded. "Feeling safe is good after what you've been through. *Nobody* involved in Last Hope would ever judge you, Vanna. We volunteer for a reason. Everyone wants to help."

I shook my head as I answered, "It's still hard to believe that such an organization even exists. Don't get me wrong, I'm grateful that Last Hope was started and continued to grow. But I have to admit the things they're capable of doing and the thought they put into every rescue is a little overwhelming."

"We have some pretty amazing volunteers all over the world," Torie informed me. "And Marshall runs Last Hope like his life depends on it. I discover something new that I didn't know about Last Hope almost every single day. It's definitely unique and pretty awesome."

"You like being a volunteer?" I questioned.

"I do," Torie replied immediately. "I think volunteering gives me a chance to turn a negative thing into a positive."

I sighed. "I wish I had a special skill I could volunteer."

B. A. Scott

Torie groaned, "Please. You have a million special skills, but this is your time to just be a rescue and recover. Let us take care of you right now."

To my horror, I felt tears filling my eyes. "Thank you. God, I hate feeling this helpless, useless, and afraid of everything. You know me, Torie. I had every minute of my day planned with work issues. I didn't have time to be idle."

"Which wasn't necessarily a good thing," she pointed out as she wrapped her arms around me. "Everything will be okay, Vanna. I promise. Getting your head back together is the hardest part."

I wrapped my arms around my best friend and hugged her hard.

"I'm not even sure if I'm the same person anymore," I muttered.

"You are the same intelligent, brave, talented woman you were before," Torie argued. "I think going through this kind of nightmare changes everyone to some extent, but you're still the Vanna I know and love. You said those same words to me when I was still recovering. I made it, Vanna. Granted, I'm a little different and slightly more wary, but even stronger than I was before. This won't change the core of who you are."

As I continued to cry, I wondered what I would have done without Torie and Chase.

I'd spent most of my adult life running around the world chasing stories, and I had no close family left.

"Do you know how lucky I feel to have you as a best friend?" I asked her tearfully.

She chuckled a little as she continued to hug me tight. "That's because I haven't really been a pain in your ass yet. You've never been around long enough for that to happen," she cautioned. "I've missed you so much, Vanna. I'm glad you're home."

I'd missed her, too. More than she'd probably ever know because she was really all I had other than my co-workers, and I really wasn't personally that close to any of them.

"I missed you, and I'm glad to be home, too," I said earnestly.

Strangely enough, I truly meant those words.

After a decade of traveling continuously, and a horrific experience that had nearly taken my life, there wasn't anywhere else I wanted to be.

Chapter 9

Chase

"I thought I heard Vanna crying when I went upstairs earlier," I said to Torie as she walked into my home office.

I'd known that my sister was with Vanna, and I hadn't wanted to interrupt, but I was concerned.

"She was," my sister said vaguely as she sat down in a chair in front of my desk. "I doubt that's something you haven't seen before. You spent a lot of time with her while she was recovering in Panama, and now here."

I shook my head, my chest tightening at the thought of Vanna being in so much pain that she was actually...crying. "Honestly, I haven't seen her shed a tear since she's been here. It was even rare during her recovery in the hospital."

I wasn't sure if I should be worried or offended that Vanna couldn't share that sorrow with me. After all, I was her advisor.

"She's fine," Torie said lightly. "She's in the gym doing her physical therapy."

I frowned. "Are you sure she's okay?"

I'd seen Vanna troubled.

I'd seen her frightened.

I'd seen every sign of her PTSD that still seemed to be bothering her.

I'd realized shortly after she'd arrived back home that I couldn't approach her from behind because it would sometimes cause a flashback.

She talked to me as her advisor about her kidnapping. I couldn't complain about her lack of candidness. But I couldn't help but think that she might be leaving out some things that didn't involve her kidnapping. Of course, I really hadn't gone there with her, either.

Torie nodded. "She will be okay, and Vanna rarely cries. You know it takes a while to work through what happened. I think she's scared."

"Of what?" I asked. "I'm doing everything I can to protect her."

She shook her head slowly. "It's not just that. You have to understand that Vanna dedicated her entire life to her career. She was starting to burn out, even before she was kidnapped. She never really talked about it before the kidnapping, but I could tell. She was emotionally and physically exhausted. Constantly being thrown into the worst things that can happen to people over and over is soul sucking, and Vanna never gave herself a chance to pause. She never experienced fun or relaxing things in her life. God, she's never even taken a real vacation since she became an adult. The only time off she ever took was to take care of me."

"I didn't know that," I told her remorsefully.

Torie's information made me wonder whether Vanna really took a few days in Vegas to sit by the pool or to go to the spa. Knowing her like I did now, I was pretty sure she probably worked in her hotel room until it was time to move to her next assignment.

"It's not your fault," she said reassuringly. "She never even admitted that to me until just now. She was sucked dry by her career, I think. Add her kidnapping on top of that, and I doubt she feels like she has *anything* left in the tank."

Fuck! I realized that her current situation had to be hard for a woman like Vanna. She'd spent her life in complete control of her destiny. She never faltered. She never flinched at any kind of challenge, regardless of the fact that she was completely wiped out. To suddenly realize that she didn't have the strength left to fight because her life had spun out of control had to be heartbreaking for her.

Didn't she realize that everyone had a breaking point?

"Then we'll just have to fill her up again," I told my sister.

"It might not be that simple," Torie said thoughtfully. "She's not just tired, Chase. I think her spirit is crushed."

"Fuck that!" I grumbled. "A woman as strong as Vanna will definitely recover. She just needs some time."

"What she needs is some happiness in her life," Torie said adamantly. "Once she's well enough physically and emotionally, she's going to want to go right back to work again. God, she's *still* working on her story for the Darien Gap, even though she's not completely recovered. Can you imagine how much that only adds to her depression right now? I'm going to do everything I can to make her remember what it's like to just have some fun before she completely loses herself to her work again."

"She doesn't have any time to relax? Not at all?" I questioned, suddenly realizing how little I knew about Vanna's life *after* childhood.

The woman had an incredibly stressful job. How was it possible to go from one assignment to the other without a break? Nobody was that superhuman.

"Never," Torie responded. "Bradley was a total jerk, and I don't think he ever cared about making Vanna happy. The other few guys she's dated seriously were in the same business as Vanna and were probably workaholics just like her. Vanna has always had zero work/life balance. And no one who really cared about her mental well-being except me. That's always bothered me. Underneath that tough exterior, she's a woman who feels enormous empathy for people who are suffering. I was afraid the way she was working would take a toll on her psyche someday."

"What else can I do to help her?" I queried huskily.

Hell, I was her advisor, but truthfully, there wasn't much I wouldn't do for Vanna, advisor or not.

"I think she'll figure everything out," Torie pondered. "I think she's reached her breaking point because of the kidnapping. At least she can admit that she's totally burned out now."

"Tell me," I said through clenched teeth.

If Torie knew how to fix things, I wanted to know, too.

"She needs something in her life other than work," Torie considered thoughtfully. "Vanna has no idea how to do something for pure enjoyment anymore, and she's really beating herself up. That needs to stop. Right now, she feels ugly because of her scars. She got a new haircut today. We ended up cutting most of her hair off because nothing we did fixed the permanent damage."

"Her scars aren't bad," I said firmly. "She'll always be beautiful. And who gives a shit about her haircut?"

Torie shot me a dubious look. "Try telling that to a woman who's been through hell and is just recovering from that nightmare. Believe me, she doesn't *feel* beautiful, and I totally get that."

I ran a frustrated hand through my hair. "Maybe I've been going about my advisor duties all wrong."

"No, Chase," Torie said softly. "This isn't about you. You've been really good to her. You've been there whenever she needed to talk about the kidnapping. This is about Vanna and what she's going through. I'm just telling you most of what I know so you can understand her situation better."

"Most of what you know?" I questioned. "What are you leaving out?"

"Only the parts that have nothing to do with her recovery," she hedged. "There are some things best friends don't share with anyone else."

"I need to know what to do to fix this, Torie," I said huskily.

Hell, I wanted Vanna to be happy, too.

"Take her outside with a glass of wine to watch the sunset," Torie replied. "Let her know that even if her scars never completely disappear, that she's still beautiful."

"I can do that," I agreed.

It had never occurred to me that Vanna might have some physical insecurities after what had happened to her. Probably because I would never be able to see her as anything less than stunning, no matter how many scars she had or how she cut her fucking hair.

Hell, ever since I'd realized how much I wanted to spend more time with her at Torie's wedding, that compulsion wouldn't leave me alone.

I'd tried to give her some space, even though we were living in the same house.

I thought she'd need time to herself in between her visits from therapists and Torie.

"She *does not* need to be alone right now," Torie mentioned as though she'd read my mind. "What she really needs is to keep her mind occupied with something other than work and the kidnapping. The last thing she needs is more time to think or work."

"I've been trying to make sure she has everything she needs," I explained.

"And you've been doing a wonderful job as her advisor," Torie agreed. "Physically, she's getting stronger every day. Sadly, I think she could use another companion. Vanna and I are too close. She went through a lot of my recovery process with me. Now that I'm ecstatically happy with a wonderful husband, I think she's worried that if she shares what's on her mind, it will trigger me or make me unhappy. I think we both know that's ridiculous, but in her mind, she never wants to see me like that again. I get that, Chase. It kills me to see her like this, too."

"Maybe you are too close to the situation," I considered.

She shot me a dubious look as she continued, "I'm not so sure you can be totally objective, either, but I think you could be one hell of a distraction to her if you wanted to be."

"I'm not quite sure what you mean by that," I answered.

"Oh, come on, Chase," she said, sounding exasperated. "I know Vanna isn't just some kind of project for you. You care about her."

"Probably more than I should," I replied, my voice graveled and rough. "But that doesn't mean that she needs me to be in her face all the time, right?"

"Honestly, I think that might be *exactly* what she needs," Torie said thoughtfully. "Vanna hasn't had anyone except me who really cares about her in a long time. She was devastated when she lost her mom. I think she's spent a lot of time running away from her loneliness. I think she became a workaholic so she didn't have to deal with the fact that she had nobody and no close family left."

"She obviously trusted Bradley," I said defensively, still wanting to tear that bastard's head off for hurting Vanna.

Torie snorted. "No, she didn't. I think he was safe for her because he didn't demand much of her emotionally. He hurt her and humiliated her, but it could have been a lot worse. She wasn't in love with him, and they spent very little time in the same place. She deserves a whole lot better."

"I'm not going to argue with you about that," I told her. "But that doesn't mean she wants to see *my* face all the time, either. I told you what happened when I asked her to spend a day with me. She couldn't get out of that hotel suite fast enough."

I wanted to be her friend, but I also didn't want to make her feel like she *had* to accept my company if she needed her privacy.

"Self-preservation," she threw back nonchalantly. "I don't believe for a single second that she wasn't tempted to accept, but she avoids any guy with a heart like the plague. Those actions are defense mechanisms, Chase. If she found a guy who was really crazy about her and *wanted* to be with her, I'm not sure she'd know how to handle that situation. She's convinced that she won't find anyone because she spends most her time wading through war zones and catastrophic situations in boots and dirty jeans. I guess she thinks all guys want supermodel partners who look gorgeous all the time."

"You're joking," I said, dumbfounded.

"I wish I was," she shared. "But you have to admit, you've dated your share of the supermodel type."

"Only because they've been pretty plentiful in the world of fashion and the luxury products that Durand is famous for producing," I shot back. "And as you've probably noticed, none of those relationships have worked out."

"I think you've just never met the right woman," Torie considered. "I'm not saying that there aren't brilliant supermodels who know how to care about someone. But I grew up in the same world you did, Chase. Genuine people were the exception and not the rule in high fashion and luxury products. It's a really competitive, cutthroat industry. Dad loved it because he appreciated quality goods, and he managed to blow off the rest of it. He played the game, but he was never emotionally invested in it."

"Wyatt and I learned from the master," I said drily. "Do you think we don't feel the same way? The only thing that matters is the products."

"I know you do," Torie said softly. "I'm just saying that maybe it's time to spend some time outside of the artificial glitz and glamor. Durand is just as successful as it's always been. You and Wyatt don't need to spend any more time proving that. I'm just saying that you may not find what you're really looking for while you're completely submersed in that world. Most of the beauty there is extremely superficial."

Like I didn't know that already?

"Maybe that's why I'm not looking anymore," I said shortly.

"You were interested in Vanna," she prompted.

"And that interest wasn't returned," I stated firmly. "Let it go, Torie. Asking her out was a mistake. I've known her since she was a child. Right now, my biggest concern is seeing her get well again."

"Don't tell me you don't care about her happiness, too," Torie warned.

I slammed my fist onto the desk, frustrated with the conversation. "Of course I care! I just have no fucking idea how to make her happy, and I'm not convinced that she *wants* to spend more time with me than absolutely necessary."

I knew something wasn't right with Vanna, but I couldn't force her to tell me what was wrong. And I wasn't about to make her endure my company if she didn't want that. She'd been through enough.

Torie folded her arms across her chest. "You can be incredibly charming when you choose to be," she told me. "Our parents taught us how to enjoy life. Show Vanna how to do that, too."

I let out a beleaguered breath before I said, "I'm not sure I remember how to do that myself anymore."

Hell, about all Wyatt and I had done for the last several years was work.

"Of course you do," Torie scolded. "It's ingrained in us because we were raised that way. You just haven't practiced it for a while. You're a stubborn guy, Chase. You've never hesitated if you wanted something. Be persistent. I think Vanna backed away from you because she was scared, not because she didn't want to spend time with you."

"I'm trying to be her friend and advisor," I protested.

"And how's that working out?" she pushed.

Fuck! I knew it completely sucked, but I didn't have a lot of options.

There were things Torie didn't know about and didn't understand, and I wasn't about to try to explain *that* to my sister.

Not now.

Probably not...ever.

"It's working out well enough," I shot back irritably.

She stood as she said, "Keep telling yourself that. Maybe you'll start to believe it."

"What in the hell do you want me to do?" I asked sharply.

She glared at me. "If the way you feel about Vanna has really changed, then nothing. But if you care about her, now's the time to show her. She could use some of that right now."

"I care, dammit!" I growled.

Torie shot me a satisfied smile. "Then be the relentless brother I know and love."

Without another word, my little sister sauntered out of my office and closed the door behind her.

I leaned back in my office chair with a groan, feeling like my guts had been turned inside out.

Maybe I *had* made a mistake by limiting the length of time I spent with Vanna.

I was under the impression that she wanted it that way while she tried to get herself back together physically and emotionally.

She already had people coming in and out of the house every day to try to help her heal.

But what if she really is lonely and needs someone beside her who gives a shit about what happens to her?

It wasn't like I didn't wonder how she was doing every fucking moment of the day right now.

So much of what Torie had said made sense. Well, except for the part where she assumed that Vanna had ran away from me in Vegas because she was scared.

Vanna Anderson had never had an issue telling me exactly how she felt.

Except…she *had* seemed a little off-kilter that day, especially after I'd asked her to spend the next day with me.

Her rejection had nagged at me ever since, but I'd never considered that I'd simply made her uncomfortable because I wasn't the kind of guy she normally dated.

Fuck it! I had promised to be her friend and advisor.

Yeah, I'd done my duty as an advisor, but I'd hesitated to push myself on her to be a friend.

What if Torie is right? What if Vanna really needs someone other than her best friend right now? What if distance is the last thing she needs at this point in her recovery? What if having a male friend to tell her she's gorgeous would actually help her?

If Vanna needed someone, I'd gladly give her everything I had.

Problem was, I just wasn't quite sure how to offer it.

Suddenly, my sister's words broke through my hesitancy.

Our parents showed us how to enjoy life. Show Vanna how to do that.

I grinned as memories flooded through my brain.

Maybe I hadn't practiced enjoying life nearly enough lately, but there were some things that a guy could never truly forget.

Chapter 10

Savannah

"Red or white?" Chase asked me after we finished dinner. My eyes shot from the dishes I'd just finished loading into the dishwasher to Chase, who was standing near the sink weighing a bottle of wine in each hand.

My heart skittered as I saw the mischievous grin on his face.

It had been a long time since I'd seen that particular smile.

It was also the first time he'd lingered in the kitchen once we'd finished dinner.

His company was always entertaining at our evening meal, but he generally retreated to his office once we'd finished.

"Oh," I said, surprised. "I really don't need—"

"Red or white?" he asked insistently. "Choose or I'll be happy to choose one for us. I know you're not a wine hater. I've seen you drink a glass or two before."

"Red?" I said uncertainly.

He nodded as he put down the white. "Good choice. I have an excellent, full-bodied Bordeaux from a small winery in France."

I watched, completely fascinated as he expertly removed the cork, put a small amount in a glass, sniffed the contents, and then swirled the liquid around. For some reason, I held my breath as he took a sip.

He continued to smile as he pronounced, "It's acceptable."

I took a large, beautiful wine glass from him that he only filled about halfway to the brim.

"Are you rationing my wine?" I asked with a small laugh.

He shook his head as he picked up his own glass that was filled similarly to mine. "Not at all," he protested. "To appreciate a wine, you have to be able to enjoy the whole experience. Swirl it, smell it, and taste it. Don't swallow the first sip right away. This one is meant to be savored."

I took a small sip and let it roll over my taste buds for a few seconds.

I'd never actually taken the time to recognize the very first burst of distinct flavors of a vintage, but I closed my eyes before I finally swallowed. "It's incredible," I informed him as I licked my lower lip.

"What did you taste?" he asked curiously.

"Black current and plums," I shared. "It's really...earthy."

He chuckled. "That could be good or bad."

I smiled at him. "It's definitely good. I drink wine occasionally. Some I like. Some I don't like. I've never really stopped to recognize specific tastes."

"I don't think I've done it for a long time, either," Chase said thoughtfully. "It's taken a while for me to remember that anything enjoyable is worth drawing out for as long as possible."

He closed the dishwasher and took my hand before I could respond to his comment. "Where are we going?" I questioned suspiciously.

"It's winter in San Diego, Vanna. There's nothing like a good wine and a beautiful sunset," he answered as he proceeded to pull me toward the sliding glass doors to the patio.

I felt the coolness of the evening as soon as he opened the door. "Chase, I don't even have my shoes on."

He took both of our wine glasses and set them on a side table on the patio between two lounge chairs. Then, he snagged me around the waist and swung me up into his arms like my weight was virtually nothing to him. "No need for shoes," he said huskily. "I'm here for transport."

He dropped me gently into a lounge chair and wrapped me up in a fleecy blanket before he took his own seat in a matching lounger on the other side of the small outdoor table.

I was still breathless as I picked up my wine and snuggled into the blanket. "I'm starting to think you've lost your mind," I muttered with no hint of criticism in my tone.

"Absolutely not true," he countered. "I'd have to be crazy *not* to want to spend time with a beautiful woman watching a winter sunset."

He was right. Sunsets seemed more spectacular this time of year in San Diego for a variety of reasons. I'd noticed that when I was a child. Since then, I hadn't really taken the time to watch a sunset anywhere.

Okay, maybe the sunset is pretty, but he is definitely missing the beautiful woman part of the equation.

"No work in the office tonight?" I asked nervously, wondering why Chase was breaking from his usual routine.

"Nope," he answered, sounding like he was perfectly content exactly where he was at the moment. "Relax, Vanna. Are you warm enough?"

"Yes," I squeaked before I took another sip of my wine.

Relaxing wasn't exactly my forte or something I knew how to do. Especially not with someone like...Chase.

"It's a beautiful night," he commented as he leaned back in his chair.

I finally pulled my eyes from him and focused on the sky.

It was alight with reds and golds that swirled together until you couldn't tell where one color ended and the other began.

I took a deep breath, noting that while there was a slight chill in the air, it wasn't exactly freezing out here.

"It *is* really pleasant," I agreed, finally allowing myself to unwind a little.

Chase had a beautiful waterfront home, and between the distant cadence of the waves and the blindingly gorgeous sunset, I felt a little mesmerized.

A comfortable silence settled between Chase and I while we drank our wine and watched the sun slowly drop out of sight.

"That was incredible," I murmured after the light left the sky.

Chase picked up a remote from the table and turned on a muted light, just enough so I could see his face as he grinned.

"It was good enough to draw out as long as possible, right?" he asked jokingly.

I nodded, still not used to this new and different Chase Durand. "It was."

"Now that it's over, tell me how you're really doing, Vanna," Chase said in a more serious tone. "Your body is healing. It's just a matter of time. I want to know how you feel."

"About the kidnapping?" I asked since we rarely discussed anything else.

"About anything and everything," he corrected.

Uncomfortable with the intensity in his expression, I turned my head toward the lights of a few boats sitting out on the water. "Chase, you're so busy—"

"Don't," Chase growled. "You said something similar when I asked you to spend time with me in Vegas. I'm *not* too busy to listen to you. I'm *not* too busy to spend time with you. I'm *not* too busy to give a shit whether or not you're okay emotionally, and that's not limited to your kidnapping, Vanna. I'm *not* asking as a CEO of Durand. I'm asking as a guy who cares about you."

I opened my mouth to protest, but ended up closing it without saying a word.

I wanted to tell him everything he was asking for, but I wasn't quite sure how to really talk to Chase about anything other than the kidnapping.

I finally responded. "I don't know how to communicate with you if we're not in the middle of a debate or talking about my issues from the kidnapping," I confessed.

"It's quite simple," he cajoled. "Just open your mouth and tell me what's on your mind. I plan on being honest with you. I wanted to spend time with you in Vegas. That desire hasn't changed for me."

I snorted. "I was alone there. You were just trying to be nice."

"If I remember correctly, I was going to be alone there, too," he corrected. "Did it never occur to you that I just wanted to spend some time with you doing something other than arguing a current events topic?"

"No," I answered truthfully.

"I did. Still do."

I shook my head. "Then I have no idea why."

"I'm not sure you'd want me to answer that question candidly," he answered. "Let's just say I prefer your company to my own. Maybe I don't like being alone all the time."

God, I could relate to that. I felt the same way.

"But you have *your family*," I disagreed. "And when is a billionaire in your industry ever really alone?"

It was ludicrous to think that a man like Chase Durand couldn't get the attention of dozens of people if he wanted it.

"Have you never been in a crowded room and still felt lonely?" he asked hoarsely. "Like something or someone was missing?"

My breath caught.

I'd felt that way more times than I could count. But Chase...

"Don't get me wrong," he clarified. "I love my family, but Torie has Cooper now, and Wyatt isn't exactly a talker. Yes, I can find company, but I doubt I'd get it for the right reasons. That day in Vegas, all I really wanted was to spend time with you. Not because I felt sorry for you. I was feeling sorry for myself because it had been a long time since I'd been with a woman who saw me and not my money."

I looked at him in surprise. "Do you really think that's all you have to offer a woman?"

He shrugged. "No. Unfortunately, that's generally the first thing they notice."

I really wanted to argue with that observation, but I didn't.

Chase Durand could reel a woman in for a multitude of reasons other than his bank account. But it was probably true that the first thing people thought about when they met him was his wealth and power.

My heart ached at the thought of Chase being as lonely as I felt sometimes. "Did you really want to hang out with a woman who spends most of her time slugging around horrible locations in mud boots and with very little makeup on unless she's on camera?"

"More than anything," he answered promptly. "You broke my heart when you ran away without looking back."

I burst into laughter. "Now you're just being facetious."

"You don't believe me?" he questioned with mock indignation.

"Not for a moment," I shot back. "But I totally get the loneliness thing. If you really want to know the truth, I think I'm experiencing severe burnout in my career."

I went on to explain what I'd talked about earlier with Torie.

Chase listened intently until I was finished.

"A person can only give for so long before they have to find a way to blow off steam and replenish the energy they've lost," Chase mused.

A tear rolled down my cheek as I said, "I think I'm completely empty. I was struggling a little before the kidnapping. Now I feel totally lost, Chase. I'm afraid of my own damn shadow now, and I hate that. I love being an investigative journalist, but I'm not sure I love running from place to place constantly. Just the thought of going on my next assignment makes me nauseous. I don't know how to fix this."

He stood, picked me up, blanket and all, and then settled back into his chair with me on his lap. "We'll fix it together, sweetheart. I'll help you work through those issues one by one. I guess we both need to go looking for our *joie de vivre*."

I laid my head on his shoulder and sighed, loving the way he could pronounce that phrase like a native French speaker. "I'm afraid that mine flew away a long time ago. You?"

"Not so long ago that I can't find it if I look," Chase said with a chuckle. "I think I probably did a better job at finding enjoyable things to do with my off time when I was in the military. There were always other guys around looking to blow off some steam or shake off the stress."

"If you think I'm going to go out and sprint for five miles with you for fun, you're out of your mind," I warned him. "I've seen you torturing yourself in the gym, and I know you go out for a run early every morning. I'm barely walking at the pace of a snail on the treadmill right now."

"The thought never crossed my mind, beautiful," he teased.

God, how I wanted to spend some time with Chase not thinking about or talking about my kidnapping, and if he wanted the same thing, the temptation was almost irresistible.

My arms crept around his neck as I finally asked, "Exactly what do you have in mind...?"

Chapter 11

Chase

"Those would look good on you," I told Vanna with a nod several days later. I took the turquoise and diamond earrings she'd been holding up to her ear and handed them to the saleswoman. "We'll take them. I told you I knew a guy who had quality turquoise jewelry."

"No, we won't take them," she said stubbornly. "They're beautiful, but they're surrounded by diamonds, Chase. If I paid that much for a pair of earrings, I'd kill myself if I lost one. And you certainly *know* a whole lot of *guys*. You knew a guy when you got us into one of the nicest restaurants in San Diego on a last minute whim. You knew a guy who had a boat, which turned out to be a luxury catamaran, when you decided to take me whale watching. You also knew a guy who could pack us a Michelin star picnic lunch when we went to the park. Exactly how many of these guys who can do miraculous things do you know?"

I winked at her as I handed the clerk my credit card. "Enough to keep you happy for a very long time," I teased.

I grew up in San Diego and I had enough money to make just about *anything* happen.

I had no shame when it came to using that power if it would get a five second smile out of Vanna.

Hell, I'd settle for a second or two if necessary.

Having seen her laugh multiple times over the last few days, I was now completely addicted to that sound and the smile on her adorable face that inevitably happened right after that.

She snagged my credit card before the saleswoman could run it. "I didn't agree to spend this week with you so you could buy me things, Chase."

I knew that.

We had fun together.

She liked being with me.

I loved being with her.

But I still wanted to buy her the damn earrings.

Why did she have to be so damn stubborn sometimes?

I plucked the card from between her fingers and handed it back to the clerk. "Stop, Vanna. You're confusing the poor woman," I said as I stepped between her and the saleswoman who would get those earrings in Vanna's jewelry box. "I know you don't need my money, and that's not why you're here with me. I *want* to buy you something you'll enjoy. Let me do it because it makes *me* happy. I don't care if you lose one. I'll just buy you another pair."

Her eyebrows scrunched in a way I'd come to adore as she replied, "You're absolutely exasperating. Do you know that? I just came here to look. I haven't actually physically shopped in a long time."

"I assume that means you're not mad," I ventured. "Come on, Vanna. They're quality earrings, but they're not exactly what I'd call expensive."

She rolled her eyes. "I think your idea of quality and mine are two very different things."

"You do realize that I own several of the most quality luxury brands on the planet," I answered. "I can make a call and get you whatever your heart desires."

"That would be absolutely no fun, and I don't buy your brands. Most of them are outrageously expensive. Who pays that much for a dress or handbag? I make decent money at what I do, but not as much as bigger name journalists. I don't have to penny pinch, but I'm a long way from having one of those black credit cards. I'm also on the market for a new home. I'd like to buy something nice in a good neighborhood that's reasonably close to the water."

I'd buy her that place in a heartbeat, but I knew I'd get kickback on that one. Besides, it wasn't like I *wanted* her to go anywhere.

"Don't hurry on that," I said firmly. "It's not like you have a time limit on how long you stay at my place. I like having you there."

She sighed as she took the bag from the clerk. "Believe me, it's no hardship to be staying there. That place would be anyone's dream home, but I need to vacate eventually."

Nope. Actually, she didn't ever need to leave.

Unfortunately, she'd feel like she had to once she was completely healed.

Physically, she wasn't as strong as she was prior to the kidnapping, but she would be.

Emotionally, she seemed to be improving as well.

She opened up to me about how she was feeling a lot more often, and she wasn't wound up as tight as a drum.

Vanna had only promised me a week of doing nothing, and I planned on making the most of the time I had.

She wasn't the only one who was laughing and smiling more often. I appreciated every fucking minute I spent with her. I'd forgotten what it was like to be with a woman who didn't give a rat's ass about my money or power. Hell, to be honest, I wasn't sure if I'd *ever* experienced that before.

I'd probably go back into the office next week, even though Wyatt had told me to take as much time off as I needed.

Vanna held up the small bag. "I'd really like to put them on, but I'm not really dressed to wear them."

I eyed her up and down as I said, "You look beautiful. They aren't exactly flashy, and even if they were, does it matter? If it makes you happy, wear them."

She smiled at me as she pulled the earrings out of the box, removed the ones she was wearing, and started to put the new ones on.

I leaned a hip against the counter and watched her, which had become one of my favorite activities.

Her new haircut actually suited her personality. It was cheeky and bold, just like Vanna.

Yeah, she had a few scars on her creamy skin, but it didn't diminish how fucking attractive she was and always would be.

She'd filled out a little since her kidnapping, so those gorgeous curves of hers were back, and they made my dick harder than ever.

"What do you think?" she asked as she faced me with the earrings secured.

"Beautiful," I said hoarsely, that word having nothing to do with the earrings.

Vanna was the kind of woman who would always look stunning—no matter what she was wearing.

Even in a pair of jeans and her bright red sweater, she took my damn breath away.

After she'd put the little bag with her other earrings into her purse, I took her hand and we walked out of the jewelry store.

That action felt as natural as breathing to me, even though we weren't in an intimate relationship.

"Thank you," she said in an appreciative tone as she bumped her shoulder against me. "That's probably the nicest thing a guy has ever done for me. Not that I'm trying to say we're dating or something," she added in a rush.

Shit! She's in a rush to correct that error.

Okay, that was a blow to my ego, but I brushed it off.

She was with me because that's where she wanted to be, money or no money, and *that* felt pretty damn amazing.

I couldn't ask for anything more. Not now. Not ever. And I needed to remember that.

"It was nothing, Vanna," I assured her. And honestly, for me, buying those earrings for her really was nothing.

"It was really thoughtful," she argued. "I still don't understand why some nice woman hasn't snapped you up, yet."

"Maybe I didn't want to be claimed by some other woman," I suggested, knowing we were venturing into dangerous territory.

We hadn't really talked much about what this week meant to either of us.

We'd basically just enjoyed each other's company.

It was going to have to be enough that Vanna wasn't running away from me like her gorgeous ass was on fire anymore.

Really, did I even have a way forward, even if she wanted something more?

Probably not.

Would it kill me when she decided to walk away and keep me stored in the friend zone?

Maybe...

But I'd hate it even more if I wasn't spending time with her right now.

She was vulnerable at the moment, and having her right next to me appeased my desire to make sure she was safe and happy.

"You're so full of shit," Vanna challenged. "If you met the right woman, you'd bend over backward to make her happy, Chase. I know you would. You've spoiled me rotten, and I'm not your love interest."

Christ! Did she really *not* know that *she* was the only woman I'd ever wanted this badly?

If not, I really did deserve an Academy Award for my performance.

"I wouldn't know," I said noncommittally as I opened the passenger door of my Ferrari and waited for her to get in.

She hesitated, and then promptly threw herself into my arms.

I caught her and held her soft, warm body against mine as I closed my eyes.

It wasn't the first time she'd done this, but it caught me off-guard every single time.

"Thank you for the earrings," she said softly near my ear. "Thank you for this week. Thank you for being here for me. I'm not feeling quite as lost as I did a few days ago."

I gritted my teeth, not sure if it was a curse or a blessing that she didn't pull away immediately.

I wrapped my arms around her and held her tightly against my body, relishing the smell of her subtle perfume and the way her gorgeous body fitted perfectly against mine.

Jesus! She was making me completely crazy, but I seemed to relish the torture.

"You know it's my pleasure, Vanna." I meant that literally.

Nothing in the world felt as good as holding her.

Yeah, I could think of a few things that might feel even more satisfying, but I wasn't about to contemplate the impossible.

Honestly, I just wanted to enjoy whatever time I could spend with her. I'd have plenty of time to wallow in my misery after she was gone.

Granted, if I could get my dick to agree to that plan, things *would* be a lot easier.

Not only did Vanna *not* seem as affected by these spontaneous gestures of affection as I was, but there were other reasons why we'd *never* end up burning up the sheets together.

There were times when I actually forgot about that when I was with her, or when she was this damn close to me.

I totally lost all rational thought when it came to Vanna, but I had to be realistic.

I had no choice but to loosen my grip when she pulled back, smiled at me, and kissed me on the cheek.

I nearly groaned with frustration.

"What's on the agenda for tomorrow?" she asked.

"Today isn't over yet," I reminded her.

She lifted a brow. "Are you trying to tell me that you don't have the day planned?"

I did, but only because I'm a glutton for punishment, apparently.

"I didn't say that," I told her. "How long has it been since you've seen snow?"

Her face lit up as she answered, "It's been a long time. Colorado. About five years ago. I was doing a piece on avalanches. Am I going to see snow again soon?"

Hell, the way she smiled *almost* made my blue balls insignificant.

I grinned as I said, "I know a guy with a helicopter and a cabin in Big Bear..."

Chapter 12

Savannah

"Okay, this is by far the craziest thing you've done for me so far," I told Chase with a sigh as I looked at the Christmas tree and the orgy of gifts that I'd opened earlier beneath it. "Christmas was weeks ago."

He shrugged as he gently pulled my body against his as we sat on the sofa, and then wrapped the blanket around me. "Does it really matter? You missed both Christmas and New Year's. You were fighting to stay alive at the time."

I snuggled beneath the blanket and put my head on Chase's shoulder.

Turned out, the guy he knew with a helicopter was *himself*, and the cabin in Big Bear we were staying in was his as well.

He'd flown us up here early, just in time to get breakfast at a little restaurant that had the best cinnamon rolls I'd ever eaten. Since my ribs and shoulder were still healing, I wasn't quite ready for snowboarding or skiing. However, there was no end to Chase's creativity. He'd simply put us on horseback to see some awe-inspiring views of winter in the mountains.

Chase's "cabin" was more like a mini estate. It wasn't quite as large or as grand as his home in La Jolla, but for Big Bear, it was pretty much a mansion.

I'd gotten back to the cabin after an already incredible day to find that Chase wasn't finished.

I'd smelled the roasted turkey the moment we'd stepped inside the cabin.

And that wasn't all…

We'd enjoyed a complete and traditional Christmas dinner while we watched the snow falling outside the gigantic picture windows.

The Christmas tree was beautiful, and fully adorned with ornaments and twinkle lights. I couldn't seem to stop myself from looking at them as we viewed the sunset and lightly falling snow outside.

"You know all those gifts were too much," I scolded.

I'd gotten a massive amount of useful gifts, all of them expensive and most of them from his own product collections. Items I would have never bought for myself because of the steep price tags.

"It wasn't me," he said with badly feigned surprise. "It was Santa. I guess he knew you were a very good girl this year."

I snorted. "Obviously, Santa has the same taste for quality that you do."

"Of course," he said in a satisfied tone.

"He also knows that I love turquoise jewelry?" I asked.

I'd gotten a beautiful necklace that nearly matched the earrings that Chase had gotten me the day before.

"Santa knows everything," he said, deadpan.

I swatted him on the shoulder. "You're completely insane, and it's totally unfair that I didn't know ahead of time. It would have been more fun if Santa had dropped you a few gifts, too."

"He did," Chase said simply as he tightened his arm around my waist. "Being here with you is the best damn gift I could get this year."

I rolled my eyes. "You're so full of shit, Chase Durand, but thank you for this. It's been a long time since I've actually been in a place where I could celebrate Christmas. Not since Mom died, actually."

He said the sweetest things sometimes, and I was never quite sure how to handle that.

Yes, Chase was naturally very charming, but there was always a note of sincerity in every nice thing he ever said.

This had honestly been the best several days of my life, but sometimes I just wasn't sure how to handle those nice things he said and did for me—or his thoughtfulness.

He had also managed to chase away every bit of loneliness I'd felt for the last decade, just because I knew he liked being with me, too.

He wasn't just being nice.

Nothing was faked.

He wasn't here because he felt sorry for me.

The playfulness and lightheartedness that Torie had said that Chase had lost was in full view.

He laughed.

He smiled.

He genuinely enjoyed my company just as I enjoyed his.

I *sensed* that he was happier, just like I was.

Did he go a little crazy on the gift giving?

Yes.

But Chase being Chase, I had a feeling that even *that* made him happy, so I didn't get on his case about it as much anymore.

Maybe it was pathetic, but this friendship meant more to me than any romantic relationship I'd ever had. No one had really cared enough about me to do something like this for me since my mother had died, and for that reason, his effort to make me happy meant more to me than he'd ever know or realize.

"You still miss her?" Chase asked in a husky voice. "I'm sorry I wasn't there for the funeral, Vanna. I would have been if I'd known. I was in a location that didn't have a lot of outside contact with the world. By the time I found out from Torie, it was over."

I nodded. "It's been a full decade and I still miss her every single day. I don't think that will ever go away. She was my whole family. If it wasn't for the fact that I was starting my first broadcasting job at the time, I probably would have been with her. Most of her work took place in the research center, but it was always an adventure when she had to go out to a location. I almost always went with her if I could."

"She was an amazing woman," Chase said earnestly. "You're a lot like her, you know."

"I'll definitely take that as a compliment," I answered. "I see quite a bit of your father in you, too. He was a pilot and loved to fly."

"He did," Chase confirmed. "Torie wasn't really interested in learning, but Wyatt and I both had our pilot's license the minute we were legal to fly solo. This was Dad's cabin before I inherited it. I have a lot of good memories here. It was our favorite getaway with our father when Wyatt and I could get leave at the same time. We'd do some fishing and drink more than a few beers while we were here. It was one of the ways I stayed grounded."

"I didn't know this cabin belonged to your father," I mused. "How often do you get up here?"

I felt him shrug as he replied, "This is the first time since he died. For a while, it was too painful to think about being here without him. I've considered coming up a time or two in the last few years, but I just never got the time. Until recently, Wyatt and I were in Paris more than we were in San Diego. Having our main headquarters back in the States means we don't have to travel nearly as often anymore."

My heart ached for Chase's loss. "I'm sorry. I know how close all of you were, and how much you must miss him."

"It gets easier with time, but as you already know from losing your mom, missing a parent never quite goes away. I probably never appreciated just how good I had it until I lost both of mine," he said, his tone full of regret.

"How does it feel to be back here again?" I questioned softly, wondering if it was painful to be here for him now.

I knew from experience how hard it was to let go of the pain of missing someone you loved. After all, it had taken me nearly a decade to sell my childhood home.

"It's good," Chase said. "I can remember the happy memories without them being painful anymore. Honestly, I think that's why

I thought about Christmas here. When we were younger, the whole family spent Christmas here a few times."

"It's a pretty magical place," I said wistfully. "I just wish Santa hadn't been so generous."

"The gifts were nothing, Vanna. Trinkets and useful things. It's not like Santa brought you a new home or a new vehicle."

I tilted my chin to send him a warning glance. "He'd better not. And it's not just the gifts themselves, it's the thoughtfulness of this entire experience, Chase. Like I said, I haven't really stopped to enjoy a Christmas tree or a holiday meal in years."

Honestly, the price of the gifts was nothing to a guy who had the kind of money that Chase had.

The sentiment was a different thing altogether.

"No intimate Christmas in the mountains with Bradley?" Chase asked roughly.

I snickered. "Oh, God, no. We were both on location that year."

"I'm sure Torie invited you to our Christmases," Chase considered. "The three of us have had very few holidays when we weren't in the same place for the holidays, even if we had to fly somewhere to be together."

"Every year," I assured him. "But I was always out of the country. I think I lost track of how important it was to be with the person who was the most important to me for the holidays. Torie is the sister I never had. Now, I regret missing those holiday celebrations with her. Tossing a gift in the mail isn't quite the same thing as spending time together. I guess I didn't know how blessed I was to have her until I almost lost her."

"You were there when she really needed you, Vanna," Chase reminded me. "Knowing how career driven you've been, I can't even imagine how difficult it was to put your own career on hold after her kidnapping."

I shook my head. "It wasn't, really. There was absolutely no question of where I wanted to be when it happened. She's been there for me, too, Chase."

He chuckled. "She wasn't happy when I told her that I was going to be your advisor, and that you'd be staying with me. The only reason she didn't give me too much grief about it was because she lives so close. She was terrified when you went missing, Vanna. The sisterly feelings go both ways. She would have been on the rescue if she'd thought she could wheedle her way onto my jet."

I smiled because that sounded exactly like my best friend. "I'm sure she would have. I'm grateful that we're close enough that she noticed I wasn't sticking to my schedule. If not for her and Last Hope, I don't think I would have made it out of that jungle alive."

"I'm not going to lie," Chase replied gutturally. "I'm sure you wouldn't have. You were already pretty septic, and the systemic infection was the most challenging part of your recovery."

I nodded. "I don't remember much about those first few days in the hospital. I just recall you being there every time I woke up scared. Did you get any sleep?"

"Enough," he said, blowing off my concern for him. "I've never really required a ton of sleep, and I learned in the military to grab an hour or two when and where I could."

"Do you ever miss your life in the military?" I asked curiously.

"Sometimes," he said candidly. "There's a comradery there that I don't think you'll ever find in another line of work. And there's rarely a dull moment. Our ops had to be planned down to the second, and there was no room for error, so the shelf life in special forces out in the field isn't generally a long one. But while I was doing it, I felt like I was part of a team doing something important. It's hard to lose that sense of having a higher purpose like that, and that instinct to save the world is hard to shake off when you become a civilian again. I guess that's why we all appreciate being involved in Last Hope. We're big and spread out now, but that comradery is still there, and it gives us a chance to do what we can to help."

"I know most of your military operations were shrouded in secrecy. You probably can't say much about them specifically, but were they really timed down to the second?" I asked inquisitively. "The investigative journalist in me has to ask."

"Most of them were top secret in the 160th SOAR," he revealed. "We coordinated with and flew other special forces units like Delta

Force and Navy SEALS to locations for specific objectives. Night Stalkers specialize in flying in the dark. And yes, my curious little friend, timing was everything. I never missed a target time, plus or minus thirty seconds. That was always our goal, no matter what kind of operation we were running."

I winced. "That's pretty brutal."

"When lives depend on not missing a time window, you get it done," he answered with a note of amusement in his voice. "We weren't known as the best of the best helicopter pilots in the military for nothing."

I smirked at his cockiness, but I supposed when someone was challenged with missions that difficult, brash confidence was probably necessary.

"So taking over Durand with Wyatt was a huge career change," I pondered.

"Yes," he agreed. "But business offers a different kind of challenge. There's a certain satisfaction in a deal well made, or releasing a new product that you know is the best quality on the market."

"Many of which were given to Santa to put under that tree," I teased.

"Of course. He knows quality when he sees it."

I burst out laughing because I couldn't hold it back. "You're obnoxious when it comes to Durand products and their quality."

"We have to be," he confirmed without a trace of arrogance. "Durand lines wouldn't be half so sought after if we weren't offering a product that will last a lifetime. Enough about me. Tell me what life is like as an investigative journalist."

I took a deep breath, but I didn't answer immediately.

Since Chase had always made it a point to be honest with me, I wanted to do the same thing.

Chapter 13

Chase

"**V**anna?" I prompted when she didn't answer. "Is this something you don't want to talk about?"

Hell, I would have nixed that question if I thought it might upset her.

She shook her head slightly before she said, "It's not that. I'm just trying to figure out exactly how to answer. It's not exactly the career I envisioned when I got out of college."

"What did you want to do?"

She took a deep breath before she answered, "I thought I was going to do groundbreaking investigations and write pieces that would earn me a Pulitzer someday. But there wasn't a lot of demand for a journalist with no real writing experience. So I took a job at a small cable news station in San Diego, hoping I could get some experience under my belt and some name recognition. For some reason, I've been there ever since. *Deadline America* got more and more popular, and it just hasn't made sense to stop doing it. My pay slowly increased until I was making decent money, too."

"But?"

I could hear the hesitation in her tone.

She lifted her head to look at me, and my gut wrenched at the melancholy expression in her gorgeous eyes.

"Don't get me wrong," she said softly. "I owe a lot to *Deadline America*. I was able to do some stories that were really important, even if I couldn't tell them exactly like I wanted. I have a producer, a director, and a lot of other people to answer to about my content. There's usually a limit on just how gritty things can be on television, and there's added sensationalism sometimes when I just want to write…"

"The facts?" I finished.

"Exactly," she said with a sad smile. "Even if those details are gritty and a little too much for television. I think that may be part of the reason why I'm burned out. I know what's real, but I don't always have an outlet to tell the ugly truth. I am doing stories worth telling, but sometimes there's way too much fluff and not enough realism. I'm writing an investigative written piece in addition to my report for *Deadline America* on the Darien Gap crisis. It's something I've done for a lot of my stories over the years, even if nobody ever reads them. The situation there in the Darien Gap is horrific, Chase. There's so many children with no place to go and so much suffering that had gone on for them even before arriving in Bajo Chiquito and some of the other reception staging areas."

"I'd like to read that article," I told her honestly. "And you're right. If you're a writer, that's probably the best outlet for you. Especially considering the topics you cover. I've marveled over every story you've ever told on *Deadline America*, Vanna, so I can only imagine how incredible those stories would be if you were writing them exactly the way you wanted."

"You can't possibly have seen *every single episode*," she scolded.

"Actually, I have. Even the earliest ones. I've also bragged to anyone who will listen about the fact that I've known you since you were a kid because I've always felt honored to know you. Maybe we haven't seen each other that much over the years, but I never stopped thinking about you," I confided.

Strangely, that was a fact I couldn't deny.

Maybe I'd never woken the fuck up enough to admit that I felt more than just friendship for Vanna, but subconsciously, I'd probably always known it. Most likely, I'd stayed in denial because I knew Vanna would always be the unattainable for me. My little sister's best friend. It had been a hell of a lot easier when I'd simply seen her as a challenging debate partner and a family friend.

I'd *never* missed a single episode of *Deadline America*. If I knew I was going to be away, I'd record it.

Granted, it was a riveting program, and Vanna was one hell of an investigative journalist, but I knew now that I'd been anal about watching because of…her.

Because of Savannah.

"I thought about you, too," she said hesitantly. "And I worried when you were flying in the military. Torie kept me posted about you and Wyatt."

Wyatt? Fuck Wyatt. Yeah, I loved my older brother just as much as Torie did, but I would have much preferred that Vanna was just thinking about…me.

For some reason, this was one instance when I didn't really want to be paired with my brother. That made me just *the other* family friend she was worried about.

Okay, back to our previous conversation. The last thing I wanted to focus on was what I *really* wanted from Savannah Anderson. "So why not give up *Deadline America* and just write freelance about whatever you want?"

Her eyebrows furrowed as she said contemplatively, "I'm not sure if *Deadline America* was a blessing or a curse in that respect. My name is definitely known, but I'm not in the upper echelon of serious investigative journalists who win Pulitzers. And I don't have creative freedom in my job. I write the stories, but they're torn apart to make them appropriate for television."

"Vanna, nothing you've ever done is pure fluff. If you wanted to make that transition, I know you could. Your name is respected. Hell, I respect you. It takes some major balls just to be in some of those locations."

Isn't that the truth?

I'd cringed repeatedly as she'd trudged through some of those deadly geographical hot spots without a thought for her own safety.

She batted her eyes playfully. "So you weren't watching just to check out how sexy I was in rubber boots and a sun hat?"

Shit! It didn't matter what she was wearing.

"How do you know I don't have a thing for women in mud boots?" I asked lightly.

To be honest, she looked sexy in anything she wore, mud boots included.

Didn't matter.

Makeup or no makeup.

Filthy dirty or clean.

Slim or curvy.

Scars or no scars.

She was the most desirable female I'd ever met.

There was no limit to the ways she could get my dick hard.

Sometimes I wanted to be inside her gorgeous body so badly that I could hardly breathe.

Mine!

Savannah was mine.

She was always supposed to be mine.

I could feel it with every breath I took, every second I was close to her.

She was the one who was always missing for me.

The one I'd been pining for in a crowded room.

I wanted to claim her elementally like a goddamn caveman and drag her off to my lair.

It had just taken me too damn long to realize it.

I tried not to think about what might have happened if I'd wised up years ago...

"Do you?" she said in breathy whisper that made my cock ache.

Okay, I'd gotten a little distracted. "Do I what?"

"Have a thing for women in mud boots?"

Not really. It was pretty much just...her. "I might," I answered noncommittally. "Now tell me exactly why you can't do what you want in your career. I think the risk is probably worth taking. You're not happy. Not to mention the fact that *Deadline America* nearly got you killed."

"I accept the dangers in every assignment," she said nonchalantly. "It's part of the job. You always know something *could* happen, but honestly, I've been in more dangerous places than Bajo Chiquito and everything was fine. I was just in the wrong place at the wrong time. Maybe I'm just afraid that I'll fail if I try to sell written stories. Not to mention the fact that I make pretty decent money in my current job. I'd be starting all over again, Chase. I'll have to think about it some more."

If money was one of her worries, I could alleviate that in a heartbeat. "What if money wasn't an issue?" I asked.

She shot me a small smile. "Money is *always* an issue for most people, Chase. I don't have a backup. I have to make a decent living. California isn't cheap. I could probably hold off on buying a house until I see how things go. I could rent a condo or a small place. I don't need a lot of space to write."

"Or…you could just hang out where you are for as long as it takes to get a new career going. You said it was no hardship to live with me," I reminded her.

She let out a stunned laugh. "Oh, my God. I said it's no hardship for *me*. I hardly think you want a semi-permanent houseguest, and I'm not exactly broke. Having a live-in female would be really hard on your love life, and Torie is getting a little impatient about nieces and nephews. I think she's about to give up hope of ever marrying off either of her older brothers."

"She's married. She can have her own kids," I grumbled. "And I already told you that I'm not seeing anyone."

"Things could change," she answered gently. "You've already done more for me than anyone ever has in my entire life, Chase, and I don't just mean monetarily. Regardless of the circumstances, this has been the happiest week of my life. It's made me realize just how buried I've been into my job, and how much I've been missing. I can never thank you enough."

Hell, the last thing I wanted was for her to thank me.

"Don't thank me," I insisted. "I told you I needed the same thing. It's been good for me. This is the happiest I've ever been, too. That offer is always going to stay open, Vanna. I want you to be happy. In the meantime, you still have healing to do. How do you feel after being on a horse half the day?"

I tried to make sure that the stables gave her a plodder with absolutely no enthusiasm to get up and go because her ribs and shoulder were still healing. But she'd seemed to enjoy herself anyway.

"I feel amazing," she said enthusiastically. "The outdoors definitely agrees with me, but I'll probably hurt in places I didn't before when I wake up tomorrow. It's been a while since I've been on a horse. Nothing some ibuprofen won't take care of, though. I wouldn't have missed it for the world."

Me, either. Just watching the happy glow on her cheeks had been worth riding a second plodder that would stay on pace with hers.

"No pain from riding?" I questioned.

"None," she reassured me. "My ribs and shoulder have only been a dull ache once in a while for days now."

"Physical injuries are usually the first to heal," I told her. "What about some of the other issues?"

"I still only remember little pieces of what happened after the first day or so," she confided. "My therapist said I may never remember more than that because I was so heavily drugged. Little pieces of my memory fall back in occasionally. I think they started pumping me with more and more drugs over time so they didn't have to deal with me. I also don't recall much of what was said between my kidnappers after I was drugged. I understand Spanish fairly well, but I wouldn't say I'm fluent enough to a have a long conversation on complicated topics."

"More fluent than me," I replied. "We grew up speaking French with Dad, but my Spanish is pretty limited. There's no hard and fast rule about what you should and shouldn't remember, sweetheart. You just have to be able to deal with what you do recall. You were drugged pretty heavily. It's not surprising that you don't remember a whole lot."

"I think I'm slowly making peace with that," she said thoughtfully. "At first, it really bothered me that I had no idea what happened to most of that week, but I'm starting to think I'm better off without those memories. My therapist is probably right. One of the few conversations I remember was when my kidnappers were trying to decide whether to kill me or keep me alive after they realized that it was going to be hard to traffic me like a normal female. I don't think I'll ever forget how damn helpless I felt, Chase. My fate was in the hands of four criminals and there was nothing I could do to save myself."

I buried my hand into her silky locks and stroked her scalp. "Fuck! Why didn't you tell me you remembered that, Vanna?"

"The conversation just came back to me a few days ago, and I haven't had a chance. Besides, I've had better things to focus on. Like finding my *joie de vivre*."

Shit! I knew I'd definitely found mine, I just wasn't sure I could keep it.

I cradled her head against my chest as I asked gruffly, "Have you found it yet?"

I tightened my arm around her, trying not to crush her.

Jesus! I felt the need to protect this woman suddenly roar through every cell in my body.

The instinct was so elemental and primordial that I closed my eyes, reminding myself that she was already safe.

No one was ever going to hurt her again.

Ever.

My fucking chest was aching when she finally murmured, "You know, I'm pretty sure that I have."

Chapter 14

Savannah

Panic filled my entire being as I opened my eyes and saw nothing but darkness.

Lights? Where are the lights?

I sat up, trying to clear my head so I could think.

I'm fine. I'm in Big Bear with Chase. I'm perfectly safe.

I nearly jumped out of my skin as I heard something rattle outside.

It's just the wind, Vanna. Calm the hell down.

I took a few deep breaths, wondering what had happened to the lights I'd left on in the bathroom.

Since the kidnapping, I never slept in the dark.

I couldn't.

Reaching toward the side table, I fumbled to open the small drawer and pulled out a very tiny flashlight I'd seen there before I'd gone to bed.

I frowned once I turned it on.

"Better than nothing," I said to myself as I scrambled from the bed.

I probably should have been cold since I was dressed in a sleepshirt that barely covered my ass, but I wasn't.

I was too busy worrying about the fact that all the lights were off.

The illumination the baby flashlight gave off was minimal, just barely enough to see the floor in front of me as I walked toward the bathroom.

"It's fine. Everything is fine," I chanted to myself as I put my hand on the bathroom light switch to turn it on.

It seemed almost impossible that I'd forgotten to turn the lights on, but I'd been exhausted by the time Chase and I had finally retreated to our rooms.

I hit the light switch.

Click. Click. Click.

Nothing.

Dammit!

The bathroom lights weren't working.

"You're fine, Vanna. Everything is fine. Everything is fine." I kept saying those words like a mantra, like by saying them, it would make everything okay.

My heart was racing, and I couldn't seem to take a deep breath.

Shit! I hated the dark.

Unfortunately, there was plenty of that here in this room at the moment.

Chase?

I should…check on him, right?

Something was obviously wrong.

My feet took me to his room as fast as the miniscule flashlight would allow.

Really, it wasn't far since he was right next door.

I pushed his bedroom door open without a second thought.

"Chase?" I called out once the door was open. "Are you okay?"

"I was all good until you decided to bellow at me," Chase said in a sleepy but teasing voice.

"What are you doing?" I said in a tense voice.

"It's nearly four am, Vanna. I was asleep. What do you think I'm doing? Having a party?" he asked wryly.

"It's dark, Chase. Really dark. I'm sorry. The lights aren't working. I know it's late. I didn't mean to wake you. I was just—"

"Wait. Stay there," Chase ordered, sounding suddenly very awake. I knew he had heard the sheer panic in my voice, but I didn't care.

"Not. Moving," I said, my entire body trembling.

Breathe, Vanna. Just freaking breathe. The darkness isn't going to kill you.

I heard Chase rustling around while he said, "The power is out. We're getting a shitload of snow overnight. It happens sometimes."

He was beside me in another heartbeat.

"I don't like it when it's completely dark," I said in a weak voice I hardly recognized.

"Then I guess we're having a slumber party," he said reassuringly as he picked me up and carried me to the bed. "Get in. Your whole body is shaking. Are you cold?"

I scrambled under the covers, finding the spot that was still warm from Chase's body. "I-I don't think so," I stammered.

"Then why are your teeth chattering?" he asked as he slid in, pulled the covers over both of us, and wrapped his arms around me. "Christ! Your feet are cold, Vanna. I knew we lost power, but I figured you'd sleep through it."

"I woke up," I told him, my voice quivering. "It was dark. I always leave the light on, Chase. It was off."

I swung my leg over him and tried to claw my way closer. I knew I was trying to crawl up his body, but I couldn't help myself.

He was warm.

He was safe.

He was Chase, and the only thing keeping me from losing it.

"If I would have *known* that you were afraid of the dark, I would have come to you as soon as I realized the power was off," he growled as he pulled my body flush against his. "Why the fuck didn't you tell me, Vanna? I'm your advisor. I should know about these things."

My heartbeat started to slow as I absorbed Chase's warmth and the hardness of his body beneath me.

I took a deep breath. "What was I supposed to say? That I was afraid of the dark like a three-year-old? It's embarrassing. But it's something that hasn't gone away after the kidnapping."

"It's perfectly understandable, Vanna. Jesus! Did you really think I wouldn't understand?" His voice sounded annoyed, but he was running a soothing hand up and down my back.

I started to relax as I pleaded, "Don't be mad. The only one who knows is my counselor. I find it absolutely mortifying that I have to sleep with the bathroom light on every night. I'm a grown woman for God's sake. I don't *ever* remember being afraid of the dark, even as a child. It's not rational. I know my kidnappers aren't coming to get me."

"Fear isn't always rational, baby," he said in his low, slow, fuck-me baritone that I adored. "But that doesn't mean it's not there. Yours was born from trauma, Vanna. You were obviously terrified. If you would have told me, you never would have woken up in the dark alone."

"That's the first time it's happened," I admitted, my voice muffled because my face was buried in Chase's neck. "I always leave the bathroom light on. As long as it's not pitch dark when I wake up, I'm okay."

My body was now completely relaxed, and the dark was no longer scary because Chase was here now.

"Or if you have company," he said, amused.

"I don't exactly run around climbing into other people's beds," I said drily. "Well, not under usual circumstances."

"Sweetheart, feel free to crawl into mine any time you're afraid of the dark," he said in a gruff baritone that vibrated through my entire body.

I blew off the flirty comment. I'd gotten used to them. I was convinced that compliments rolled off Chase's tongue pretty easily.

Not that I didn't want to think he was attracted to me, but I knew he wasn't.

I slowly loosened the choke hold I had around his neck as I asked, "Can you breathe? I'm sorry."

I wasn't sure what he was wearing, but he was covered. I was pretty sure he'd been hastily putting something on when he'd jumped out of bed.

J. A. Scott

It felt like a soft cotton thermal shirt and flannel bottoms.

God, did I really want to think about the fact that he might sleep naked?

No. No, I probably shouldn't.

Even though I appreciated his tantalizingly masculine scent and every hard muscle of his body, I felt guilty for flinging myself over him.

I started to pull my leg off him.

"Don't," he said huskily as he put a hand on my bare thigh to keep me from backing off. "Stay. I'll take care of you, Vanna. Do you want me to start a fire in the fireplace? I'm not sure why the damn generator didn't kick in, but I'll check on that tomorrow. It probably needs to be replaced."

"No," I said in a sleepy voice. "I'm fine now, and you throw off plenty of body heat."

The house was warm enough. The power hadn't been out that long.

"Are you really okay?" he questioned suspiciously. "Is there anything else you need to tell me?"

"No. That's it. I only get terrified when I wake up in the pitch dark all alone," I said with a sigh. "You know everything else."

And, oh yeah, by the way, you're the most amazing man I've ever met and I'm dying to get you naked.

Okay. Yeah. That was the one secret he was *never* going to discover.

My body ached with a desire that only Chase could satiate, but I wasn't willing to give up this kind of closeness with him, either.

Not yet.

I couldn't.

Even though my addiction to being with him was getting rawer and rawer.

I was attracted to more than just his hot body and gorgeous face.

Even though I'd spent a lot of time with him this week, he still fascinated me.

Honestly, maybe I was never going to completely understand him, but I *felt* him. I got him, and in some ways, I was pretty sure he got me, too.

Even when I was afraid of the dark.

"Sleep, Vanna," Chase rasped beside my ear. "The weather should clear up in the morning. In the meantime, I'm not going anywhere."

"Thank you," I whispered fiercely. "Thank you for being here for me, even when I'm feeling like a three-year-old."

"I'm not going to let you be embarrassed in the morning about this," he said in a warning voice.

I smiled into the darkness.

Yep. He definitely got me like no other guy ever would.

Chapter 15

Chase

"I heard Vanna's apartment hunting," Wyatt said several weeks later as we finished up on some work issues in his office. "How are you feeling about that?"

I lifted a brow. "Torie told you?"

He nodded. "Who else?"

"Honestly, I fucking hate it," I replied. "But I've run out of excuses to keep her with me. The doctors have released her physically, and she really doesn't need me as her advisor anymore. She stays on top of her counseling herself, and she goes into the studio every day now to finish the Darien Gap project narration, so she's back to work, too."

Vanna had decided to return to *Deadline America* for now since she was feeling better about her job and life in general.

She was going to try to write pieces on the side to see if she could get them published.

She'd also decided on an apartment for the time being, until she knew exactly where her career was headed.

While I hadn't been thrilled with those decisions, I under-stood them. I just hoped she got out of *Deadline America* sooner rather than later. It would kill me to watch her go out on another assignment.

Hell, I didn't want her to go, but I couldn't force her to keep living with me if she wanted her own place.

The two of us had fallen into a pleasant routine, even after we'd spent that memorable week together.

I'd gone back to my office, and Vanna had spent her time writing her piece after our week together. She'd spent the rest of her recovery time writing her story about the Darien Gap that she thought no one was ever going to read or publish.

She'd taken over the responsibility of planning dinner during that time because she was home.

I was pretty sure I'd never been so eager to leave the office on time to get home for dinner.

We ate, drank our wine on the patio, played an occasional game of chess or watched movies neither one of us had gotten a chance to see after dinner every night.

Things hadn't changed much since she'd gone back to work at the studio.

Whoever got home first started dinner.

On the weekends, we still played. Either with family or on our own, but we never forgot how to drop work for a time and just enjoy life.

"How about you tell her that you're crazy about her?" Wyatt suggested gruffly. "That should work."

"She doesn't feel that way about me," I snapped. "We're close. As close as two people can be without sleeping together. But she still thinks of me as an honorary big brother, Wyatt. A *friend*."

Fuck! I was starting to hate that word.

"Bullshit," he answered firmly. "I was at that impromptu barbeque that Torie threw last weekend. I saw it. Hudson, Jax, and Cooper saw it. You two might as well be sleeping together judging by the longing in Savannah's eyes. There's a hell of a lot more than friendship there, brother. I think you're the only one who *doesn't* see it. And you know it has to be punching *me* in the face for me to recognize it. I'm not exactly intuitive when it comes to romance."

I smirked. "Some woman is going to come along some day and knock you on your ass. Then you won't be so damn cynical anymore." He shot me a doubtful look. "Almost forty. Hasn't happened yet. I'm not exactly holding my breath. I'm not cut out for long-term relationships, and I'm happy that way. If I had to walk around with a despondent expression like yours because I was crazy about someone, I'd probably want to kill myself. I'll skip that kind of misery, thanks."

Sometimes I really preferred it when Wyatt was quiet instead of being a sarcastic asshole. "Then why are you pushing me to confess how I feel to Vanna?"

He raised a brow. "Because you're pathetically depressed that she's leaving and I don't like to see you or Torie unhappy. Just marry the woman and get it over with. Torie seems perfectly content in her wedded state of bliss."

"You can't just fix everything that easily, Wyatt," I rumbled. "These are human emotions we're talking about. I know you have a few of them underneath all that bullshit."

"It was a perfectly good solution," he replied. "You're crazy about her. She's crazy about you. You've already done the trial run of living together, so you know the two of you can cohabitate without making each other insane. What else is there to know?"

I shot him an irritated look. "It's not that easy when you're crazy about someone who doesn't feel the same way. Yes, I admit, Vanna is fond of me. But that's where it stops."

"Has being in love affected your intellect, too?" Wyatt asked drily. "*Look* at the woman once in a while. She doesn't want it to stop. When it comes to you, I'd say she's more than willing to take things to the next level. I have to wonder if it's really her slamming on the brakes, or if it's you."

"She hasn't said a word—"

"Have you?" Wyatt interrupted. "She's been through a lot, Chase. She's scarred. No doubt she's still trying to get her head together, even though she seems okay."

"I don't give a shit if she's scarred. She's still the most beautiful woman I've ever seen. Fuck! Do you really think I'm that superficial, especially after what happened to me?" I asked him, my body almost shaking with anger.

"Not at all," he said as he shook his head slowly. "I think I made the point I wanted to make. You're right. Vanna is beautiful inside and out. She always has been. You'd be damn lucky to have her."

I slammed my fist down on the desk. "I can't have her. That's the whole point."

"You probably could if you'd get out of our own way, little brother," Wyatt said pointedly. "And you're sure as hell not going to know until you ask."

I looked at him, feeling desperately cornered as I confessed, "I'm not sure if I can. She's not like any other woman I've ever known, Wyatt."

"No," he agreed. "She isn't. She's better. As Dad used to say, anything worth having is worth the risk."

"Yeah, well, he never mentioned how badly it will rip your guts out if you have to go through the rejection. Sometimes it might be easier just to not take that risk."

Wyatt glared at me as he said, "Now that's total bullshit. You've never been a quitter in your entire life, Chase. Don't start now. If you want Vanna to stay, find a way. I've never seen you this damn happy with a woman."

"She's the one," I said in a defeated tone. "Maybe she always has been. Dad also said that we'd know when the right one came along. He was right."

"Taking your obsession with never missing her show into consideration, I'd say you're probably correct," Wyatt observed. "Luckily, if I have to have a sister-in-law, Vanna would be tolerable. I've always liked her. And Lord knows that Mom and Dad adored her."

"Maybe if I was the man I used to be, I'd do everything I could to make her stay. I'd bust my ass to make her mine."

"You're still that same *man*, Chase," Wyatt said solemnly.

I held up a hand. "We're not getting married, Wyatt. She's looking for her own place, remember? Does that sound like a woman who wants to stay exactly where she is right now?"

He was silent for a moment before he shot me a deliberate glance. "Sounds like a woman who hasn't been asked to stay. It's not like you're a guy who has nothing going for himself, Chase. You're intelligent, one of the richest men in existence, and you're a much slicker talker than I'll ever be. You have a prettier face, too. If she isn't already, make her fall in love with you."

I grinned. My brother was far from unattractive. It wasn't like women hadn't vied for his attention since he'd gotten out of the military. He'd just chosen to ignore it most of the time. He probably did frighten some people away with his abrupt mannerisms and his dry sarcasm. If Wyatt liked someone, he was either quiet or cuttingly derisive with his humor. If not, he simply didn't talk to them. His hair was darker than pitch, and he was built like a heavyweight prize fighter. I was a big guy, but Wyatt was enormous and all muscle. When a guy like that almost never cracked a smile, he could be pretty damn intimidating.

Thing was, those of us who knew him were very well aware of how much he loved and cared about his family and the people closest to him.

It was the ones who didn't know him who found him a little bit scary.

"Vanna's not impressed by my money, my pretty face, or my charm, unfortunately. She blows off my compliments like I throw them out to every female I know," I shared.

"Then maybe you should make them a little more…personal," Wyatt suggested. "Vanna's no fool. She's known you most of her life. You're not exactly known for dating women with advanced intelligence."

"What the hell does that mean?" I asked grudgingly.

He shrugged. "I'm just saying that most of your past love affairs haven't been with investigative journalists. Granted, you've had some beautiful women on your arm—or should I say draped over your body—but I doubt you were attracted to their brains."

"That was a long time ago," I answered defensively. "And those relationships didn't last very long."

"Not exactly surprising," Wyatt replied. "But has it ever occurred to you that Vanna might not feel like she can compete with the kind of women you may appear to like? Look, I know beautiful women are everywhere in our orbit. I'm not saying I haven't very briefly dated a few of those women obsessed with haute couture, too. But, quite frankly, Vanna might feel like she's not your type. She did get cheated on by an A-list movie star."

"He was a prick and a complete idiot," I said indignantly. "He had *her*, Wyatt. And he threw Vanna away to sleep with another woman."

I would have killed for a chance to be that asshole, to have Vanna committed to me and our relationship.

The bastard had no idea what he'd given up.

"Lucky for you that he *was* a major dick. If he wasn't, she probably wouldn't be with you right now," Wyatt commented. "And she definitely deserves better. I'm just saying that maybe you should let her know exactly how you feel."

I swallowed hard before I said, "You realize I haven't had a real date in years, and I think you know exactly why I haven't."

"I know," Wyatt said agreeably.

"I'm definitely out of practice," I told him.

Wyatt rolled his eyes. "What in the hell do you call what you've been doing with Vanna? It looks like dating without the sex part to me. You've taken her everywhere. You've wined her and dined her. Hell, you even took her to Big Bear. I'm almost jealous that I wasn't invited. Haven't been there myself for a long time."

"There was no beer drinking or fishing," I said with a snicker.

"Okay. Then never mind," Wyatt said stoically. "Maybe I'm not jealous."

I took a quick glance at my watch. "I better get going. Vanna's making lasagna tonight."

"Send me the leftovers," Wyatt ordered impassively.

"Not happening," I said adamantly. "If I have to be miserable, *I'm* getting the leftover lasagna."

Wyatt and I knew how to cook, but most of our cooking skills didn't reach the world of Italian food.

While I could make a good burger on the grill and a fairly wide selection of French dishes, that was where my cooking talent stopped.

Overall, Vanna was a much better cook than me, and I had no problem admitting it and appreciating the fact that her talents were broader than mine.

I stood, and then stacked the folders we'd been reviewing before I headed for the door.

"Chase?" Wyatt called.

I turned. "Yeah?"

"You haven't been miserable with Vanna until you found out that she was moving out. You've been happy. Keep it that way," he said shortly before he reached for a folder and went back to work.

I frowned as I exited his office.

Easy for him to say. He wasn't the one who was going to have to put his balls on a chopping block to get the woman he wanted.

Chapter 16

Savannah

"So, is that your final decision?" Torie asked as she savored a bite of her chocolate chip cookie.

The two of us had been sitting at the kitchen table going over the rentals I'd seen so far.

"The condo in the Gaslamp Quarter would work for now," I said resolutely. "It's not like I'm buying a place at the moment."

Torie wrinkled her nose. "Traffic will suck."

"It's highly walkable," I countered. "I wouldn't have to take my car out if I was going local."

"It's much nicer here," she suggested with a smile. "And you're really close to your best friend."

God, she had no idea how much I wished I could stay, but I couldn't take up space in Chase's home forever, and now that I felt better physically, it was getting hard for me not to want…more.

I couldn't be this close to Chase, closer than we'd ever been, and not want to get the man naked.

It was just too…painful.

The two of us were so connected it was almost scary.

But I didn't really need to lean on Chase anymore, and now that I was healed, I ached for something far different from him, something that would *never* happen between the two of us.

Yeah, we were so close that there were times that I'd been tempted to tell him how I felt, but that would only ruin the friendship we'd built. Things could get very awkward, and I'd come to value our close relationship. A lot.

What other choices did I have but to go?

"It's not like I'm moving across the state, Torie," I teased. "And I can't stay camped out at your brother's ridiculous mansion forever."

"I don't think he'd mind," Torie badgered. "In fact, I think he'll be pretty devastated if you do decide to leave him for the Gaslamp Quarter."

I watched as she picked up her wine glass, swirled it, and then took a breath in before she finally took a sip.

Funny, I'd known Torie forever and I'd never really noticed that she drank a good glass of wine the same way Chase did.

"There's something seriously wrong with drinking a glass of wine with chocolate chip cookies," I said jokingly as I took a sip from my own glass.

"No way," Torie argued. "They're both amazing. My brother has good taste in wine."

"He has an entire wine cellar," I reminded her.

She wriggled her eyebrows. "Just think about how much help he'll need consuming all of that wine."

I snorted. "You're not exactly being subtle, Torie."

"Never say I didn't offer you one of my brothers wholeheartedly," she said with a mock pout. "Honestly, Vanna, Chase is crazy about you."

"He's fond of me," I corrected. "But that kind regard only goes so far. I need to give him his house back."

"Savannah Anderson, we've known each other for most of our lives. Please don't try to tell me you aren't attracted to Chase. I know you. I've seen it. Last week at my barbeque, you looked like you'd much rather devour Chase than your food."

I took in a sharp breath. "God, was I really that obvious?"

I wanted to deny what she'd said because she was Chase's sister, but I also wanted to confide in my best friend.

She shrugged. "Maybe not to everyone, but I've seen you with every boyfriend you've ever had. I've never seen you look at any other guy the way you look at Chase. Open your eyes, Vanna. He looks at *you* exactly the same way. I call bullshit on the whole fondness thing. You two want to rip each other's clothes off. I should know. I look at Cooper the same way. It's not only that, though. I know you two adore each other. It's obvious."

Oh, I adored *him*. I was far from convinced that he wanted me the same way.

Yes, he could be flirty. But Chase was a natural charmer.

"Okay. Yes. I'm attracted to him. Are you happy now?"

"Not yet," she said slyly. "But at least we're getting somewhere. Why in the hell do you want to leave then?"

I gave up all attempts at pretending when I answered, "Have you ever tried to live with a guy you're crazy about but know you can never have? I love every moment Chase and I spend together, but it's never going to turn into anything more. He dates women who are ten out of ten on the hotness scale, Torie. I was average at best *before* the kidnapping. Now I'm average with scars on my face. Not to mention a few other parts of my body."

"Please, Vanna," she replied, exasperated. "Yes, he has dated a few models—"

"Not just models," I interrupted. "Supermodels. Every one of them ridiculously perfect."

Torie swallowed a sip of her wine. "Vanna, that was a long time ago, and when you're involved with a company like Durand, you're surrounded by those women. That's the kind of women he met when he first got out of the military. And yes, he dated a few in college and in the military, too. Honestly, I haven't seen Chase with anyone for...well, it's been a long time. I swear to God, I don't think either he or Wyatt has gotten laid in years. They're both workaholics."

"Not so much now," I said with a smile. "He usually makes it home for dinner on time."

"Because of you," she said firmly, stressing the phrase. "*You* made that happen. He finally found somewhere he'd rather be than at Durand. He finally found someone he cared about more than his company. I'm not trying to be a nag. I just want to see both of you happy. And you have been. Screw the women who are supposedly a ten out of ten physically. I guarantee he never looked at them the way he looks at you. There's a hell of a lot more to attraction than platinum blonde hair and a tall, thin body that fits into a doll-sized dress."

"I know that," I said solemnly. It was definitely time for me to come clean with my best friend. "And this attraction to Chase isn't exactly…new."

She eyed me warily as she crossed her arms over her chest. "What exactly does that mean? How long, Vanna?"

I cringed. "Do you remember that party your dad threw for you when you earned your PhD?"

Her eyes widened. "No way."

I nodded. "We've been sparring like debate participants ever since. I never wanted things to get awkward. I thought it would just…go away. I know he's your brother, but he's also an attractive guy for many reasons, and I'm not talking about his gorgeous body and handsome face. I noticed at that party, and it never really went away. I could forget about it when he wasn't around, but the moment I saw him again, it was there. We spent a lot more time in the same place when you were recovering from your kidnapping. By the time I saw him at your wedding, it was pretty much unforgettable."

"He did mention that he asked you to spend time with him in Vegas. Why didn't you take him up on that?" Torie asked curiously.

"He wanted to catch up," I explained. "I wanted to get him naked. I was way too afraid I'd say something I'd regret."

"Oh, my God. I want to bang both of your heads together," Torie said in a frustrated tone. "Have you ever considered that the two of you might want the same thing, but you're both too afraid to say it first?"

I shook my head. "God, no. Chase has always been a fantasy for me, Torie. Let's get real. Men like Chase do not have girlfriends like me."

"Vanna, you were dating an A-list movie star."

"Not the same thing," I explained. "He was a good-looking man with muscles who got lucky doing action films that required very few acting skills. You can't even compare him with a man like your brother. Chase is brilliant, highly educated, sophisticated, incredibly thoughtful, and he didn't act in movies where he pretended to be a hero. He *was* a real special forces hero. Oh yeah, and he's a billionaire with more money than God. Not that I give a crap about his money, but overall, my dear friend, Chase *is* a fantasy."

"He also used to leave his dirty underwear and towels on the floor in the bathroom when he was a teenager," she said sarcastically. "Hopefully, he's outgrown that habit. He's just a man, Vanna. And really, I have Cooper. He's gorgeous, filthy rich, more intelligent than most people in the entire world, and also very highly educated. Plus, he's also a billionaire. To have your conclusion make sense, we'd have to say that Cooper should be married to a supermodel, too, rather than an average woman like me."

"Newsflash," I said. "You're a gorgeous genius, too. You're also a billionaire who was raised in the world of the ultrarich."

"I'm passably attractive if you can get past my weird eyes," she said adamantly. "And I couldn't have cared less about the world of the ultrarich. I have money, yes. But you know I never lived in that world. Move on to the next excuse as to why you aren't perfect for my brother, because I honestly do think he's mad about you. I also think he believes you're too good for him and that you're not interested. Otherwise, he would have made the first move already. Trust me. I know both of my brothers. I also know you, although I have to admit that you hid your attraction to Chase pretty well."

"I'm sorry I never told you," I said remorsefully. "It's about the only thing I just didn't feel like I could share. It's just…weird. Tell me you wouldn't have felt the same way if Cooper was my brother."

She grinned. "Awkward, yes, but I still would have found a way to get him naked anyway. Weird as it might sound, Cooper and I just…clicked."

I smiled back her. God, she looked so happy. After everything that Torie had been through, she deserved a man like Cooper.

I shook my head distractedly. "No, I get it."

She lifted a brow. "So are you going to tell him?"

I squirmed in my chair. What were the chances that Chase wanted to be more than friends?

Was I willing to take the chance?

"Do you actually want me to try to seduce your own brother?" I asked nervously.

She shrugged. "I don't think it would take much. He'd be pretty easy. All you'd have to do is tell him the truth and then stand there and breathe."

"I'm not completely convinced he'd be on board," I confessed.

"Stop, Vanna," she said in a disgusted voice. "I think you're running away because you're scared. I get it. But wouldn't you always wonder if you didn't try? I know it's harder because you two have known each other forever. But feelings change and evolve as you get older. When I look at the two of you now, it feels like the two of you should have always been together."

"I had a little more confidence before the kidnapping and these stupid scars," I revealed.

"They fade a little more every day, and any guy who can't see beneath them is a fool."

I chuckled. "You have to say that because you're my best friend."

"No, I know it's true because I'm your best friend," she replied smugly.

"I'll think about it," I said cautiously.

There was really nothing holding me back but fear anymore. I'd just shared with Torie earlier that I'd gotten back all of my health screens and they were negative.

If there was even a small chance that Chase wanted what I wanted...

My phone started ringing.

I picked it up and looked at the caller ID. "It's my producer," I told Torie. "I better take it."

Torie rose and snatched another cookie. "I have to get going anyway. Cooper will be home soon. He's bringing Chinese for dinner. Call me and let me know how it goes."

"I didn't say I was definitely going to do it," I called after her.

Torie didn't answer as she sailed out the door.

I sighed as I pressed the button to take the phone call.

Chapter 17

Chase

I heard Vanna crying the second I opened the door, and it scared the shit out of me.

Savannah Anderson wasn't the type of woman to cry over small events.

My heart was already racing by the time I got to the kitchen.

One look at her tearstained face nearly gutted me.

"Vanna?" I questioned as I kneeled in front of her. "Baby, what's wrong?"

Her eyes locked onto mine and she slowly shook her head. "I just got canned, Chase. I was just let go from *Deadline America*."

"I don't understand," I answered as I took her hand. "How and why in the hell did that happen?"

Were they completely insane? There really was no *Deadline America* without Savannah Anderson. She was the face of the show.

She pointed her finger at her face. "They think my scars will be distracting, and they're not sure they can always stay covered with the makeup. They're probably right. I don't work in the studio where I'm in a controlled environment. In some climates, it might be difficult to make sure they're completely unnoticeable. But I didn't really think it would matter. I guess it *does* matter to the higher ups. They're assholes who think appearance is everything. My producer and director went to bat for me, but the corporates were adamant that they needed a new face for *Deadline America*."

"Christ!" I cursed. "They're completely out of touch then. People who watch that show don't give a damn about your face, Vanna. They watch it for the way you present the issues."

She sniffled. "Corporate has never really understood what their watchers want. They're only worried about the image they present."

"Which is probably why they're still a fairly small cable channel," I grumbled. "Your show was the most popular on the network."

She swiped a tear from her cheek. "I can't really complain. They're paying out my contract for the rest of the year. I think they just want to get rid of me because I'm damaged in their eyes."

"Bastards!" I snarled, unable to control my anger. "You made that fucking program. I hope they enjoy watching their ratings crash and burn. *Deadline America* was popular because you made people want to give a shit about issues that they didn't even know existed before they watched it. They'll regret it."

She shrugged. "Well, right now they think it needs an overhaul, and that means a show without a woman with scars on her face."

My blood was boiling with every tear that trickled down Vanna's cheek.

"They're hardly noticeable," I said gruffly. "And they sure as hell don't affect your talent for storytelling."

She looked at me with sad, liquid eyes as she replied, "I want to believe that, but I see the scars in the mirror every single day when I get out of bed, Chase. They aren't invisible, and in television, looks matter sometimes. They're ugly."

My temper boiled over, and that was something that rarely happened, but I was royally pissed that anyone had made Vanna feel like she was less valuable just because of a few fucking scars.

"They are *not* ugly, and they don't have a goddamn clue," I growled as I stood up, grabbed my tie and ripped it off. I then took off my suit jacket and dropped it into the chair next to Vanna's. "Those are not scars, sweetheart. They're tiny little marks that are barely there."

I started to unbutton my dress shirt.

She swiped the tears off her face again as she asked, "What are you doing?"

"Showing you what scars actually look like," I answered as I pulled my shirt out of my pants and finished unbuttoning it.

I didn't care what it took anymore to make her realize that nothing about the scars on her face were unattractive.

Hell, I knew what repulsive *really* looked like.

I saw it every time I took off my shirt, and I'd seen it reflected in a woman's eyes when she saw them.

But that didn't matter anymore.

I was trying to prove a goddamn point that might make Vanna feel better about her gorgeous face.

All that really concerned me at this point was…Vanna.

"I was doing one last operation before I was due to be discharged from the Army four years ago," I said stoically. "My crew and I were going over last-minute details near the hangar out on the airfield when we came under heavy RPG fire. It came out of fucking nowhere and it took us all by surprise. I don't remember much of anything that happened after that. I nearly bled to death from shrapnel wounds by the time I was carried to safety. One of them nicked a blood vessel in my leg. My co-pilot was also injured. Unfortunately, my crew chief didn't make it. My face was spared, but that's about the only part of me that didn't get littered with shrapnel."

I pulled open my shirt and shrugged it off, fueled only by the need to make Vanna understand that *her* scars weren't ugly at all.

I heard her swift intake of breath as her eyes settled on my torso, but I still didn't stop. I was too fucking angry to stop.

"Oh, my God, Chase!" she said in a strangled, distressed voice.

My chest ached at the dismay and shock in her tone, but I wasn't about to cease just because she was repelled by the way that I looked.

Most women would be.

My body wasn't exactly a pretty sight.

I unbuckled my belt and let my pants drop to the floor.

I picked them up, tossed them beside my shirt and then held my arms out. "Now *these* are scars, Vanna. Take a good look. And don't ever tell me that your scars are ugly again. You're fucking beautiful. If anyone tells you anything different, they're completely full of shit."

I turned around slowly, covered only by a pair of boxer briefs, the rage that had consumed me a few minutes ago starting to slowly cool.

I knew where every piece of skin was missing, and just how deep some of those wounds had been.

Yeah, over time, some of the scars had faded, but not a single one of those ugly bastards were ever going to disappear.

Maybe they didn't show in my everyday life because I made a deliberate effort to cover them, but I knew they were there, and I'd seen a woman flip out when she saw them.

That's why I'd never bothered to inflict them on another female.

I didn't look at Vanna as I gathered up my clothes. "I think you probably get my point," I said in a graveled voice. "Let me take a shower and we'll talk about what happened today. I think those short-sighted, superficial assholes probably did you a favor, Vanna. You can take your exceptional talent somewhere else where it's appreciated."

Without another word, I exited the kitchen and sprinted up the stairs.

My rage level had lowered to a simmer as I pulled out a pair of jeans and a sweatshirt.

Hell, in hindsight, I probably should have prepared Vanna for that strip show, but I'd been livid at the thought of her agonizing over something so unimportant and so out of her control.

I wanted to tear the heads off every asshole at the network for hurting her feelings.

I couldn't handle seeing her cry for *any* goddamn reason.

My heart sank as I tossed my clothes into the hamper and strolled into the master bathroom.

So much for revealing the way I felt about her to Vanna.

There probably wasn't a woman on Earth who'd want to go to bed with a guy who looked like me when he was naked.

I'd known that since the very beginning.

But it hadn't stopped me from wanting Vanna anyway—every single fucking moment of every day.

I'd told myself that I could live without a woman in my life. *Until her.*

Until the moment I'd realized in Vegas that the woman I'd always hoped to find had been staring me in the face for years now.

In some ways, it probably should have been a relief when she'd ran away in Vegas after I'd given into a compulsive instinct to ask her out.

Unfortunately, even though I'd been at peace with swearing off relationships before I'd seen her again, Vanna's rejection had eaten my guts out.

"Fuck!" I growled as I slammed my fist against the wall. What in the hell was wrong with me? Why couldn't I just accept that Savannah Anderson was *never* going to be mine?

She hadn't said another word after her initial shock of seeing my torn-up body, but her horrified reaction and then her silence had spoken pretty loud and clear.

I yanked open the shower door and turned on the water.

"Tell her how I feel, my ass," I rumbled out loud as I shucked my briefs. "There isn't a woman on the planet who wants to go to bed with this body every night."

I tensed as I heard a voice behind me as she said, "Oh, there are probably dozens of them, but I'd fight them all off to have that chance myself."

I turned to see Vanna leaning against the doorjamb, tears pouring down her face as she said, "I think I'd do just about anything to get into your bed, Chase. I've fantasized about it for a very, very long time. I just wasn't convinced you wanted the same thing. Do you?"

Jesus! My heart started to pound so hard that I could hardly think.

I locked eyes with her because I couldn't help myself.

There wasn't even an iota of revulsion or disgust in her gaze.

It was bold and...hungry.

"You have no fucking idea how much," I answered, my voice rough and disbelieving.

She folded her arms across her chest. "Was that whole strip show thing you did just for me?"

"Yes," I said, my jaw clenched.

"Good. Because it was pretty hot, and I'd prefer you didn't do it with anyone else but me. You're a beautiful man, Chase. You work out like a fiend, and it definitely shows," she said softly. "But do you know what turns me on the most?"

I gritted my teeth. Fuck knew I definitely *wanted* to know. "No."

"The fact that you cared about me enough to do it in the first place. God, do you have any idea how much that means to me? You wanted to make me stop crying. You wanted to please me. I'd really like to know what it would be like to be with a man who cares whether or not I'm satisfied."

"Then I'm your man," I informed her tightly.

"Yes," she purred. "I believe you are. Either you come here or I'm coming to get you. Choose. Or I'll choose for you."

I knew she was using some of my own words lightheartedly about her choosing a wine for us that first night, but I couldn't otherwise wrap my head around what was happening. "You. I'm not quite sure if this is even real."

"Okay," she said amiably. "But fair warning…once I touch you, I may not stop for hours. I've wanted you naked like this for a very, very long time."

My dick had been hard from the second she'd said that she actually wanted me. She hadn't even said a word about my scars. What the fuck?

"Vanna," I warned her hoarsely. "Don't start something you don't want to finish. You have no idea what kind of monster you're messing with right now."

I hadn't gotten laid in years, and I'd never wanted a woman the way I wanted Vanna. Not even close.

Christ! If she checked me out one more time with that fuck-me look in her eyes, she was going to end up getting more than she bargained for in about two seconds flat.

She didn't seem to be even a little bit daunted as she batted those gorgeous eyes of hers and asked in a sultry tone, "Are you getting into the shower?"

I swallowed hard and nodded.

She sauntered her beautiful ass over to me and wrapped her arms around my neck. "Kiss me first," she demanded.

Jesus! I couldn't resist. I didn't even have the will to try.

Savannah Anderson had been my favorite fucking fantasy for way too long.

I fisted her silky hair and wrapped an arm around her waist before I lowered my head.

I hoped she knew what she was doing, because the monster wasn't going back into his cage anytime soon.

Chapter 18

Savannah

I moaned as Chase's mouth finally connected with mine because his kiss was even better than anything I had ever conjured up in my imagination.

He was a man who took complete control and kissed a woman with very clear intentions.

I opened to him as I speared my hands into his hair, feeling freer than I'd ever felt in my entire life.

I could taste his desire, and it was the headiest thing I'd ever experienced.

Chase wanted me. That need pulsated in the air around us as he devoured my mouth like it was the only morsel of nourishment that he needed to survive.

I savored his fierceness as he nipped my bottom lip and then stroked over it with his tongue.

"Chase," I whimpered as we came up for air.

"Is this really what you want, Vanna?" he said huskily beside my ear.

"Yes," I whispered breathlessly. "It's what I've wanted for a long time."

I moved back from him to pull my lightweight shirt over my head and dropped it to the floor, nearly panting with the need to get closer to him.

"My scars—"

I held up a hand before I unzipped my jeans and shoved them, panties and all, down my legs. "Don't," I cautioned him. "It upset me when I saw them, but only because I hate to think about how painful they must have been for you, but you still have the hottest damn body I've ever seen. They're part of you, Chase. Part of your history. Part of the sacrifice you made to serve this country. If you think that makes you less attractive, you're out of your mind."

Yes, the scars were deep and some of them were long and jagged. I'd cringed thinking about how close he'd probably come to losing his life because of them. But there was nothing about those marks that made Chase less appealing. The fact that he'd been willing to bear them for me so I'd feel more normal had made me want to sob like a child.

The fact that he'd done something so totally selfless just to make me feel more normal had just made me adore him even more.

I hadn't been able to stop myself from coming after him. Nothing would have kept me from racing up the stairs to talk to him.

However, once I'd seen him naked, my plans had changed to something considerably more…carnal.

When he'd muttered that comment about no woman wanting his body, I'd known that it was time to take a chance.

After all, he'd done the same with me, leaving himself completely and utterly vulnerable in the process.

I unclipped my bra and let it fall to the floor as I eyed his muscular body, my gaze finally dropping to the largest, hardest cock I'd ever seen.

My core clenched hard with a need I'd never experienced before.

I looked up, and my heart skipped a beat when I recognized the look of pure, primal lust in his gorgeous gray eyes.

"I never thought I'd ever see you look at me like this," I said, stunned by the way it made me feel.

"Were you serious when you said that you've always been with guys who didn't care if you were satisfied?" he asked gruffly.

"Completely serious," I said honestly.

"I care," he told me roughly.

I shuddered in anticipation. "I know," I answered simply.

The muscles in his neck contracted and relaxed. He appeared to be fighting for control as he rumbled, "Vanna, I haven't been with anyone for years, but I want you so much that it's killing me."

I wrapped my arms around his neck. I nearly purred as my nude body slid against his bare, fiery skin. "I'm pretty sure you'll remember exactly what to do," I teased softly. "I want you, too, Chase Durand. So badly I can hardly think. Take a shower with me?"

"I think you already know you're going to get a hell of a lot more than just a shower, sweetheart," he rasped as he put his hands on my ass and lifted my body.

I wrapped my legs and arms around him as he stepped into the shower and pulled the door closed.

The enclosure was enormous, but it was already full of steam as Chase pressed me against the wall and buried his face in my neck.

I let my head drop back as I savored the feel of his mouth against my skin.

"I got my results back today on all my screenings," I panted. "They were all negative."

"You protected?" he asked, his baritone muffled against my skin. "I know I'm clean, too."

"Implant," I said breathlessly. "Now fuck me."

He chuckled as he ran his hands down to my hips. "Not so fast, beautiful. I'm not eager to sprint across the finish line. Not after wanting you for so damn long. And I *never* want you to be able to say you weren't completely satisfied. Not with me."

Holy crap! I was fairly certain I wasn't *ever* going to be able to say that about Chase.

He kissed me as he released his grip and let my feet touch the ground.

I then watched in fascination as he swept a strong arm across the long bench seat and sent all of the bottles of shampoo and bodywash flying through the air. They landed across the enclosure, but I didn't really care where they went.

He picked me up and dropped me gently onto the now empty space as he said huskily, "I'm going to get to know every inch of this gorgeous body, sweetheart."

"Chase!" I squeaked as he moved his large body between my open thighs.

He nudged my legs wider as he ran his hands slowly down my entire body. "Christ! You're so fucking beautiful, Vanna. I don't know how any guy could not want to see you come over and over again."

At that particular moment, I felt like the sexiest woman on the planet. It was hard not to as I watched the hot, covetous look in his eyes.

Any hesitation I may have had about not having a model's body melted away. Chase definitely liked what he saw, and there was no denying that he wanted...me.

I gasped as his mouth came down to my breast and he bit lightly on my hardened nipple. I sucked in another breath as he soothed it with his tongue.

I closed my eyes, lost in a sensual world where only Chase and I existed.

"Chase, please," I begged as he teased the other nipple with his fingers. "I need..."

"I'll give you exactly what you need, sweetheart," he assured me as he moved lower.

Oh, sweet Jesus! I was sure he would.

"Oh, my God," I hissed when his tongue finally found my needy pussy.

I thrust my hands into his damp hair to try to keep myself grounded.

I couldn't believe any of this was happening, and it was so much better than any fantasy I'd ever had.

Longing overwhelmed me as I cried out, "Yes. Please."

I moaned as his mouth devoured me leisurely but thoroughly, like he had no plans of stopping any time soon.

"Chase," I said insistently as I tugged on his hair, my body screaming to be satisfied.

I was on fire with a nearly painful, primitive desire I'd never felt in the past, and it was eating me alive.

I moaned as he finally stopped teasing and focused on my clit, his tongue flicking across the sensitive, engorged nub over and over again until I was ready to lose my mind.

I was surprised when my orgasm started to build, each wicked pass he made over my clit stoking my desperate need for release.

I was frantic to come, but Chase was completely in charge of when that happened, and he seemed hell-bent to draw out the event as much as possible.

"Now," I pleaded.

He moved a little bit faster, but he didn't quite push me over the edge.

"Oh, God, I can't take anymore," I said, my voice shaky with desperation.

All I wanted was the release my body craved.

Immediately after I spoke those words out loud, Chase sped up the pace.

When he slipped two fingers into my channel and started fucking me while he was still tormenting my clit, I completely shattered.

My climax consumed me as I lifted my hips and tried to press my pussy harder against his hungry mouth.

Chase lingered like he was trying to make sure he drew every drop of pleasure he could get from me.

The climax went on and on, lingering for so long that I didn't think it was ever going to stop.

My whole body trembled as I slowly came back down to Earth.

"Wrap your legs around me and hold on," Chase said in a demanding voice.

I'd barely lifted them into position when he rose and my back suddenly hit the wall.

Instinctively, my arms went around his neck.

"I can't wait any longer, Vanna. Not this time. I want you too goddamn much to go slow right now," Chase growled as he lifted me higher and brought me down over his rock-hard cock.

"I don't want you to wait," I whimpered, my body responding to his urgency.

It was exhilarating to know how much Chase wanted me, and I was ready to take the wildest ride possible with him.

Even though I'd already had an orgasm, my body wasn't fully satiated. I knew it wouldn't be until Chase was inside me.

Some primordial, elemental desire for him to join our bodies was so strong that it was painful.

I sucked in a breath like I was oxygen deprived as he buried himself to the hilt inside me.

"Yes!" I screamed, urging him on.

He was big, but I wasn't going to complain about the momentary twinge of pain that I felt before I was absorbed in the complete bliss of finally having him inside me.

I nipped his earlobe as my body stretched to accommodate his size, frantic for him to soothe the ache that wouldn't leave my body alone.

I'd craved this ultimate closeness with him, and now that I had it, the carnal satisfaction was almost more than I could take.

"I need you, Chase," I told him, my voice raw with emotion.

"You have me, Vanna," he said roughly as he started to move. "Fuck! I'd love to stay like this forever because you feel so damn good around my cock, but I can't."

"Then fuck me. I need it, too," I said in a sultry tone I'd never heard come from my lips before.

He started to move, slow and deep at first, but his movements got more and more fierce as I submerged myself into erotic bliss all over again.

This was what I'd craved, this tumultuous, obsessive possession that rocked my body until I was in a frenzy.

"Good. So good," I chanted, knowing the words couldn't begin to explain what he was doing to me right now.

Chase grasped my hair and pulled my head down so he could ravage my mouth as our bodies undulated to an insane, frenetic beat that only the two of us understood.

"Yes. Yes. Yes," I said in a hoarse, agitated voice after he released my lips. "Harder."

He wanted to possess me, and I wanted to be claimed by him.

"Come for me, Vanna," Chase urged as he slammed inside me over and over again.

My legs tightened around him and I felt my climax looming. It was like a tightly wound knot in my stomach that slowly started to unfurl, reaching out to encompass every nerve cell in my body. It was a pure and utter ecstasy that sent me reeling.

"Chase!" I screamed as my orgasm began to move through me so powerfully that it was almost frightening.

The pulsations were intense as I reached the pinnacle.

"Fuck!" Chase groaned as my release set off his own. "You're mine, Vanna. Say it. I need you to tell me."

"I'm yours, Chase," I said obliging, panting my way through those words, my breath harsh and my emotions raw. "I have been for a very long time."

That was a truth that made me realize that no matter how long it had taken, this kind of passion was always meant to be, but could *only* happen with him.

I collapsed into his strong form, trembling from the sheer force of what had just occurred.

I felt wrecked, but freer than I'd ever been in my entire life.

I laid my forehead against his shoulder and closed my eyes, my body still humming from the ferocity of my climax.

If this was what post-coital bliss felt like, I wanted to experience it over and over again.

"Okay?" Chase asked, his breathing still slightly ragged.

"More than okay," I replied, not ready to move as I smiled.

"Baby, that was…" his voice trailed off like he didn't quite know what to say.

"Unexplainable?" I suggested.

"Exactly," he rasped.

Yep. This man got me—he really, really did.

Chapter 19

Chase

"Are your scars the reason you blew me off whenever I asked if you wanted to use the hot tub with me?" Vanna asked as the two of us lounged lazily in my outdoor jacuzzi several hours later.

Luckily, Vanna had turned the oven to warm before she'd followed me upstairs, so we'd still had edible lasagna for dinner. We'd both devoured the food like we hadn't eaten in weeks. Not surprising since we'd moved to the bed after the shower and hadn't surfaced for hours.

I was certain we'd satisfied that ugly problem of her never being satisfied by a man. I wasn't sure what kind of guy *wouldn't* care about her pleasure, because watching her come was a beautiful thing that I could never get enough of myself. I'd wanted to see it over and over again.

"Yeah," I confessed. "I don't exactly get naked with women anymore. Haven't in a long time."

I had to admit that it was surreal to be nude in a hot tub again. Especially when I was holding the only woman I really wanted against my bare-assed naked body.

Hell, if I was dreaming, I hoped nobody ever woke me up again.
I still had a hard time believing that Vanna had accepted my scars
like they didn't even exist.

All this time, I'd been a fucking idiot to think she'd react any
other way.

I knew her, yet I'd almost let my insecurities chase her away.

Her happy sigh washed over my battered soul like a healing balm
as she said, "I wish you would have told me. I could have reassured
you that you're still the hottest man on the planet. Obviously, some
other female missed that opportunity."

I winced, but I confessed, "I tried dating about a year after I got out
of the military. Without thinking about the possible consequences,
I changed my shirt in front of the woman I was dating at the time
because we were going out to dinner. She was so horrified that we
never did make it to the restaurant."

Vanna turned her body until she was straddling me on the seat
and we were face-to-face. "She must have been a total nitwit," she
said in a scalding tone. "I'm not going to lie to you because you've
never lied to me. Your scars are definitely visible, but I'm not sure
what woman could resist the body underneath them. Are you going
to tell me more about what happened?"

I threaded a hand through her hair and pulled her head down to
kiss her because I couldn't resist. *Fuck!* This woman could undo me
with a couple of words.

She wasn't filling me with a bunch of bullshit, either. I could see
the genuine adoration in her eyes every time she touched me. And
every fuck-me look she sent me made me absolutely insane.

She laid her head on my shoulder after I released her mouth,
waiting patiently.

There was only so much I could tell her, but I could do a lot better
than my previous explanation. "I wish I had seen it coming for even
a second or two, but I didn't," I disclosed. "One minute I had my
head down discussing the operation and the next it was lights out.
One of the RPGs slammed into a junk vehicle nearby where we were
standing. My helmet, and the fact that I had my head down, probably

saved my life. I didn't even know the fate of my crew members until I finally woke up in Germany. Wyatt was there. I don't know how in the hell he knew what happened or how he got there so fast. Torie was on a hiking trip in a remote location. She didn't find out until I was actually able to talk to her on the phone a few weeks later, after multiple surgeries to try to remove all the shrapnel from my body. She wanted to come, but I asked her to just wait until I got back home. I never got to do another mission. I was discharged soon after I got out of the hospital and back to the States."

She stroked a hand over my jaw. "I'm so sorry you lost a teammate."

I swallowed hard. "Me, too. He was a good man with a couple of kids back home. I didn't make it to the funeral, but I stopped to see his ex-wife and the children once I was back home to see if there was anything I could do to help. My co-pilot made out a little better than I did. He got back to his wife in relatively decent shape. We still talk once in a while."

"So Torie doesn't really know how bad it was? She mentioned that you were injured not long before you were discharged, but she didn't sound like she knew the full extent of it," she said contemplatively.

"Hell, no," I balked. "What guy wants to tell his little sister about every scar on his body and how it affects his sex life? She knows I was injured in a blast, and I generally stick with long sleeves so no one asks a lot of questions. Do you remember how mortified you were to be afraid of the dark?"

She lifted her head and nodded.

"I feel the same way about having my younger sister seeing my shrapnel scars. She thinks I'm a goddamn hero, and I like to keep it that way."

"I think you're a hero, too," she murmured as she ran her hands down my chest. "And I've seen all of your scars."

Even though I loved to hear her say that, I knew it wasn't true.

"For fuck's sake, I wasn't even engaged in the operation at the time. Like you said, I was just in the wrong place at the wrong time," I grumbled.

"Wherever you were, you were there because you were getting ready to go fly a helicopter into a dangerous situation. Please don't downplay what you did in special forces, Chase. Or the importance of what you do in Last Hope. I would have died out there in the jungle if you hadn't come after me," she said irritably. "And I'm sure you did it without a single thought to your own safety."

"I'd come after you a thousand times if that's what it takes to keep you safe, Vanna," I answered hoarsely. "Knowing you were out there somewhere being held against your will made me half crazy. Once I knew the whole situation, I wasn't even sure if you were still alive."

"I was, and you saved me," she said shortly. "So don't try to tell me you're not a hero. It's bullshit. I'm also certain I was one of many people you saved."

I grinned at her because she was getting adorably testy, and I knew it was because she was trying to defend me.

"I sure as hell hope I never fall off that pedestal you have me on, sweetheart. I'm really just a guy who went after a woman he cares about," I drawled. "It was a gut instinct that would trigger most men into action."

She punched my shoulder. "Only the ones who think they can save the world singlehandedly. I'm not sure if that's arrogance, ego, or insanity, but I'm pretty glad you've got it, whatever it is. I can't complain because it saved my life."

My grin got even larger. "Hate to say this, but I don't think it's really cockiness. It's confidence. We all just know what we're capable of doing after intense training. Our limits are being tested almost constantly in special forces."

"You've always been a little bit cocky," she informed me. "You hate losing a debate when you think you're right. But your kindness keeps you from being totally obnoxious. Honestly, maybe it was that effortless confidence that was one of the things that made me so attracted to you."

"Damn!" I said with pseudo chagrin. "I thought it was my handsome face, hot body, and my status as one of the richest guys in the world."

"Stop it," she said with a delighted laugh. "I'll admit, there was that, too. Well, not the billionaire thing. I've never really cared about your money. That's not what made me flustered every time I saw you again."

It was bizarre to have a woman say she didn't care about my money, but in Vanna's case, I knew it was true.

She'd been Torie's best friend for a long time, and she was accustomed to being around people who had an obscene amount of money. Never once had she treated me any differently just because of my wealth, nor would she let me win an argument just to appease me.

"Tell me what else gets you flustered, and just how many times have you had that affliction when we met up in the past?" I asked, wondering exactly when she'd realized I was a guy she wanted to get naked.

Fuck knew she'd never shared *that* knowledge with me.

If she didn't need or want my money, I wanted to figure out how to keep her happy.

She seemed to have no problem being blunt as she answered, "It's been a while. Probably since the party your dad had for Torie when she finished her PhD. That's probably when I noticed that my best friend had a brother who had grown up to be incredibly gorgeous. Back then, I didn't have a lot of problem brushing it off. You *were* my best friend's brother, a guy I'd known for most of my life, and I didn't want to make a fool of myself."

"Why didn't you tell me, or at least give me some kind of hint?" I questioned, wondering what I would have said to her back then if she had.

"Please," she said drily. "I was still like your honorary little sister. You would have thought it was pathetic."

I mulled that comment over for a moment before I replied. "Honestly, I'm not sure I would have. Maybe I wasn't ready to admit that you were the most remarkable woman I'd ever met, but I probably would have with a little encouragement."

"I wasn't ready to take that chance," she admitted.

"And when we saw each other at Torie's wedding? What really happened there, Vanna? By that time, I *knew* I was attracted to you. I think you felt that connection, too. But you ran away and broke my heart."

She shrugged and ran a gentle hand through my hair. "I got scared. I thought I was imagining it, and I didn't want to lose the only people who were like family to me. I didn't think you'd ever really see me as anything else except Torie's best friend. And you know I didn't break your heart."

"Oh, I saw you," I informed her. "And I'm not gonna lie, I was a little heartbroken. You took off that day like just the thought of spending time with me was off-putting, and you hadn't even seen my scars. It was pretty deflating."

"I'm sorry," she said regretfully. "I had no idea you offered for any reason except sympathy that I was on my own in Vegas."

"And if you had known that wasn't the reason?" I asked huskily.

Our eyes locked and hers were full of a romantic affection that made my chest ache as she answered, "I'm not exactly sure. By that time, I wanted to be with you so much that I might have thrown caution to the wind. I almost did. If I'd known you felt the same way, it might have been different. I wasn't really worried about Torie not approving. She's been begging me to take one of her brothers off her hands for a long time."

I raised a brow. "Has she really? Wyatt, too?"

Hell, I didn't like that idea. At all.

"Absolutely," she said with a smile. "Whichever one I was willing to take. She wasn't picky."

"Brat!" I grunted with very little animosity. "She didn't need to offer up Wyatt, too. I don't think I would have handled that very well."

"I adore Wyatt. But there was always only one Durand brother that I really wanted," she purred, her voice suddenly as sultry as a temptress.

"Which one?" I asked gruffly.

Yeah. Okay. Maybe it was pathetic that I was asking for reassurance, but I was still stunned that Vanna wanted me at all after seeing all the damage my body had suffered.

I tensed as she moved her hand down my body and wrapped her fingers around my stiff cock.

"The slightly cocky, argumentative, gorgeous one with a very large appendage that I desperately want to taste right now," she whispered against my ear.

"Dammit, Vanna," I groaned as she stroked me. "I wanted to discuss what happened to you today."

I honestly did, but I'd known I was screwed the minute she'd wrapped those clever fingers around me.

Not that I was complaining.

But I didn't want to talk about me anymore.

I needed to make sure she was okay with the stunt *Deadline America* had pulled today.

She nipped my ear, and ran her tongue down the side of my neck as she murmured, "Later. I'm busy with something *very* important right now."

I swallowed hard and closed my eyes, knowing that every day that I'd waited for this woman was all worth it.

Being adored by Savannah Anderson was mind-blowingly incredible, and I was still a little worried that I was in the middle of some fucking fantastic dream.

"Ride me," I ordered roughly.

"You're not getting your way. Not this time," she argued as her mouth skittered across my chest. "My turn to get to know this gorgeous body."

Jesus! That was likely to kill me.

"Vanna," I cautioned, my voice heavy with lust.

"Up," she insisted.

I pulled myself onto the edge of the hot tub, my lower legs still in the water.

She looked up at me as she pronounced softly, "I think you're the most beautiful man I've ever seen, Chase."

Our eyes met, and the sensual, scorching gaze she shot me sent my pulse out of control.

Sure, she was going to kill me, but damned if I wasn't going to die a happy man.

I watched when her eyes left mine and she wrapped those gorgeous lips around my cock.

"Holy fuck!" I rasped as she took as much of my cock as she possibly could, and then backed off as she sucked.

My balls tightened as she found a slow, hypnotic rhythm that drove me nearly mad.

Her lips…

Her hot, hungry mouth…

The way she seemed to be thoroughly savoring my cock was so damn heady and erotic that I nearly exploded on the spot.

"Vanna," I said, my voice throaty and hoarse. "Dammit, Vanna!"

Never in a million years could I have imagined being this intimate with a woman after my injuries, much less being laid bare and raw emotionally and loving every damn second of it.

I fisted her hair and guided her mouth exactly where I needed it.

She shifted, accommodated, and devoured.

She wanted to please me, and she didn't seem to care how that was accomplished.

I wanted to relish every single stroke of her tongue, but I knew I wasn't going to last very long.

I tried to slow it down.

I was afraid if I got too enthusiastic, she'd choke.

She was having none of that.

Vanna Anderson was determined to make me lose my mind, and once I realized that, there was no way I was able to control the frantic pace.

"So. Fucking. Good," I groaned, fisting her hair harder than I should have.

When her fingers started to play gently with my balls while her mouth sucked me at an almost frenzied pace, I completely lost it.

The tension that had been building reached a level so intense that every muscle in my body was tight.

My balls tightened to the point that it was almost painful, and the tingling in my groin spread to the base of my spine.

My heart was pounding like I'd just run ten miles uphill with a ton of weight on a sweltering summer day.

Son of a bitch! I had zero control when Vanna went after something she really wanted, especially when that something was me.

"Point of no return is happening in about two seconds," I warned Vanna as I tried to hold onto the feel of her mouth on my cock and the all-consuming pleasure it was giving me.

My dick was so fucking sensitive that every movement she made was euphoric.

I'd never felt anything like it, before or after the scars.

"Fuck! Vanna!" I growled when I suddenly detonated and realized that she wasn't going anywhere.

She stayed, apparently relishing the task of swallowing every drop she could possibly wring from me.

I loosened my death grip on Vanna's hair, my chest heaving as I felt the most exhilarating rush of testosterone I'd ever experienced in my entire fucking life.

I felt like I was literally floating, my legs and arms almost numb as I lowered myself back into the water and pulled Vanna on top of me.

"You almost did me in," I said hoarsely before I pulled her head down to kiss her.

Truthfully, I was annihilated, physically and mentally, but I didn't give a flying fuck.

Vanna could massacre me every day and twice on Sunday if this was what it was going to feel like.

After that, I'd start another week feeling like the luckiest bastard on Earth.

Chapter 20

Savannah

"Stay with me, Vanna. Screw those assholes at *Deadline America*. Finish your article on the Darien Gap crisis. Do whatever makes *you* happy. Hell, I'll buy that fucking network if you want your show back."

"Oh, no, you won't," I said firmly.

I picked up a piece of cheese and eyed Chase to figure out what he was thinking.

Once we'd gotten out of the hot tub, we'd taken another shower. After that, we'd come downstairs because Chase had declared he was still hungry.

He'd cut up some fruit, cheese and pulled out the crackers before pouring us both a glass of good wine.

We were currently seated at the kitchen table in the middle of the night sharing the food and wine. I'd explained that I wasn't really that horribly upset about the way I'd been treated by *Deadline America* anymore.

Yeah, it had been painful to get dumped by the executives simply because they wanted a prettier face, but I'd been in television for a decade. I knew we were always at the mercy of the whims of corporate, even if they were clueless.

Nothing lasted forever in television, that was certain.

Just the fact that I'd been doing *Deadline America* for so long was unusual.

My career was going to be in flux, but it was an inevitable move that was eventually going to happen at some time or the other.

I'd been mourning the sad ending to one phase of my career when Chase had come home from work.

He'd actually put my pain into perspective by stripping down to his underwear right in front of me.

Maybe it hadn't been intentional, but his bold actions had made me realize how small my scar insecurities were compared to someone who'd really gotten kicked in the teeth.

He'd not only went through the horrific pain in the hospital and nearly lost his life, but he'd also been rejected by a woman he was dating. I couldn't blame him for not wanting to try again with another woman who might or might not be quite as superficial.

Not once had Chase ever considered my scars hideous or ugly.

Did it really matter what some stuffed shirt in the corporate office of a small cable news channel thought about the scars on my face?

I chewed the piece of cheese and swallowed it with a sip of wine before I asked, "Do you really want me to stay? Chase, I have enough saved to get me through to my next career. I need to know exactly what and where that new career will be, but I certainly don't *have* to stay here."

"Then do it because you want to," he said insistently. "If you want me to get what I really want, you'll stay. Is there a single question in your mind about what I want right now, Vanna? I'm asking you because I know exactly what I want. I'm looking at her and hoping to hell she wants the same thing. I'm happier than I've ever been in my entire life. As different as we may be, we fit, Vanna. I want you to stay with me and be my partner in everything."

Our eyes locked and my heart skipped a beat.

Longing welled up inside me as I fell into his beautiful gray eyes.

It was definitely what I wanted.

I'd spent the majority of my adult life wandering the planet, continually restless and horribly lonely after I'd lost my mom.

I'd known something was missing.

I knew exactly what it was like to be in the middle of a crowd and still feel alone.

But I didn't feel that way anymore and probably wouldn't as long as Chase and I were together.

He was that something that had been missing, and I finally felt like I was exactly where I was supposed to be.

For the first time, I wanted to stay in one place because I'd finally found that absent part of my soul.

Was it a risk because caring about this man was as elemental as breathing for me?

Yes.

It was terrifying.

But I was addicted to being whole and dizzy with excitement about staying here with him.

"I'm happier than I've ever been, too," I confessed breathlessly.

I watched as something that resembled relief crossed his face. "Thank fuck!" He took my hand. "I'll do everything humanly possible to make you so damn happy that you'll never want to leave."

His vow made tears fill my eyes, but I blinked them back. "I want you to be happy, too."

Chase had spent enough time serving his country and other people. Somebody needed to work on pleasing him for a change.

He squeezed my hand. "Just looking at you makes me fucking ecstatic. I've never wanted you to go, but I couldn't make you stay if that wasn't what you wanted, too."

I sighed. I couldn't say he was a flowery romantic, but everything he said came from the heart, which was even better.

"I want that, Chase. I want to be with you, too. It might take a while, but I'm going to apply to be a freelance writer for the paper here and maybe a few other bigger publications. I just need to make sure there won't be any conflict with *Deadline America* if I try to sell my article on the Darien Gap crisis before I seriously try to sell it," I shared. "I have a ton of other written stories from previous episodes I'd love to update and sell, too, if there's no conflict."

He grinned. "Sweetheart, I have a whole legal department that isn't all that busy with Durand issues. And as far as newspapers go, I know a guy—"

"I'm sure you do," I interrupted. "You know a lot of guys who could probably solve every one of my problems, but I'd like to do this on my own merit. I'm perfectly capable of putting a portfolio together and submitting. But I might take you up on that legal advice. I'm sure you have the best attorneys on the planet."

His eyes sparked with humor as he answered, "You bet your beautiful ass I do. Quality is important, baby, and Durand employs only the best."

I rolled my eyes. "I think it might take a while to get used to your idea of quality," I said drily. "I'm not used to consuming a bottle of wine that costs more than my automobile."

"Not all of them are that expensive. Only the rarer ones. And I'm not really a collector. Everything in my cellar is meant to be consumed and enjoyed. I buy them because I like them. When it comes to wine, quality isn't always synonymous with being pricy," he explained.

"Well, thank God," I teased as I held up my wine glass. "This one is delicious by the way. I probably don't need to know if I'm drinking thousands of dollars' worth of alcohol for a late-night snack."

I took a sip of wine and rolled it around in my mouth.

He lifted a brow. "Then maybe you shouldn't ask. I consider this a very special occasion."

I nearly choked on my wine before I swallowed.

"Then I really don't want to know," I said in a rush.

He shrugged, unconcerned. "If you like it, then it was money well spent. I'm a very wealthy man, Vanna, but don't get hung up on that. It's only money. I work hard for our company, and I buy what I can afford, just like anyone else."

It's only money? How many billionaires say that?

I eyed him contemplatively, suddenly thinking about the comment Torie had made about Chase leaving his dirty underwear on the floor as a teenager. "There are instances where I have a hard time reconciling the Chase Durand that I know with the powerful billionaire that I know you are."

Truthfully, maybe that's what made him an enigma sometimes. He was so down-to-earth most of the time, but there was also a part of him that wielded a lot of power in an ultrawealthy world I knew very little about.

Torie was a billionaire, but she didn't work or spend much time in that world.

Strangely, Chase managed to exist in both the real world and the circle of the ultrarich without even thinking about it.

He could wear an outrageously pricy custom suit like it was a second skin, or he could hang out in a pair of jeans and a sweatshirt at home.

There was an endless amount of facets to his personality, and every single one fascinated me.

"You know who I am," he objected.

I did.

He was the guy who had bandaged up my knee when I'd fallen off my bicycle as a child.

He was the guy who had openly wept with profound grief when he'd lost each of his parents, but had still managed to be strong for his siblings.

He was the guy who would have gladly taken his little sister's place rather than see her suffer when she was in such bad shape from her kidnapping.

He was the guy who had rescued me in a jungle when I had very little hope left.

He was the guy who had stripped down to his underwear, making himself vulnerable just because he hated to see me cry.

He was the guy who had just given me multiple orgasms until I couldn't move.

He was the guy who was now sitting at a table with me in the kitchen, wanting to help because I was switching careers.

"You're the most incredible man I've ever known," I told him honestly. "Maybe I'm just a little worried that I won't fit into that ultrawealthy world when it's necessary."

"You don't have to fit in, Vanna. It doesn't matter. Occasionally, I do attend events when it's important to Durand. You don't have to go if you don't feel like playing that game. I'd love to have you with me, but you have to remember that it's work, not my personal life," he said gently.

"I think I'd like to be with you," I confessed. "It's not like I'm completely naïve. I've had to do some of those work events myself. They were snobs, but not quite the same wealthy crowd you circulate in."

"Those parties are incredibly boring. You'd be saving me if I had some company," he teased. "You know who I hang out with when I have the opportunity. My older brother is probably my best friend, even though he's a cantankerous, sarcastic asshole some of the time. Torie is your best friend. You also know Hudson, Jax, and their wives. And Cooper is your best friend's husband. That's pretty much my inner circle."

I'd gotten to know the Montgomery brothers a little better at a barbeque, and I really liked Taylor and Harlow.

"Sadly, Torie is pretty much it for me," I told him. "I mostly hung out with my crew because we were always in the same place at the same time. Globetrotting around the world isn't really conducive with making a circle of good friends." I paused for a moment before I added, "I'd like to be a Last Hope advisor someday, Chase. I think I'd really like to be part of something that important. I just need some time to get my career nailed down."

"Take all the time you need," he agreed wholeheartedly. "When you're ready, you can learn the ropes. I'm sure Marshall would be happy to get another advisor to help our victims. It's a commitment that not all previous victims want to make. In the meantime, I'll take you into our headquarters and show you what we do and how we do it when you have the time. Now what else can I do to help you?"

I shook my head as I smiled. "Don't you think you've already done enough? You've been there for me for months now as an advisor. I've stayed here at your place like an honored guest, too."

"It's *our* place now, and you don't need me as an advisor anymore. I want to support you the same way you want to support me, Vanna," he said earnestly. "Remember, I promised I'd make you so happy that you'd never want to leave."

"Right now, I think I'd be *very* happy if you take me to bed." I held up a hand when I saw the hopeful look on his face. "Oh, no. We need sleep. We both have to work in the morning. I need to get moving on that portfolio."

He stood and then pulled me up with the hand he was still holding. "I called Wyatt a long time ago and told him I'd be late coming in. Probably very late."

My entire body shivered and heat crept directly between my thighs as he kissed me, and then nuzzled those sensual damn lips of his against my neck.

How in the hell was it even possible that I could still crave this man after the gluttony of sex we'd engaged in all evening and half the night?

One simple touch and I was ready to throw reason out the window.

I squealed as he picked me up and started toward the stairs.

"I suppose I could probably sleep in, too," I said, caving in almost immediately.

I'd wanted this man for what seemed like forever. Maybe one day wasn't going to even quench my thirst for him.

"Excellent idea, baby," he agreed as he sprinted up the stairs like he was afraid I'd change my mind.

Chapter 21

Savannah

"Oh, my God, Vanna. He's really beautiful," Torie said as she sat watching my new protection trained German shepherd play with her dog, Milo.

His name was Axel because he had a very long, unpronounceable registered name, and he *was* gorgeous.

"Chase wanted me to accept a bodyguard," I told Torie. "Axel was a compromise."

It had been nearly a month since Chase and I had made the decision to live together and be a couple. During those weeks, I'd learned that compromise was necessary when a woman lived with a very stubborn man who was obsessive about her safety.

Torie raised her eyebrow at me from her side of the sofa. "Was it really a compromise? Axel looks at you like he worships you already and vice versa."

"Not really," I confessed. "I haven't had a dog since I was a child, and I've really missed being a dog owner. I absolutely adore him, and he's good company. I'm still working with the trainer to make sure

I have all the commands down, but it is nice to have a companion who doesn't talk when I'm working."

Chase had insisted on remodeling one of the downstairs bedrooms into an office for me, and he'd gotten it done in record time. Of course, he knew a guy who did quality work and could complete the task with a large crew inside of a week.

In the last month, I'd also quickly learned that almost nobody said *no* to a billionaire Durand, especially one as charming as Chase.

I loved having my own space decorated just the way I wanted it. Everything about my office inspired my creativity.

"Get used to the protective instincts," Torie warned me. "If Cooper could get away with it, I'd have a bodyguard with me whenever he wasn't around. But we leave for work at the same time every day. I'm generally not home alone unless he has to work late. And he has a state-of-the-art security system here."

"Chase does, too," I said. "But he's still concerned, more so very recently."

Torie nodded. "He told Cooper and me about the weird letters he and Wyatt have been getting at the office so we'd stay alert. Judging by the content, Chase and Wyatt think it's actually the son of one of Dad's old enemies, Gerald Kruger. My father started speaking out about Kruger's company not long before he died, when they started stealing designs. Not so much for his own good, but to hopefully help smaller and independent designers who were losing their livelihoods. Dad was one of several big luxury brands that was sick of watching this other company blatantly copy other's designs. Items were made cheap with those stolen designs and then sold in mass quantities at a bargain price. Dad came out a lot stronger than some of his competition."

Chase had told me about what happened, but he'd been light on the details. "Couldn't they be stopped by patent or copyright laws?"

Torie sighed. "Intellectual property laws for apparel and accessories are complicated. Usually, my father didn't get all that worked up about companies making dirt cheap products that resembled his. But this was a creepy company that was known for using a lot of very young child labor with horrible conditions overseas, too. Between that and the smaller designers and artists who couldn't make a living because of the design theft, I think he reached his limit of what he could tolerate without saying something. Eventually, Kruger's company failed, not just because of their reputation but their practices, too. Their goods were so poorly made that they were almost disposable. I think people just got tired of the poor quality, even if the merchandise was dirt cheap. It's tragic because Gerald Kruger committed suicide, and Wyatt and Chase think his son is out for revenge because they lost everything."

Chase had explained something similar. "Do you think they're right?" I asked Torie.

She shrugged. "It's possible. There are all kinds of crazy personalities in the fashion and luxury brand world. That's why I was never eager to stay that close to the industry."

"Do you think Chase and Wyatt are in danger?" I asked. "What about you?"

"Half the time, I don't think anyone realizes that a female Durand exists. I stayed out of the limelight, and I've never had anything to do with the brand. You're a lot more high profile than I am. It's no secret that you're close to Chase now that you're his live-in girlfriend. You just did that charity gig with him last week where he was representing Durand, so everyone knows. I won't say I wasn't concerned when Chase told me what was happening, but I wasn't surprised, either. My father had his life threatened more than once in that industry, which is why he protected his kids. My brothers both have a concealed carry permit, and I guarantee they're both carrying at the moment."

"Chase is," I confirmed. "I know that he knows how to take care of himself, but anything can happen."

Torie laughed. "Now you sound like him when he's trying to protect you. In the past, Chase would have blown off the nasty letters. Neither of my brothers are that concerned for their own safety. Like you said, they can take care of themselves. Having a *girlfriend* is a whole different story. Honestly, Chase has never had to worry about something like this before while he was a CEO of Durand. He hasn't had a serious girlfriend since he and Wyatt took over the company. Be patient with him. If he gets too overbearing, put your foot down like you did with the bodyguard thing. He might not like it, but if he wants to be with you, he'll have to understand that you've handled your own life just fine for a long time now."

"I can't live in fear of something that will likely never happen. I never have," I said.

"That's my philosophy, too, but Cooper will always try to protect me. I think it's in his DNA."

"Chase's, too," I commiserated. "It's like this whole situation has kicked his protective instincts into overdrive. He said the police are trying to investigate, but they've got no proof so far, and the son swears he had nothing to do with those letters. They can't arrest someone for content alone. It could be any crazy person pretending they're someone else."

"I know," Torie acknowledged. "I wish it would stop. It has Cooper on edge, too."

"Me, too. Not that I minded getting an awesome dog out of this situation, but I don't like seeing Chase so worried."

Torie snickered. "All you would have had to do was mentioned that you might like a dog in passing, and Chase would have brought you one home the next day. He's crazy about you, Vanna. I'm surprised he hasn't asked you to marry him, yet."

I let out a surprised bark of laughter before I said, "We just started living together. I don't think he's going there."

"He loves you," Torie said confidently. "He'll ask."

"He hasn't said so," I said firmly. "And I don't expect those words. It's way too soon."

"But you do love him, right?" she asked, her voice slightly anxious.

I wasn't about to lie to my best friend.

I'd already learned that once in a while I had to watch what I said to her so I never disclosed anything that Chase wouldn't want me to tell. But these were *my* feelings. "Yes. I think you already know that, but you can keep it to yourself for now, please."

"I'd never say anything that would betray our friendship, Vanna. Nor would I ever want to hurt Chase. I might hint or something when I want to knock your heads together, but I'd never want to do anything to overstep my bounds as your future sister-in-law."

"Torie," I said in a warning tone.

"Alright, alright," she said jovially. "I'll behave since you're the woman who has made my brother happier than I've ever seen him. Now, if I could just get someone to take Wyatt."

I chuckled. "I have a feeling he doesn't want to be taken."

I really liked Wyatt, but I'd known him since childhood. I knew that he had a heart underneath all that cynicism, but it was going to take a very smart, very brave woman to get to really know him.

"He has absolutely no interest in dating anyone," Torie said, sounding thoroughly disgruntled.

"Maybe he's happy that way," I suggested.

She shook her head slowly. "I don't think he is. He's just never found anyone who really wants to get to know him. I think we both know that Wyatt is a softie beneath that rough exterior."

I snorted. "You think that because he would always do anything for *you*."

"He'd do anything for the right woman, too. Mark my word on that," she replied smugly.

She was probably right. I'd certainly watched Torie wrap both of her brothers around her little finger as a kid. Although I wasn't certain I'd exactly call Wyatt a "softie."

"So tell me about work," Torie requested. "Are you really feeling okay about leaving *Deadline America* now?"

"Better every day. I just sold my story on the Darien Gap to the paper here in San Diego," I informed her. "Actually, I had multiple offers from publications that have already accepted me as a freelance journalist. I'm going back and updating pieces that are still really hot issues. I was really nervous, but I think I can publish most of the stories I write, Torie. Chase was an enormous help with the legal issues."

Torie frowned. "Was there ever any question about your ability to sell that story and any others that you write?" she asked, sounding confused. "Vanna, you're probably the most talented journalist I've ever read. That story was so heartbreaking that I cried when I read it. You present the facts, but it all comes from your heart. You have a gift that you've worked at and honed over the last decade. There's never been a single doubt in my mind that publications *wouldn't* be fighting each other for your work. Do you think you'll still have to travel?"

I smiled at her, grateful that Torie was my best friend. "Probably," I replied. "But in a world where I can do interviews and research by computer, I doubt it will happen often or for very long. It depends on what the story is about. I'm throwing around some interesting ideas for local and regional issues to work on once I finish updating my previous stories. Who knows? I might decide to write books about the stories that mean something to me someday."

"I think that would be amazing," Torie said enthusiastically. "I think you were meant for even bigger things than *Deadline America*."

"For now, I think I'm pretty burned out on traveling around the world."

I had a whole beautiful new life with Chase that I just wanted to enjoy for a while before I even thought about traveling for a story.

Torie snorted. "Well, at least you can travel by private jet now when you do have to go. You don't think for a single second that Chase would have it any other way, do you?"

I smiled. "No. We've already had that discussion. I might be independent, but I'm not crazy. If it makes him feel better, I'd take him up on that offer. The bodyguard issue is a whole different thing. I'd go crazy having someone watching me all the time. I understand his concern because of the crazy letters he's getting. I'm worried about his safety right now, too, but the human bodyguard is a no-go for me."

"You can't blame the guy for trying," Torie said.

"Chase can be stubborn sometimes. If I didn't know better, I'd think my name was 'Dammit Vanna' when we disagree. Did Cooper try?" I asked curiously.

"He already knows I'd never go for that, either," she responded. "And Cooper really isn't as high profile as Chase. Mining and luxury brands are two completely different industries. Now that Chase and Wyatt are the faces of the company, they are front and center when it comes to publicity. Especially Chase. Since Wyatt isn't exactly social, Chase has willingly taken on the role almost singlehandedly. It makes sense that he's a little worried about you. Not to mention the fact that you almost died when you were kidnapped in a foreign country not long ago. I think that experience is still pretty fresh for him, Vanna."

"I know," I said. "He still asks me every day how I'm feeling about the kidnapping. I still have times when I'd like to remember more of what happened, but I'm pretty okay with not knowing now."

I'd also managed to conquer my fear of the dark with Chase's help. If I had to sleep alone now, I doubted that I'd need a nightlight anymore.

Torie was silent for a moment before she said in a quiet voice, "I saw a few of Chase's scars the other day, Vanna."

My eyes flew to her face and noticed the sorrow in her expression.

She continued, "He stopped by after one of his morning runs to have a quick word with Cooper about some Last Hope equipment. He was wearing a short-sleeved T-shirt. Looking back, I realized that I hadn't seen him in short sleeves for a long time. I could see a small portion of a few of those scars and I asked him what happened. He told me more than he's ever admitted about those injuries. He also told me how some idiot he was dating hyperventilated over how ugly they were. He's never been that open about what he suffered. I never knew. I think he was so self-conscious that he didn't really share with anyone, not even his sister. By the time I talked to him on the phone after the incident, he was very lucid and said he'd be home in a few weeks. He did come home, but he's been distant about it ever since. Until a few days ago. Considering what happened, I'm going to assume he has the same scars all over his body."

I paused for a moment, not quite sure how to respond. I'd known Torie for too long not to understand what she was trying to ask in a roundabout way. "It's never mattered to me, Torie. I love him. He accepted my scars like they didn't exist before I even knew about his. I hate what he went through, but to me, he was and always will be the man with the hottest body on the planet."

I'd encouraged Chase to wear short sleeves again and not to be so self-conscious because he had no reason to be. I'd also told him that he should consider telling Torie more about what happened since Wyatt had physically been there and knew more about the whole incident.

It was time for Chase to stop feeling like he needed to hide his scars. Spring was here and summer was coming. There was absolutely no reason for him to hang out in long-sleeved shirts when he loved water sports so damn much.

I hadn't known that he'd started shaking off his uneasiness about his scars.

He hadn't told me yet that he'd decided to take my advice about Torie, but I knew he would when we had a chance to talk about it again.

My heart swelled at the thought that he was finally getting past what had happened years ago.

Because of that early rejection, I was pretty sure that Chase saw those scars as far more horrific than they were in reality.

She held up a hand as she said, "I won't ask for too much information. All I wanted was to thank you for loving my brother so much. He really needed you, Vanna. I just don't think I realized how much."

The dogs started to bark as they chased each other around the house.

As we laughed at their antics, I thought about what Torie had just said.

She really had no idea how much I'd needed Chase, too, or how damn easy he was to love.

Chapter 22

Savannah

"I'm ready," I told Chase as I opened the door of the master bathroom.

He'd insisted on taking me out for dinner tonight to celebrate the sale of my first independent piece of work about the Darien Gap.

I'd put on a cute black dress that could be dressed up or down with three quarter length sleeves and a V-neck. It probably hugged my ass, hips, and thighs a little bit more than was completely comfortable for me, but I loved that it worked for almost any occasion. It wasn't blatantly sexy, but it was different from my normally relaxed and casual attire. I'd finished it off by adding a pair of black thigh-high stockings and pair of dress heels.

I'd gone heavier on my makeup to diminish the scars on my face, and I was wearing the turquoise earrings and necklace Chase had given me.

"You look stunning," he said in a low, throaty baritone as his gray eyes assessed me.

"You're looking pretty gorgeous, yourself," I said as I smiled at him, taking in the lightweight cashmere sweater and slacks he was wearing. The sweater was a lovely shade of blue that made his gray eyes pop.

Really, Chase seemed to know exactly what colors to wear that suited him. He looked incredibly handsome in anything he chose to wear.

"Do you have any idea how beautiful you are?" he asked as he snaked an arm around my waist.

My heart tripped as I saw the appreciation in his gaze.

Nope. I didn't think I was beautiful, but he never forgot to tell me that *he* thought so.

Really, no one else's opinion mattered anymore. Not to me.

"Thank you," I said softly as I looped my arms around his neck.

The expression in his eyes was breathtaking.

Explosive.

Heated.

Hungry.

Intense.

And all of those emotions were focused directly on…me.

I swallowed hard as I tried to get my emotions under control.

Chase Durand could make me feel like a wicked temptress with a single look, and I'd never felt this way before.

I'd never had *any* guy look at me like this, much less the one that really mattered the most.

God, it was no wonder I was so damn happy that it was almost scary.

"How in the hell are we going to make those reservations on time?" he asked.

"You know you hate to be late," I reminded him teasingly.

Unless otherwise stated, Chase was always ridiculously prompt, like he still expected himself to arrive on the dot, give or take thirty seconds.

"I'm not sure I give a shit today," he said as he lowered his head to kiss me.

The embrace was demanding and sensual, a claiming of my mouth and lips like they belonged to him.

Just the kind of kiss that made me half crazy, and he knew it.

His hands moved down my lower back to my ass. He pulled my body against his with a forceful tug so I could feel exactly how much he wanted me.

"Chase," I whimpered as he released my mouth.

"Turn around and put your hands on the dresser, Vanna," he demanded as he moved back a step. "Stay there and don't move."

My nipples hardened until it was almost painful, and incendiary heat flooded between my thighs.

I immediately recognized his tone, and it almost sent me melting into a puddle at his feet.

There were times when Chase really wanted to be in control in the bedroom, and I certainly didn't mind how bossy he got. It aroused and captivated me, and I trusted him completely.

I trembled with anticipation as I started to turn, stepping forward so I could bend over.

The dresser was actually a sleek, contemporary gray table with drawers that sat lower to the ground than most normal dressers.

My rear end was almost even with my shoulders by the time my palms hit the surface.

I let out an audible sigh as his hands moved over my ass, up my back, and then underneath me until he was cupping my breasts through the material of my dress.

I bit back a moan as he found my nipples and pinched just enough to send a needy jolt through my entire body.

"Chase," I whispered desperately.

"Do you know how long it took for my cock to get hard when I saw you come out of that bathroom?" he asked in a graveled voice.

"No," I squeaked as he began to pluck the hardened peaks over and over again.

"A millisecond," he informed me before stopping his sensual assault and moving his hands to right above my knees where the hem of my dress rested. "That's exactly how long it takes for my dick to get hard whenever I see you."

The small amount of spandex in my dress stretched as he lifted it slowly up my thighs and over my ass.

At that moment, I was vulnerable, but completely unafraid.

Chase cared about nothing but my satisfaction, and I already knew he'd take care of that…after he had me so worked up I was begging.

"That's really…fast," I finally answered.

He slipped a finger under the elastic in the leg of my black bikinis, and I shivered as that finger caressed the full length of my damp slit.

"You're wet, baby," Chase informed me in a low voice dripping with lust. "But not wet enough."

Oh, God. I could tell by the tone of his voice that he was hell-bent on making me crazy.

I let my head drop, and my body tensed as I waited…

And waited…

And waited…

Anticipating his stroking touch over my clit.

I needed that…right now.

"Tell me what you want, Vanna," he insisted as a few more fingers invaded my slick heat.

"Touch! Me!" I panted, my body strung tightly.

"Like this?" he questioned as he finally found the hard nub.

"Oh, God, yes," I whined, my hips starting to move involuntarily. "Make me come, Chase. Please."

That was exactly what I needed.

"Not yet," he said patiently as he slapped my ass firm enough to send a jolt of fire through my pussy. "I need you to want me as much as I want you right now before I fuck you, Vanna."

"I'm there, Chase. I'm there, dammit!" I told him, my voice needy. "Please."

In my desperation, I started to rise up, but Chase quickly covered my body, putting his hands next to mine as he bent over me.

"Don't move. Spread your legs wider," he ordered.

I complied, my entire body on fire.

"Hope these aren't your favorites," he growled. "If they are, I'll buy you a truckload of them tomorrow."

He gave my panties a hard yank, and they separated from my body, giving under his strength.

Now that he had better access, those talented fingers were every-where, and I was so ready for him that I rocked back against him.

"Easy," he growled into my ear. He kept a persistent, light, teasing pressure on my clit as he stroked back and forth. Over and over. Until I was ready to lose my mind.

"I can't take much more," I moaned, my body screaming for sat-isfaction. "Please, fuck me."

He slid a finger inside my channel as he asked roughly, "You want my cock, Vanna?"

I nodded, my breath sawing in and out of my lungs and my heart pounding like it was going to escape my chest. "Yes," I hissed.

He buried his face in my neck, and licked upward until he reached my ear.

He nipped, and then traced my earlobe with his tongue, his breath heavy, warm, and aroused as it wafted over my ear.

I quivered, barely able to keep my arms from giving out from under me.

"You're fucking mine, Vanna. Say it!" he instructed hoarsely.

"I'm yours, Chase," I whimpered. "Now fuck me and prove it. Take me if I'm yours, dammit!"

"Whatever you need, baby," he said in a low, carnal voice as he gave my clit one last stroke before he straightened.

I knew that he sensed that I was on the edge.

In a matter of seconds, I felt the velvety tip of his hard cock poised at my entrance.

"Now, Chase!" I mewled, my core throbbing with need.

I gasped as he buried himself to the hilt with a tormented groan. "Christ, Vanna. You feel so fucking good."

"Yes!" I cried out, my body shuddering with relief, and stretching hard to accommodate him at this particular angle.

He was so damn big and hard, but I was so far gone that I didn't feel the very brief discomfort that I normally did.

There was just him.

Everywhere.

Surrounding me.

Insisting on everything I could give.

Playing my body like an instrument.

I didn't care because I knew he was starting to come apart at the seams, too.

He was coming undone, and he didn't give two shits if I knew that.

He grasped my hips and started to move.

There was no slow start, no savoring this time. We were both desperate and greedy, wanting and primal.

I moaned helplessly as Chase pummeled into me, every muscle in my body tight. Something fierce was building with every stroke, and I made no attempt to stop it.

It was like this between us every single time he touched me.

Untamed.

Wild.

And so powerful that all I could do was ride the waves of pleasure.

"Time to come, sweetheart," Chase said huskily as he moved his hand in front of my body and found my clit.

I imploded almost immediately.

My climax sent me reeling, and my legs began to shake as the overwhelming climax reached its peak.

I put my head back as I screamed his name, "Chase!"

I wanted to tell him I loved him, and that instinct was so acute that I had to bite on my bottom lip to keep from blurting it out.

The hand gripping my hip squeezed my flesh harder, and Chase surged one last time as he found his own release.

My legs gave out, but he caught me as I went, picked me up, and held me as he moved into a sitting position on the dresser.

I straddled him as he held me tightly, stroking my back, his heated breath on my temple as he rested his lips there.

We stayed just like that, wrapped up in each other as we recovered our breath.

He threaded a gentle hand in my hair and pulled me down for a kiss a few moments later, an embrace that made me blink back tears because it was so full of reverence and devotion.

"I think we're definitely going to be late," Chase said in a lazy baritone after he released my mouth.

"That's what you get for being so bossy," I said with a snicker.

"Had to," he said with feigned defensiveness. "You and that ass-hugging dress almost destroyed me. If you *had* touched me, it would have been over."

I smiled softly as I ran my fingers through his hair, savoring every second of that raw intimacy before we finally had to get up to salvage dinner.

Chapter 23

Chase

"That was probably the most incredible dinner I've ever eaten," Vanna said with a sigh as she pushed away her empty dessert plate. "Thank you for the beautiful flowers you gave me earlier, and for this gastronomic delight this evening. I think I've been to every really nice restaurant in San Diego now. Is there any eatery in this city that you *haven't* been in yet?"

She'd suggested dinner at home because we were going to be late for our reservation, but I wasn't having it.

Maybe I couldn't keep my damn hands off her, but I wasn't missing a dinner this important.

I was so damn proud of Vanna, and I wanted her to know that I supported every aspect of her career.

It was a big deal for her to sell her first independent piece of work, and I wasn't going to let my horny ass spoil it.

I'd read that story on the Darien Gap several times, and it was so incredible that I wasn't surprised that she'd sold it almost immediately with multiple offers.

In the end, I'd called for a later reservation, and since I knew the guy who owned the restaurant, it hadn't been an issue.

Vanna loved every restaurant we'd been to so far. Because she'd been traveling for years, she usually asked me to choose, so I'd taken her to most of my favorites.

"Probably not," I admitted. "From fast food and cafés to Michelin star, there's not many I haven't tried." I liked my food, and since I was unattached, I'd eaten out a lot. Wyatt and I also ordered out for lunch most of the time, too. "I'm glad you liked this place. That's probably high praise since you've been all over the globe."

She shook her head slowly. "I've never really gotten to see the sights or experience the cuisine during a lot of the assignments I've done. Either the location was too remote, or we were on a tight time schedule because of the budget. We arrived, we worked, and then we left. We usually ate whatever was available. I would have gladly spent my own money if I'd had time to explore some of the countries I've visited, but we were usually due at another location right after the previous one. It never stopped, really. That's why I rarely got home to San Diego."

I really hated the fact that they'd pushed Vanna so hard that she'd never gotten a chance to enjoy the places that she could. Cheap bastards!

"We can go anywhere you want just for fun," I told her. "Make a list, and we'll make sure we find time for those vacations. Even though we relocated our headquarters back to the States, there will be occasions when I'll need to go to France, too. I'd be happy to introduce you to my second home."

Her face lit up, which automatically made my damn chest ache. It was humbling how open she was with me now, and how eager she was to do almost anything if it involved the two of us together. Vanna had the same amount of enthusiasm, whether I suggested a trip for ice cream or an excursion to Paris. It didn't matter to her.

"I'd love that. I've been to Paris, but I never even got to visit the Louvre, much less the Eiffel Tower," she said with regret.

I had no fucking idea how someone could send an employee to Paris and not give them a little time to enjoy the City of Lights. It seemed downright criminal to me. However, that did mean that I'd get to see her face when she saw all of those places for the first time. "I'll take you all over the country," I promised. "I love Paris, but there's other places that you should see in France, too."

She swallowed the last sip of her wine and put her empty glass beside her discarded dinner plate. "You do realize that you're going to spoil me, right?" she asked teasingly. "Actually, you already have."

Spoil her? Hell, I planned on ruining her to the point where she wouldn't ever consider being with any man but me for the rest of her life.

Vanna was a woman who deserved to be treasured wholeheartedly, and I was the perfect man for that job.

"It's about time that someone does," I grumbled after I'd drained my own wine glass.

I wondered how I'd gotten lucky enough to capture and keep Vanna's attention, but I wasn't going to question the best damn gift I'd ever been given. All of those other idiots who had dated her before me and let her go had to have a screw loose somewhere.

Miracle or not, Vanna *was* mine now, and there was nothing I wouldn't do to keep it that way.

"I hope Axel is okay at home by himself," Vanna fretted. "I've never left him alone this long before."

"He's fine. He's a trained protection dog, Vanna," I reminded her, secretly pleased that she cared about the canine so much since she'd gotten Axel to appease *my* concerns.

"But he's still a dog that's being left alone for the first time in a new home," she protested.

I grinned. "I think you've fallen in love with a dog."

Lucky. Fucking. Dog.

She smiled sheepishly. "Maybe. He's such a good boy, Chase. All he really wants is to play, be near his people, and get a bunch of cookies every day."

"Sounds like the perfect life to me," I said wryly as I signed the receipt the waiter had brought me and put my card away. "Do you want anything else before we go, sweetheart?"

Actually, the mutt and I had similar goals and needs, so I guess I could sympathize with him if he was missing Vanna right now.

Hell, I missed her, too, when we weren't together.

Axel and I both wanted to protect Vanna and keep her safe.

We'd never turn down treats if she offered them.

And we both wanted her to pet us, albeit in far different ways.

"No thanks," she replied.

I waved the waiter away before I asked, "So I'm forgiven for insisting that we get Axel?"

I had to admit that I really liked the mutt, too, but my main purpose in getting him had been to add an extra layer of protection to Vanna.

The way she adored him was just a huge bonus.

"Of course," she said softly. "I'm perfectly willing to compromise, but I can't do the human bodyguard thing, Chase. Ever. It would drive me completely crazy."

Honestly, I couldn't blame her. I wouldn't be able to tolerate it, and Vanna had her own life. Normally, I wouldn't have given this much credence to an obvious lunatic, but something in my gut was nagging me about this one.

This person was excessive and obsessive. They wanted Wyatt and me to pay because, in their twisted mind, we were responsible for their father's death. That meant the people we cared about could be in more danger than we were.

Something didn't feel right, and even Wyatt agreed with me.

Cooper was taking every precaution possible with Torie.

Which pretty much just left...Vanna.

Fuck! I couldn't stand the thought of her being vulnerable.

I had no problem admitting that both Vanna and Torie were my Achilles' heel.

Now I just had to make sure they were safe until this psycho wasn't a possible danger anymore.

"I understand, Vanna, and I don't want to stifle you," I answered truthfully. "Just be careful right now. Don't let your guard down."

Christ! I wasn't even willing to consider what my life would be like without Vanna in it anymore.

It was highly likely that nothing would ever happen. I'd tried to remind myself of that every single day since those letters had started to arrive, but then the apprehension would inevitably show up.

What if something happened to Vanna?

What if this person was serious?

What if I couldn't protect her?

"Are you ready?" Vanna asked as she stood.

"Yeah," I said distractedly as I rose from my seat. "Let's go home."

I took Vanna's hand as we exited the restaurant and headed for the parking lot, my eyes scanning the area to look for anyone hanging around outside.

It was actually pretty quiet since we'd had a late dinner just before the restaurant had closed.

Still, I couldn't shake off that damn gut feeling...

What happened next occurred so fast that I never had a chance to draw my weapon.

A dark figure came out of the bushes next to the sidewalk, tore Vanna away from me and snarled, "Make a move and I'll slit her throat right now."

Suddenly and without warning, Vanna was put in a position that made my blood run cold.

She was pulled against a madman with a very large knife to her throat.

Knowing the guy was certifiable, I kept my hands to my sides.

Stay calm! Don't lose your shit! That's not going to help Vanna right now.

Vanna was only about six feet away from me, but if this asshole decided he was going to use that knife, I'd never get there in time to save her.

He could cut her throat in less than a heartbeat.

"Your beef isn't with her. It's with me," I said, trying to keep my voice calm when all I really wanted to do was tear the bastard's head off. "Let her go."

The man was big and unkempt. His dark hair was dirty, and his eyes were bloodshot and devoid of any emotion except madness.

Christ! I'd seen dead eyes like his, and it never turned out good. "Do you have any idea what it's like to watch someone you love die?" the man barked. "My father shot himself right in front of me. The only thing I could do was watch as the life in his eyes just drained away. He was all I had. He took care of me. I think you should know how it feels to watch someone you care about die right in front of you."

I was honestly terrified at the thought, but I couldn't take my mind off of my goal, which was to get that goddamn knife away from Vanna's throat.

Obviously, his father *hadn't* taken good care of his son if he'd blown his own brains out right in front of him.

The man was mental, and there was nothing left in his eyes but vengeance and wrath.

I locked my gaze with Vanna's as I quickly contemplated my options, knowing I had only seconds to decide, and that her life was probably going to depend on that decision.

I saw terror in her tumultuous gaze, but there was also something else...

Fucking resignation.

She knew this maniac was going to kill her.

We both knew it.

I also had a feeling that she had decided that she wanted to go down fighting.

She made her move quickly, and I was ready for it.

Bam! Bam! Bam!

One right after the other, she slammed her head back and hit him in the face, then the solar plexus with her elbow, and finally she slammed her heel down onto his foot and ground down before letting her body drop.

I flew across the space as he howled with pain and I coldcocked him, adding a few extra punches as he fell—just in case.

I didn't bother giving him another glance once he hit the ground and was out cold.

Immediately, I crouched by Vanna's side where she lay on the sidewalk.

She was pale.

Her eyes were closed.

And there was blood trickling from a wound on her throat onto the sidewalk.

"The police and ambulance are on their way, Mr. Durand," the owner of the restaurant said breathlessly as he came to a stop behind me. "I wasn't far behind you. I called 911 as soon as I realized what was happening."

I was relieved that help was coming, but I didn't even look at the voice that had told me that. I simply waved at the perpetrator and growled, "Keep an eye on him. She's hurt. Vanna!" I bellowed as I felt for her pulse and put a hand on her chest.

Her pulse was fast, but strong, and I could tell that she was breathing.

I checked the wound at her neck, relieved when I realized it was fairly superficial.

"Wake up, Vanna. Open your eyes," I pleaded.

My heart thundered in my ears as I watched her eyelids flutter for a moment before she completely opened her eyes. Her expression was full of confusion until she saw my face and apparently remembered what had happened.

"Chase!" she choked out on a sob as she sat up and flung herself into my arms.

I wrapped my arms around her protectively. "Vanna," I said with relief.

I knew basic first aid.

I knew I should have kept her quiet on the ground in case she had a back or neck injury.

But the chances of that were slim, and I couldn't fucking let her go. Not after I'd almost lost her.

"Everything is going to be okay, baby," I reassured her.

She openly sobbed against my shoulder. Her entire body was shaking like a leaf, so I simply held her, trying to soothe her by gently rocking her over and over until the ambulance finally arrived.

Chapter 24

Savannah

"**A**re you sure that you're okay?" Torie asked as she sat at the side of my hospital bed several hours later.

"I'm fine," I said as I took her hand and smiled. "It's just a superficial cut on my neck. The only reason they're keeping me overnight is because I lost consciousness briefly when my head hit the pavement. It's just for concussion observation. All of my tests were fine."

It was after one am in the morning, but the whole gang was here in my hospital room.

The nurses had allowed it because I had a private room, and I'd just gotten upstairs from the ER a short time ago.

Hudson, Jax, and Cooper had arrived with Taylor, Harlow, and Torie, but apparently, Wyatt had been the first one to arrive soon after Chase and I had gotten here by ambulance. I wasn't sure if Chase had called him, or if Wyatt just knew about everything the second something happened to his family. Everyone had been waiting for me in my room when I'd arrived a short time ago. The ER was packed, so no one had been allowed to visit me there since

Chase had been with me, and the police had been interviewing both of us.

"I was so worried," Torie said, her voice still reflecting concern.

"I'm glad that asshole is dead," Cooper chimed in from his place behind Torie.

Truthfully, I was relieved myself. The perpetrator *had* been Jeffrey Kruger, the son of the late Gerald Kruger.

The police had just informed us before we'd come up to my room that Jeffrey was dead. They'd taken him to a holding cell at the jail, and he'd immediately found a way to hang himself.

I shuddered, still not quite over my initial shock.

Maybe he was a tormented soul, but he would have killed me without a single ounce of remorse. He'd been *that* crazy.

I didn't remember anything about the short time I'd been unconscious, but I'd seen Chase flying into action right before my head had connected with the pavement.

I'd known that I either had to try to escape or I was going to die. The lunatic's intention had been extremely obvious.

I'd also been aware that all Chase needed was a second or two *without* that knife at my neck to take the man down.

As it turned out, he hadn't even needed an entire second. He'd dove for the perpetrator immediately after I'd let my body drop.

"I'm glad, too," Torie said adamantly. "He was evil and twisted. God, if I'd had any idea that he was that nuts, I would have encouraged you to agree to that bodyguard. At least for a while."

"Nobody knew," Chase answered from his place at the foot of the bed. He was obviously tuned in to our conversation, even though he was conversing with Wyatt, Hudson, and Jax about what had happened.

"You must have been terrified, Vanna," Taylor said gently. "We had to know if you and Chase were okay."

Taylor and Harlow were standing right next to where Torie was sitting on the bed.

The two of them had already asked if I minded company.

I'd thanked them both for their concern and told them I didn't mind at all.

Honestly, I welcomed the distraction, and I was touched that they were worried.

Both Taylor and Harlow were very easy to like.

"I was, but it happened so fast," I explained. "I was even more scared after it was over, I think."

"That's probably natural," Harlow mused. "Once you have a second to think about it and the initial danger is over, you can finally process the incident. Can we get you anything?"

I shook my head as I replied, "I'm fine now. I am a little worried about Axel."

"Your dog is fine," Torie informed me. "I hope you don't mind, but I have a key and the alarm code, so Cooper and I checked on him while we were waiting for you to get to your room."

I let out a sigh of relief. "I'm glad."

"I wasn't sure if he'd let me in," she said. "But he recognized my smell and probably Milo's scent on me as well, even though he was hesitant at first. Cooper waited outside in the front while I let Axel out in back, got a change of clothes for you, and then left the gorgeous beast with a very large cookie. The bag with your clothes is on the chair in the corner. I can check on him until you get home if you want. I'm assuming that Chase will be staying the night."

"I'm staying," Chase answered before I could.

I nodded. "Please check on him. They said I'd be discharged after breakfast in the morning."

"No problem," Torie agreed. "Maybe I'll take Milo with me in the morning. It's Saturday, so we could go for a walk. Text me when you're getting ready to leave so I know you're on your way home. I suppose we should all bail so you can get some rest."

Taylor and Harlow agreed and then both women hugged me before they joined their husbands.

Hudson and Jax wished me a goodnight before they left with their spouses.

I embraced Torie and Cooper next before they exited.

I raised my hand at Wyatt to say goodbye as he broke off his conversation with Chase to depart.

Wyatt strode over to the bed and he scooped me up in a huge bearhug as he said gruffly, "I'm glad you weren't seriously injured, Savannah."

I was taken aback for a second before I put my arms around his very large body and hugged him back. Wyatt wasn't normally a hugger with me, even though I'd known him since I was a kid.

When Wyatt straightened up, he said to Chase, "Call me tomorrow. Both of you get some rest."

Wyatt left without saying another word.

"I think that's the first time I've seen Wyatt hug anyone other than Torie," Chase observed as he pulled up a chair next to the bed and sat. "You definitely scared him. Scared me, too."

He looked almost unaffected except for the anguish I could see in his eyes, but that expression spoke volumes.

"I'm fine," I assured him as he took my hand. "I'm sorry I had that meltdown after I woke up. I'm not sure why, but my adrenaline was still pumping. Harlow was right. I don't think I even processed what happened until I woke up and realized how scared I'd been. Thank you for saving me—again."

"You were so fucking brave, Vanna," Chase said, his voice almost like a supportive caress. "And you actually saved yourself. I just finished the bastard off."

Chase was so full of it. "If you hadn't been there to knock Jeffrey senseless, I would have been dead."

"If you weren't with me, you wouldn't have been in danger in the first place," Chase rasped. "Where did you learn to fight back like that?"

"I've had some self-defense classes. I used to go to some dangerous places. I thought it would be a good idea," I told him. "I wasn't sure what to do. I knew if I could just get that knife away from my neck, I'd have a chance. How's your hand? What happened to the ice pack they put on it?"

Chase's knuckles were pretty swollen from boxing without a glove, but they'd X-rayed it, and nothing was broken, thank God.

"I'm good, Vanna," Chase replied, blowing off my concern. "I'm more worried about you. I don't think the visions of you with a knife at your neck and about to die are going to leave my brain anytime soon."

"You felt it, too, didn't you?" I asked in a shaky voice. "He *was* ready to kill me. He wasn't bluffing."

Chase stood, kicked off his shoes and climbed into bed beside me. He cradled my body against his before he answered, "I told you I wouldn't lie to you, so yeah, I felt it. He was a madman, Vanna. I could tell you knew it, too. That's why I was ready when you made a move."

A shiver ran through my body.

I didn't really want to think about how close I'd come to dying.

The thing that had actually saved me was probably the close connection I had with Chase—so close that we could almost hear each other thinking in a dire situation.

"Is it horrible that I really am glad he's dead?" I wondered aloud in a hesitant voice.

Chase buried a hand in my hair and pulled my head gently to his chest. "Fuck, no. Who knows how much time he would have gotten in the end, and that bastard was dangerous. I've seen people who were already past the point of no return. He was there. I've had a bad feeling about this situation for a while. It didn't feel right. I should have never taken you out. It's ironic that I got you a protection dog and this happened when you couldn't even have Axel with you."

I could tell he was really troubled. "I had you. It's over, Chase. It's not your fault. You never could have anticipated something like this happening."

I knew he was feeling guilty about the whole situation, and he had no reason to feel that way.

"I should have anticipated it," he answered harshly. "Jesus! I nearly got you killed just because you're my woman, Vanna. You've been through enough."

"I'm not dead, Chase," I said softly.

"Let's not talk about this right now," he said abruptly. "Let's just focus on you getting well. You sound tired."

"I feel like my brain is still a little scrambled, and I'm exhausted. I think it's probably more emotional than physical. I'm a little over-whelmed," I admitted.

"I'm not surprised," he said morosely. "You've had two near-death experiences in the last six months."

"True," I said as I released a big breath.

"Sleep, Vanna," he said gently. "It's been an insane day."

"For both of us," I added with a yawn.

I was exhausted, and I knew my head would be more together after I slept.

I burrowed into his body, trying to get comfortable, still feeling like something wasn't quite right with Chase.

"Are you sure you're okay?" I asked him.

"I'll feel better when I can get you home," he confessed. "I hate hospitals."

My heart fell as I thought about how much time he'd spent in the hospital after the attack in the military. "I wasn't even thinking about how much you must dislike being in one. I'm sorry."

"Relax, baby. You haven't had the best experiences with hospitals yourself," he said huskily. "It's not going to kill me to stay here tonight. I'll just be more relaxed when you're back in a normal environment with Axel."

My eyes fluttered closed.

I felt exactly the same way.

Chapter 25

Savannah

"I'm not sure that Chase really wants to be with me anymore," I told Torie two weeks later on a Saturday afternoon. "I swore I'd never discuss any problems Chase and I ever had with you, but you're my best friend. I wanted you to know that we might not stay together."

I'd lamented for a week over mentioning something to her, but in the end, I knew I needed to talk to *someone*.

Chase certainly wasn't talking, and Axel wasn't good with romance advice.

Torie and I were so close, and I felt so incredibly miserable. We'd always been there for each other at the best and darkest times of our lives. Right now, mine was the latter.

Chase had gone to a rare Saturday meeting at Durand, and Cooper was out running, so Torie had stopped by with Milo to chat.

I had pulled some snacks and soft drinks out of the fridge and we'd sat down at the kitchen table as Axel and Milo played outside.

Her eyes were dark with concern as she answered, "Vanna, we've been best friends almost our entire lives. Chase might be my brother, but he's also your boyfriend. Talk to me. Did something happen?"

I shook my head slowly as I shared, "I'm not even sure what happened. We didn't argue. He just put up some kind of wall between us. He asks me how I'm doing every day, but he's really distant, emotionally and physically. Chase hasn't touched me since I got home from the hospital. I've never seen him like this, and the more I try to talk to him, the more he backs away."

Tears filled my eyes and they began to flow steadily down my cheeks. Having Chase step back from our relationship instead of forward was killing me. Especially when I had no idea why it was happening. I couldn't fix something I didn't understand.

And God, I really *wanted* to fix it. I missed him so much that it was tearing my heart to shreds.

"Wait," Torie said as she frowned. "So nothing weird preceded this distance at all?"

"Nothing," I said as I pulled a handful of potato chips from the bag. "We didn't even have a small disagreement. He still eats dinner with me when he gets home from work, but he's quiet. Once he's done, he goes into the gym while I stress eat in the evening. At the rate I'm consuming junk food, I won't be able to fit into my jeans anymore within a day or two."

Torie popped the top on a Diet Coke. "When guys work out excessively, they're either cheating or frustrated," she said thoughtfully. "Since I'm positive Chase *isn't* a cheater, I'd say something else is bothering him."

My eyes flew to her face as I swiped the tears from my cheeks. "You don't think there's someone else?" I asked, knowing even as I asked that question that there almost certainly wasn't.

Chase wasn't the type. At all.

I may not know what was wrong, but I still trusted him.

Torie rolled her eyes. "Are you joking? He loves you in a way that's pretty much obsessive. There's no room in his brain for another female. I'd say he's definitely frustrated."

I swallowed the chips I'd stuffed into my mouth before I answered, "I'm starting to feel the same way."

(T. A. Scott)

"He won't talk to you about it at all?" Torie questioned.

"Nope," I said after I'd washed down those chips with some soda. I instantly grabbed another handful. "He says everything is okay when I ask him what's wrong. But everything is *not* okay. He usually talks to me about everything. Which tells me his problem is with *me*."

"Not necessarily," Torie mused. "Or at least, not directly. I honestly don't think Chase has ever been in love. Yeah, he's been fond of other women in the past. But I'm wondering if he just doesn't know how to handle all this. Give him some time, Vanna. If he doesn't snap out of it, smack him upside the head to knock some sense into him. You're the best thing that's ever happened to him, and I think he knows that."

"He hasn't ever said that he loves me, Torie," I confided.

She nearly choked on her Diet Coke. She coughed before she shot me a seriously-are-you-joking expression. "I'm surprised he hasn't," she shared. "But no one can look at Chase when he's with you and doubt that he loves you for even a single moment. Have you told him how you feel?"

I shook my head. "I've wanted to, but it always felt like it was too soon. And then he started putting this distance between the two of us. When I got home from the hospital, I'd all but decided to just tell him that I love him. If there's one thing I learned from that attempted murder experience, it's that life is too short not to tell someone you love them. But I'm pretty certain it isn't something he wants to hear right now."

Torie snorted. "I doubt that. I think he just feels guilty about what happened. You know my brothers are always willing to take the blame for anything that happens to someone they care about. First, you were kidnapped and nearly died. Then, you were almost killed because of a madman with a vendetta against Wyatt and Chase. My brothers have always been the type of guys who analyze things a little too much."

I opened the bag of chocolate cookies and took a few. "If that's true, then I'm not handling the way he's pushing me away while he does that," I grumbled and took a bite out of a cookie.

"Then make him listen to you, Vanna," Torie suggested. "You're far from a meek and mild type of woman. Get in his face and make sure he's hearing you."

No, I generally wasn't the kind of female who hesitated to make my opinions known when it was important. Then again, I'd never been in love like this before. I wanted to respect his space, but enough was enough.

"He either wants me or he doesn't," I considered aloud.

"Or he wants you *too much*," Torie said, her tone slightly amused. "I have a feeling he's trying to decide whether he's good enough for you right now, or whether he should be putting you at risk by being with him."

I eyed her for a moment before I inquired, "Are you being absolutely serious right now?"

She swallowed a sip of her Diet Coke. "Completely," she informed me. "Both Wyatt and Chase have a habit of taking on the responsibility for anything that happens to someone they care about. God, they still blame themselves for my kidnapping, which we both know is entirely ludicrous. I'm a woman with a doctorate degree and I'd already traveled the world by that time in my job with the UN. I was perfectly able to take care of myself, but I was still their little sister, and they felt like they should have watched out for me better. And it's not just my brothers who feel that way. Cooper beat himself half to death over me getting kidnapped the second time, even though he rescued me and got me to safety when he was horribly injured himself. Alpha men like Cooper and Chase have a very hard time dealing with the fact that someone they love could get injured under their watch. It's not really ego. It's the overactive sense of responsibility they feel for taking care of someone they love."

"That's totally insane," I told her, astonished. "They can't control the actions of other people."

Torie smirked. "Don't tell them that. In their minds, they should be able to protect us from anything that makes us even the least bit uncomfortable. I guarantee that's where Chase's head is right now.

It's not that hard to figure out since I'm married to a man who has a lot of the same reactions."

"I've already told him that he wasn't responsible," I objected.

Torie lifted a brow. "I've tried to convince the stubborn men in my life of the same thing. Do you think that matters to a guy who has an overinflated sense of guilt and responsibility?"

"To be honest, that really makes me...angry. I'm very able to take care of myself, too. What happened was a fluke. It was the result of someone with a very sick and twisted mind. Chase isn't all powerful, nor does he think like someone who is mentally ill."

"But you love him anyway," Torie pointed out. "Be warned that guys like him are always going to think they should be able to keep you safe at all times with no excuses. They don't cut themselves a break on that and probably never will."

"How do you handle that?" I asked, still trying to process what she'd just said.

She shrugged. "I don't, because I know I'm never going to change Cooper when it comes to his protective instincts. Honestly, I hate to see him hurting for any reason, too. I don't really *want* to change him. I just have to draw the line when it's too much to handle. Otherwise, I accept it as part of his personality. Part of me loves that part of him, unless he gets too pigheaded."

"Like asking if you'll use a bodyguard?" I asked drily before I took another bite of my cookie.

She chuckled. "That's when you start setting some boundaries so their obsession doesn't completely take over your life."

"I can handle that," I explained. "But I can't deal with being completely shut out. It's killing me, Torie."

"Then tell him that's a defense mechanism that you won't tolerate," she advised. "I don't blame you. I wouldn't stand for that, either. I don't think he consciously realizes he's hurting you, but it's selfish."

"You do realize that you're talking about your own brother here, right?"

"Look, I love both Chase and Wyatt, and I know they're two of the most amazing guys on Earth, but I also know they aren't perfect," she said with a sigh.

"I didn't want to intrude on his space," I reasoned. "But I don't think he's going to listen unless I do. I've waited for him to snap out of this for two weeks now. I've had about as much of the silent treatment as I can take. This isn't like him, Torie. He's never been like this. God, he knows he can tell me anything."

"Most likely, he doesn't understand this issue enough to talk about it," she observed.

"Or he just wants me to leave him alone," I said wistfully. "I'm seriously thinking about moving out, Torie. That condo is still available. I checked. All I have to do is sign the lease. It's empty. I could move in within days."

"Is that really what you want?" she questioned.

A tear leaked from the corner of my eye as I confessed, "No. But I can't be the only person in this relationship who wants to communicate."

"I promise that you're not," she said sadly. "But my brother is acting like a jackass."

"I used to know what he was thinking most of the time. I don't anymore."

The silent understanding that Chase and I used to share felt all but dead. He barely looked at me anymore.

Although I wanted to believe that all of this was coming from an overreaching sense of responsibility, I just wasn't sure anymore.

Why wouldn't he talk to me?

Why wouldn't he tell me if he was just plain…worried?

Every single day, I got more and more concerned that he didn't really want me around anymore, and it was tearing me apart.

"You're a woman who has always known what you wanted," Torie contemplated as she got up and crouched beside me. "I'm not going to interfere, and you know I'm going to support what you do either way. Just think about confronting him before you make that move, okay? At least you'll know you tried."

I nodded right before I hugged her tightly, beyond grateful once again that this woman was my best friend.

Chapter 26

Chase

"I can't fucking do this," I said to Wyatt after the CEOs we'd been meeting with had all filed out of the conference room to go home.

He lifted a brow. "What? You mean sign this contract that you've hardly even looked at over the last few hours?"

Okay, I knew I'd been inattentive all afternoon. It was because all I could think about was... "Vanna. I can't do this."

Wyatt was sitting directly across from me at the conference table. He leaned back in his chair before he said, "Yeah, I figured. You certainly weren't here at this meeting today. Don't be stupid, Chase. Of course you're going to keep doing it. You love her. Maybe I don't understand that kind of extreme lunacy. But I recognize it. I've seen it all over Hudson, Jax, and Cooper's faces over the last year or two."

"I nearly got her killed, Wyatt," I said sharply, every muscle in my body tight. "Do you have any idea how I felt when I knew Kruger was going to slit her throat at any second? I can't do that again. I can't live with the fact that she's in danger every day that she stays with me."

I'd been like this for two weeks. Wondering whether Vanna would be safer if she *wasn't* my girlfriend. Thinking that if I'd just let her go, she'd wouldn't be in that kind of danger.

Wyatt let out a disgusted breath. "Oh, for fuck's sake, you're not an idiot, Chase. Pull yourself back into the real world for just a moment. Neither one of you are going to die. If you've been this distracted at home, she's probably ready to kill you herself."

"We haven't really talked since she got home from the hospital," I admitted. "I've been working out. A lot."

He snorted. "So you retreat to the gym like a recluse every night to try to work off your frustration? Now I'm really shocked that Vanna hasn't slapped you silly. I suppose you haven't said a word to her about this plan to leave her alone."

"I can't...exactly tell her. I've tried to work up the guts to do it," I answered. "Fuck! It's nearly impossible for me to give her up."

"You won't have to if you keep treating her like this," Wyatt grumbled. "She'll leave your sorry ass if you keep ignoring her for long enough. She's not the kind of woman who will put up with that bullshit forever. What in the hell is wrong with you? There's a risk in being with anyone. You inherit any crazy friends or family they might have."

"She almost died, Wyatt," I said, my voice harsh and irritated.

He rolled his eyes. "She almost died when some assholes decided to kidnap her, too. Was that your fault—was that because she was your girlfriend? No. No, it wasn't. You're being totally unreasonable, Chase. Just marry the woman and get it over with. I have a theory about the whole marriage thing."

"I actually have an engagement ring," I muttered. "I was going to ask her when we got home from the restaurant the night of the attack. Do I really want to hear this theory?"

He picked up an ink pen and rolled it around in his fingers. "Probably not, but I think I'm right after watching three other men lose their minds over a female before you. Every one of them calmed down a little *after* they got married. Before that, they were a mess. There's something about the uncertainty *before* they make that final commitment that makes them lose their minds. Fuck knows that I couldn't wait until Torie and Cooper got married so they could just get down to the business of everyday life again. Just marry Vanna and get it over with. You won't be happy until you do."

I let out a bark of laughter without a hint of humor in it. "You really think it's that easy?"

"I do," he returned smugly. "Apparently, this madness doesn't mix well with any kind of indecision. Marry her, make a vow that you'll always be together etc. etc., and the torture will be over."

"You're wrong," I informed him. "I wanted Vanna to marry me because I wanted her to know that I was ready to commit to her and only to her. Okay, maybe I just selfishly wanted her to be mine, too, in the most permanent way possible. I suppose it's not always a life decision because divorce would always be an option for her, but I would have felt better if she'd said yes. I don't fucking know why. Hell, maybe I was afraid she'd wake up one day and realize she made a huge mistake. Or that all that happiness would be fleeting for her. Or that she didn't really care enough about me to even make a lifelong commitment. It *is* torture. I feel like a Neanderthal who's determined to keep his mate, come hell or high water, which is why I can't fucking let her go. That's not attractive in a modern male, but I can't seem to fight those primitive instincts, even though I know she'd probably be safer without me."

"Would she?" Wyatt questioned in an irritatingly dry tone.

"I think so," I said defensively. "There's no end to the enemies we've made in the past. Maybe there's even some we don't know about. And then there's still Dad's enemies, too."

"She was kidnapped in the Darien jungle, Chase, and she nearly died," he reminded me. "Vanna also suffered far more injury with that kidnapping incident than she did from that momentary situation with Kruger. And unless I'm mistaken, which I never am, you two weren't even dating at the time of her kidnapping. In fact, she would have been dead already if you hadn't risked your own ass to go in and save her. Like I said, be reasonable."

"I can't," I said tightly. "I'm fucking paralyzed with fear that something will happen to her after the Kruger incident."

"We've been through a lot of life-threatening situations. We were special forces. You've never flinched at the thought of throwing your ass into a dangerous situation."

"This isn't about *me*," I said angrily. "It's about *her*."

"Really?" Wyatt said with feigned astonishment. "Because it certainly sounds like you're being a selfish dickhead. Did it ever occur to you that what you're doing *right now* is hurting Vanna? Go ahead and push her away, but you'll end up being the sorriest bastard on Earth when everything is said and done. Much as I hate to say it because I don't believe in all this sentimental bullshit, you two obviously belong together, and if you lose her to this craziness, you'll always regret it."

"Don't you think I know that?" I questioned as I shot him a withering glance. "She's always been the one for me, but I'm not so sure that I'm the guy *she* should end up with."

"Because you're not good enough? Because she'd be safer with someone else? Because she might be happier or more secure with a guy who has a lower profile?" he inquired. "I rest my case on my theory. Marry her."

I glared at him. "I told you there's more to it than that."

"And I gave you a simple solution, whatever the reason. Think for just a second. How are you going to feel a few years down the line if she's with someone else? And you *are* going to see it. Torie and Savannah will be best friends for the rest of their lives. In your eyes, no one will ever treat her well enough or be good enough for her. The only way you're going to guarantee her happiness is to marry her yourself. Because fuck knows you'll always treat her like the most important person in your life."

I cringed at the thought of another guy being by Vanna's side. Wyatt was right. No one would ever treat her well enough for me. Most certainly not an asshole like…Bradley.

My blood boiled every fucking time I thought about how that asshole had hurt her.

"Don't start thinking you're better than any of those other guys," Wyatt warned. "You're hurting her right now, and she's the best damn thing that ever happened to you."

"What in the hell would you do?" I asked bitterly.

He shot me a self-righteous grin. "I really wouldn't know. I'm never going to put myself in that situation. It's easier that way."

Egotistical asshole!

Maybe he thought that right now. I'd been confident I'd never fall for a woman like Hudson, Jax, and Cooper had, too.

"Then how in the hell do you think you're qualified to give me any advice at all?" I asked furiously.

He dropped the pen back onto the table and leaned forward. "Because I know you, Chase. First, you thought you'd never find a woman who would accept you, scars and all. Now you're trying to find a way to dump that woman you've always wanted just because you're terrified of the way you love her. Doing that would be an enormous mistake. I think you want Vanna more than you want to give yourself some kind of relief from those conflicting emotions. You just haven't realized that yet. You can protect her better than any man I know if she needs protection. You're definitely not short of the resources. You've already taken measures to ensure her safety, like giving her Axel. She's never going to be completely safe out in this crazy world we live in, Chase. But she's safer with you than without you. What if something happens like her previous kidnapping, and you aren't there to save her? What happens then? Christ! You're obsessed with her happiness and her security. I have a hard time believing anyone else will be just as protective."

"She saved herself from getting her throat slit," I choked out, my voice rough and raw.

Wyatt's eyes widened. "No, she did *not*. She helped you by being a woman who thinks on her feet, but she went unconscious from those actions. Do you think she would have survived if you hadn't been there? Have you totally lost it?"

I ran a frustrated hand through my hair. "I don't know. I can't think straight."

"You have definitely lost it," he verified. "And you better snap out of it before you fuck up so badly that the situation can't ever be fixed."

"I *never* meant to hurt her," I mumbled.

"Of course you didn't," Wyatt rumbled. "You're temporarily insane because you're in love and probably haven't told her that yet. Since you've been completely unhinged for the last two weeks, you probably haven't given her the opportunity to tell you that, either."

I nodded. "You're right. I haven't told her yet."

"Then do it," Wyatt demanded. "I'd like the old Chase back again, please. Although I very much doubt you'll ever be the same. But at least you won't be a moron that screws something up because he thinks it's for the greater good or some such ridiculously altruistic notion."

"Vanna is everything to me. I just want her to be happy," I said fiercely.

"No offense, brother, but that is not obviously apparent at the moment. You're acting like you're demented," he drawled. "I'm a little worried about Vanna's safety now. Maybe I should pack up her stuff and have her come stay with me. I think I like her more than you do right now."

I sent him an enraged glare as I asked hoarsely, "Are you trying to piss me off?"

"If that's what it takes to make you see some sense, then maybe I am."

"I love her," I professed vehemently.

"Then act like it," he insisted. "You're never going to succeed at pushing her away completely, and you can't keep on like this. Either decide that you're going to love her forever, marry her, and treat her like a queen, or let her go for good. I've always considered Savannah family because she's so close to Torie. I feel that way now more than ever because of everything she did for Torie after her kidnapping. She's like the sister Torie never had, and I do not like to see *any* of my family hurting."

Hell, I *would* love Vanna forever, no matter what happened. That was inevitable, and if I really was hurting her, I hated myself for *that*, too.

"I'll figure it out," I grumbled.

"Good. I'm glad this whole fear and self-loathing episode is resolved. Now let's look at this contract you didn't read earlier this afternoon," Wyatt grunted like the whole ugly conversation we'd just had never even happened.

Chapter 27

Chase

I was doing rounds with a punching bag later that evening when Vanna walked into the gym.

I hadn't talked to her yet because I didn't know what the fuck to say.

I'd been considering my options, and ultimately, I knew damn well there was really only one.

Letting her go was out of the question.

I couldn't.

It wasn't possible, no matter how long or hard I'd considered it.

No one would ever love her or keep her safer and happier than I would.

I was done trying to figure things out beyond those simple facts. All it did was screw up my head.

I'd decided I had to come clean with the way I felt, the sooner the better if I'd really hurt her.

Judging by the wary look in her eyes at dinner tonight, I'd already done some damage that I'd never intended to inflict.

Fuck! What in the hell had I been thinking?

Obviously, I hadn't been using my brain at all, and my damn heart had completely betrayed me.

I had the most amazing woman in the world, and I was completely blowing it.

All because I was afraid I'd cause her an even greater injury that was never likely to happen.

Yeah, some of Wyatt's annoying comments *had* gotten through to me.

"I'm moving out, Chase," she stated firmly as she stopped beside me. "The condo I was looking at is still available. I'm signing a lease tomorrow. I'll be out by Friday, if not sooner. I'm sorry if I've over-stayed my welcome."

I stopped swinging abruptly.

The punching bag swung back and hit me in the head, but I didn't even feel it.

What? Wait!

I met her gaze directly for the first time in two weeks.

She was deadly serious, and I'd brought this on myself, Goddammit!

It was all there in her gaze.

Uncertainty.

Sadness.

Anguish.

Anger.

Along with a longing mournfulness that made my blood run cold because it told me she'd already accepted this decision.

Oh, fuck, no!

She wasn't leaving.

I *had* hurt her. Badly. And that was the most painful realization I'd ever experienced.

Screw the fear of her getting *physically* hurt.

I'd wounded Vanna's spirit, and if I never saw this look in her eyes again, it would be much too soon.

"Vanna," I said hoarsely. "We need to talk."

She folded her arms in front of her obstinately. "About what, Chase? About the fact that you don't even want to be with me long enough to eat dinner? Or about the fact that you haven't touched me or even kissed me in two weeks? Or maybe about the fact that you don't even seem to acknowledge that I exist in the same house that you do? Or possibly about the fact that you barely speak to me anymore, even though I've tried repeatedly to get you to tell me what's wrong?"

Okay, there was the fury, and I could handle that a lot better than the sadness.

I'd rather she be pissed off than hurt any day of the week.

But then, a single tear rolled down her cheek, and it broke me.

I felt completely gutted.

I couldn't fucking ignore the pain I'd caused her, and I didn't want to. I had to find a way to make it right somehow.

"You can't leave," I croaked as I reached out for her hand.

She pulled away and backed up.

That hurt, but I knew I more than deserved her disdain right now.

"I doubt you'll ever even notice that I'm gone," she bantered furiously.

"Bullshit!" I bellowed. "I'm fucking in love with you, Vanna. I'll admit it, I got scared. After what happened with Kruger, I had no idea if I could keep you safe in the future with my high-profile name and face. Don't you know that if something happened to you, I wouldn't want to live on this Earth anymore? But there's a problem with that, because I don't want to live *without* you when you're still on this Earth, either. So I'm totally fucked."

Her expression softened ever so slightly, but she wasn't about to give in. "You think you love me?" she asked cautiously, her expression still wary.

"No! I *know* I love you, Vanna. Probably have since Vegas. Hell, maybe it was even before that and I was in denial," I corrected.

"You certainly haven't acted that way for the last two weeks," she said suspiciously.

"I know," I said remorsefully. "And I'm more sorry about that than you'll ever know."

"Are you?" she questioned, her gaze still livid. "Do you have any idea what all of this has done to me? I've turned myself inside out, wondering what in the hell was wrong with *me* because you wouldn't even talk to me—"

"Jesus, Vanna. There's nothing wrong with you. You're so goddamn perfect that it scares the shit out of me sometimes—"

She held a hand up. "Stop! I'm not done. I've always been an *all in* or *all out* kind of woman. Sometimes it takes me a while to commit to something or someone, but once I do, I'm going to give it everything I've got. I was scared, too, in the beginning. I held back. I didn't want to hope for things that would never happen between the two of us. But the moment you made yourself vulnerable to me by taking off all of your clothing in the middle of the kitchen to show me those scars, I was *all in*, dammit! Did it ever occur to you that I might not want to live in a world without you in it, either?"

I shook my head slowly, both stunned and ensnared by her passionate wrath.

Oh, she was entitled to it and more, but I'd never seen Vanna quite this upset and furious before.

"Well," she said, her voice starting to waver. "I did feel that way. Furthermore, I've also gained eight pounds from stress eating a truckload of junk food over this situation, and I'm about to lose the ability to button my jeans. So I need to give it up before I need a new wardrobe. Even poor Axel is gaining weight because he has no problem commiserating by eating those cookies with me. That's why I really…need to go."

"You look beautiful," I told her, and I meant it. "Don't go, Vanna. I love you."

Hell, I'd buy her whatever size new wardrobe she wanted as long as she stayed.

Tears began to pour down her face as she asked hesitantly, "Do you really mean that? I don't even know anymore."

I felt sucker punched that she actually doubted me, but I'd brought that distrust on myself.

Vanna *had* given me everything, and in return I'd given her reason to be this damn uncertain.

Fuck it!

I pulled the ring I'd gotten her out of the pocket of my sweatpants and handed her the box. "I've had this ring for almost a month now. I was going to ask you to marry me when we got home from dinner the night of the attack. I had to wait a while to get it custom-made from diamonds that came from the best Montgomery mine. They're quality, and I couldn't give you anything but the best."

There wasn't a turquoise center stone that would do her justice, but I'd mixed a few in with the smaller accent diamonds. The center stone *had* to be a big ass diamond. Well, at least it had to be for *me*.

If she wanted something else, I'd be happy to accommodate her.

Anything she wanted.

Everything she wanted.

If she'd just say she was fucking mine and put me out of my misery, I'd make damn sure I never saw that mournful, broken look in her eyes again.

It was so quiet you could hear a pin drop as Vanna stared at the box.

My heart was pounding so hard that I wasn't sure that I wouldn't have a heart attack and keel over in another minute or two if she didn't say something soon.

She'd be perfectly justified if she told me to fuck off after I'd been such a dick for the last two weeks.

But Christ! I really hoped that she wouldn't.

"You'll never be able to save me from every single bit of pain or danger in my life, Chase," she mentioned in a less angry tone.

"Maybe not, but I'll sure as hell give it my best shot," I said stubbornly. "If I can't prevent the pain, I'll be there with you, Vanna, good or bad. I know I've acted like an idiot. I guess I was terrified that you were in danger because you were with me. I hate what happened at the restaurant."

She raised a brow. "So you were planning on dumping me because of that?"

I swallowed hard. "Yes! No! Oh, fucking hell! I didn't know what I was doing. I'm crazy in love with you. My head wasn't on straight after that happened."

She kept holding the box tightly in her hand but didn't open it.

Vanna took a deep breath as she whispered, "I was in love with you, too."

Was? She was in love with me?

Oh, hell, no. That wasn't going to fly. She *still* needed to love me.

"Do I take it you're not in love with me anymore?" I asked hoarsely, that possible heart attack starting to look more like a reality.

"Chase, you can't just close me off when you're worried or upset. We're supposed to be partners."

My gut rolled as her tears just kept coming.

"Vanna," I said huskily, really needing to hear the answer to my question.

She held up a hand. "Wait. This is really important to me. I thought you didn't want me anymore. I thought you wanted me to go. I thought you realized that you made a mistake when you asked me to stay. It hurt me, Chase. I never want to feel like that again. It ripped my heart out. I'm not afraid of being *with* you. I'm afraid of being *without* you."

I got exactly what she was saying.

It was crystal clear.

I felt the same damn way.

I was also now completely aware that she *still* loved me, but just hadn't uttered those words...yet.

I knew because Vanna and I were connected.

Yeah, I'd damaged that connection for a short time, but it was still there.

"It won't happen again, sweetheart. I swear," I vowed, meaning every single word. I'd learned my lesson about just how many mis-understandings could come from silence.

She raised a brow. "Promise?"

I started to sweat. "I promise."

"Then I guess I can finally tell you that I love you, too, you crazy man. I've wanted to say that for a very long time."

My breath released in a giant *whoosh* of relief.

"Marry me?" I asked, my voice hoarse with relief. "This isn't the way I planned on doing this. I stink, and it's not exactly romantic, but I can't wait another second to ask."

"You haven't touched me in two weeks," she reminded me.

"Believe me, I've felt every moment of that," I grumbled. "There will never be a time when I look at you and don't want to be touching you, Vanna."

"Is that why you barely looked at me?"

"I haven't analyzed it yet, but I guarantee if I *had* looked at you, I would have had you naked so fast that you wouldn't have even seen it coming. I guess that's why I didn't. At the time I didn't want to cave in. I wanted to do the right thing," I said openly. "Can I kiss you now?"

"Wait," she insisted as she slowly opened the box.

I nearly groaned out loud, but I was also impatient to see how she liked the ring.

"Oh, dear God," she whispered as the velvet box popped open.

I wasn't exactly sure if that exclamation was good or bad, so I waited.

"It's enormous," she gasped as she gingerly touched the large diamond center stone.

Any other time, I'd welcome that comment, but I still wasn't certain that she was happy with *the ring*.

The center stone and surrounding diamonds set in platinum amounted to a fairly high carat count, but not so big it made her a target from a mile away. Besides, big and gaudy just wasn't Vanna's style, so I'd settled for...quality.

"The workmanship is incredible, Chase," she said, her tone reverent.

"It's custom. I know a guy who does really nice work," I told her.

She looked at me with tears in her eyes as she replied, "Of course you do. I love it, especially the little turquoise accents. It's perfect."

I finally relaxed as I saw the joy that had seeped into her beautiful eyes.

She handed me the box as she asked, "Are you going to put it on my finger?"

I snatched the box before she could change her mind.

Hell, yes, I was putting it on her finger.

Right. Fucking. Now.

Chapter 28

Savannah

"You're not mad at me anymore?" Chase asked as he slipped the stunning ring on my finger.

I shook my head as my heart skittered inside my chest. "Not now that I know you were reacting out of fear. I didn't like it, but I understand. Please remember that I love you the same way, Chase. I never want to see you hurting, either. *But...*if you *ever* do that again for any reason, I swear I'll take your sister's advice and smack you upside the head until you're sensible again."

He probably didn't know I was serious, because all he did was shoot me a shit-eating grin.

He kissed the ring on my finger when he was done putting it on. "Then say you'll marry me. I wholeheartedly agree with you smacking me if I ever act like that again."

I'd obviously said *yes* by asking him to put it on, but I knew he wanted to hear it. "Yes," I said in a breathy, delirious tone. "I love you so much." I wrapped my arms around his neck. "Kiss me."

He moved forward and put his arms around my waist. "I can't resist that invitation, but I really do stink, Vanna. I need a shower."

I inhaled his musky male scent as he lowered his head.

Yes, he was all sweaty, but it was actually kind of sexy.

He kissed me slowly, his emotions present with every touch of his lips.

I felt adored.

I felt wanted.

And I definitely felt…loved.

I was breathless by the time he lifted his head.

"I plan on making you pay for making me wait for so long to hear that you love me," he teased in a sexy baritone against my ear.

I shivered in anticipation. "I can hardly wait."

He pulled back with what seemed like severe reluctance. "I have to shower first. Come with me?" he asked as he held out his hand, his low baritone vibrating with emotion.

He wasn't just asking me to shower with him.

His question meant so much more, and I knew it.

Chase Durand was asking me to stay with him forever, and I didn't hesitate to accept all that he wanted as I took his hand.

I knew he'd suffered as much as I had—maybe even more—over the last two weeks.

Next time, if there was one, I wouldn't hesitate to get in his face because I knew that he loved me.

"Need somebody to wash your back?" I offered teasingly.

"Only if that someone is you," he grunted.

I smiled and followed him upstairs to the master bathroom.

When we were both naked and ready to get into the shower, I looked hesitantly at the gorgeous ring on my finger as I wondered aloud, "Maybe I should take it off."

It was the most beautiful piece of jewelry I'd ever owned, and last thing I wanted was to mess it up. I knew it was going to become the most precious item I owned, not because of the monetary value, but due to the love that was put into the ring.

"Don't," Chase urged, pulling me into the shower. "It was made to last a lifetime, Vanna. You don't ever need to take it off unless you need to for some reason. It was made to withstand anything."

"Just like us," I said teasingly as I picked up his bodywash and poured a liberal amount into my hand.

"Just like us," he confirmed in a more serious tone.

I ran my hands over his muscular body as he stood willingly and let me simply touch him. He winced a little as my fingers stroked over his fully erect cock.

"Keep that up and I'll never make it all the way through this shower," he rumbled in a warning voice. "Jesus, Vanna! It's been two weeks. I know that's my fault but try not to torture me. When in the hell are you going to marry me and put me out of my misery?"

I took pity on him as I moved to his six-pack abs with a small smile, tracing each one of those defined muscles as I went.

For now, I was happy just to touch Chase, to have that kind of intimacy back after what had happened.

I loved every inch of his rugged male form.

"I haven't exactly had time to think about that yet," I told him, bemused.

Everything had happened so fast, and he'd only told me that he loved me a few minutes ago.

Did we really have to think about that right now?

"Think about it," he instructed hoarsely. "I want you to be my wife, Vanna. If you want a big wedding, we'll arrange that, but I'd rather not wait any longer than absolutely necessary. Well, unless you need more time to get used to the idea."

I started to quickly clean myself up while he rinsed off and washed his hair, not particularly picky about my shower since I'd already had one earlier. "I'm not going to have second thoughts, Chase," I reassured him. "When I said *yes,* I meant it. All in, remember?"

Like I was going to second-guess my answer?

I'd be marrying Chase Durand, the man I knew was the *only* guy for me.

He wrapped an arm around my waist and drew me to him the moment he finished rinsing his hair. "You're still all in? Even though you know that there will probably always be crazy people who might try to get to me through you?"

I pushed the wet hair back from his face tenderly as I looked at him, the fierce protectiveness in his tone making my heart race.

He'd always be worried about my safety and my well-being, and that fact touched me more than I could express in words. "Yes, I'm still all in. I love you, Chase. The chances of something happening again like the last incident is ridiculously minute. You understand that, right?"

"Unlikely or not, just the thought of ever seeing you in that position again guts me, Vanna," he rasped as he pushed me back against the wall of the shower enclosure.

"It won't," I said in a soothing tone as I ran my fingers along his stubbled jawline. "But I'm willing to take my chances if that means I'm with you."

I knew his fears were very real to him after what had happened, but almost anything in life was a risk. Marrying him certainly didn't feel daunting to me.

"I'll do everything I can to keep you away from the less pleasant aspects of my business," he promised.

"I know you will," I said softly as our eyes locked.

My breath caught as I saw the bold possessiveness in his gaze.

"Then marry me soon," he insisted.

"How soon?" I asked as my heart tripped.

"Next month?" he said hopefully.

I let out a startled laugh. "If we're going to have a wedding at all, I need longer than that."

I didn't need a huge, pretentious affair, but it was San Diego, and we were quickly approaching the tourist season.

He threaded a hand into my wet hair as he asked, "How much longer?"

I shook my head. "I don't know. I've never planned a wedding before, but I'd think even finding and reserving a venue might take a while. Unless you want to run away to Vegas."

I was perfectly okay with that idea. Torie's wedding had been beautiful.

He shot me a cheeky grin as he replied, "Not necessary. I know plenty of people."

I rolled my eyes playfully. "I'm sure you do."

"Do you doubt my ability to give you whatever fairytale wedding you want within a short amount of time, woman?" he asked in a lighthearted voice. "Tell me what you want and I'll make it happen."

I sighed. I was happy to get my slightly cocky, confident man back. Chase really didn't do anxious and remorseful all that well, and it had killed me to see him that way.

I had no doubt that he *could* make just about anything happen. He was stubborn that way. Chase Durand would always make sure I was spoiled rotten and loving every minute of it.

I wrapped my arms around his neck. "All I really want is you. I'm not exactly picky about exactly how that gets accomplished."

"You've had me for a long time, sweetheart."

He lowered his head and gave me a heart stopping kiss, an embrace that told me just how much he loved and cherished me.

My nipples hardened and heat engulfed my body as Chase did a thorough exploration of my mouth with his tongue.

I was straining for breath by the time he released my lips. "I need *you*, Chase," I told him honestly. "I think we can wait and discuss the wedding later."

"Later," he agreed succinctly as he slammed his hand against the controls to turn off the water. "I'll probably never understand why you want this scarred up body of mine, but I'm fucking glad you do."

He pulled me gently from the shower and started to towel us both dry.

I'd probably never be able to convince him that he was and always would be the most beautiful man I'd ever seen.

So I'd just have to keep showing him instead.

I squealed with laughter as he picked me up and tossed me in the air to get a more solid hold.

"I could walk," I told him as I gripped the back of his neck. "The bed isn't very far away."

"I'm a very willing transporter right now, baby," he said huskily. "And I'm too close to getting exactly what I want to let you get away."

I let out another happy sigh as he carried me to the bedroom.

My body was clamoring for his, and I wanted to crawl inside him right now and never come out again.

Chase Durand was my everything, and I didn't care if he knew that, because I had no doubt that I was *his* everything, too.

"I think what you want is precisely what I want," I whispered into his ear.

There was only the muted light from the small lamp on the bedside table as he dropped me carefully onto the comforter and came down on top of me.

"Then I'd say it's my lucky day, sweetheart." He twined our fingers together and lowered his head.

Chapter 29

Savannah

It felt so good just to kiss him like this again that I moaned into his embrace.

He devoured my mouth like it had been a lifetime since our lips had met rather than just two weeks.

"I love you, Vanna," Chase said in a graveled voice as he lifted his head and met my eyes. "No matter how much of an idiot I may be in the future, I never want you to doubt the way I feel about you for a single second."

I fell into those beautiful gray eyes as he stared at me.

The sincerity...

The longing...

The naked vulnerability...

It was all there in his gaze.

If I would have forced him to talk to me sooner, I knew I would have seen the very same things.

I never would have questioned his feelings from that moment on, either.

Maybe deep inside, I'd always known, even when he wasn't talking. I'd just been so afraid of losing him that I'd let that insecurity get to me.

I swallowed hard. "I love you, too, Chase."

"Were you really going to leave me?" he asked.

I nodded slowly. "If that's what you wanted."

No matter how much I loved him, I wouldn't want him beside me unless he wanted to be there, too.

"I would have found you," he replied. "I've decided that you're better off with me since there isn't another idiot on the planet who will love you as much as I do. Or one who wants you to be happy more than me."

I beamed up at him as I teased, "There's no idiot I want to be with more than I want to be with you."

"Then I think you're stuck with me for life, sweetheart," he growled as he lowered his head to the tender skin at my neck.

I whimpered and leaned my head back, giving him better access. That was a life sentence I'd blissfully accept.

"Chase," I breathed out, molten heat flooding between my legs. "I need you."

He rolled me on top of him. "Take what you want, Vanna."

I scrambled to get into a sitting position on top of him while I watched the blatant arousal on his face.

He wanted me.

He could have satisfied both of us any way he wanted to, yet he was letting me decide what I wanted this time.

I licked my lips. "I want to lick every inch of this amazing body," I said as I ran my hands down his chest.

"Jesus Christ!" he cursed. "I said take what you want. I didn't say you could kill me off while you were doing it. It's been two weeks, Vanna."

I laughed as I kissed my way down his neck and then ran my tongue over his chest. "You didn't specify," I murmured.

I moved lower, tracing every muscle in his abdomen, relishing the way touching Chase like this made me feel.

I finally wrapped my fingers around his cock.

"Don't, baby!" he said harshly. "I'll be completely screwed."

I moved back up his body and placed the tip of his cock against my heat. "You'd rather be screwed this way?" I asked in a sultry voice.

"Oh, fuck, yeah," he agreed wholeheartedly as he gripped my hips. "Ride me, beautiful."

I slowly lowered myself onto his enormous cock one inch at a time until I'd taken him to the hilt.

I was still for a moment when he was finally buried completely inside me, reveling in the sense of being this connected with Chase.

I craved him, and that urgency eventually made me start to move.

"You feel so fucking good, Vanna," he said in a harsh, aroused voice as he gripped my hips harder.

I knew he was trying not to lead, which was probably difficult for a guy like Chase because he definitely liked to be fully involved in the bedroom.

I lifted my hands to my breasts and pinched my nipples as I gyrated slowly on top of him.

I could feel him watching me, which made my pleasure so acute that I could feel it down to my toes.

My body now on fire, I tossed my head back and released a throaty moan.

I felt possessed.

Ensnared.

Consumed.

Yet so incredibly free that I could barely contain the elation that bubbled up inside me.

"You're the sexiest woman I've ever laid eyes on, Vanna," he said in a voice that told me he was barely retaining his control.

I moved faster, but couldn't get quite what I wanted.

Frustrated, I cried out, "Chase, I need..."

He gripped my hips hard and started surging upward. "I know what you need, gorgeous. Come here."

Chase reached his hand up and pulled my head down.

My whole body started thrumming with a ravenous yearning that was nearly impossible to bear as our mouths crashed together in a hungry embrace.

I gave up all illusions of having control as Chase hammered into me deep and hard.

This was exactly what I'd needed, this fierce possession that satisfied my desire to be connected with Chase.

I panted as I came up for air, riding the sharp need that coursed through my body.

I speared my hands into his hair. "Fuck me harder," I pleaded, lost in our frenzied need for each other.

He complied, and I felt my climax approaching.

"You're mine, Vanna. Say it!" Chase demanded in an out-of-control tone.

"I am yours, Chase, just like you're mine," I answered.

Joy and love for this amazing man inundated my soul until tears were pouring down my face because I was overwhelmed with emotion.

Waves of pleasure rolled over me, and my heart practically beat out of my chest as I reached the top of my release.

"Chase! I love you so much!" I cried out, the happiness of saying those words out loud almost unbearable.

He buried himself inside me with one more powerful thrust as the spasms of my release milked him of his own. "I love you, too, baby," he groaned as he wrapped his arms tightly around me.

My body continued to shake as I buried my face in his neck, feeling completely spent.

Chase stroked a hand down my back, and it landed on my ass in a deliciously possessive manner as I tried to recover my breath.

I relaxed completely, wallowing in my ecstasy as I cuddled into Chase's warm body.

He moved a hand down my hair and along my cheek in a soothing touch. "Hey, sweetheart. Are you crying?" he questioned, obviously puzzled.

"Yes," I confessed. "I've never had that happen before. I guess I was just too happy."

I shivered a little as I started to cool down, but I wasn't chilly enough to move from my comfortable resting spot.

"No such thing as you being too happy," he said in a relieved voice as he swiped a tear from my cheek with his thumb.

He reached to the other side of the bed, pulled the covers down, and then rolled both of us between the sheets.

I sighed as he reached for me again after he'd pulled up the sheet and comforter around our naked bodies.

I burrowed into his side as he put his arm around me and pulled my head onto his shoulder.

"Better?" he asked.

"Yes," I replied, surprised by how quickly he'd reacted to such a small body movement. "I think I'd really like to have a child someday, Chase."

I wasn't quite sure why I'd brought *that* up.

Maybe because we were getting married and it was probably an important subject to discuss.

Honestly, I'd never given a lot of thought to having kids or whether or not I wanted them.

Not until Chase.

Since I was approaching my mid-thirties, it was a decision we probably shouldn't wait forever to decide on.

His entire body froze. "Are you sure that's what you want?" he asked.

I sat up a little so I could see his face.

He didn't exactly look repulsed at the idea of us having a child. His expression was more terrified than unwilling.

I frowned. "What? You don't want kids? It's not something I've really thought about until now. It's not a deal breaker for me if you don't."

Chase was always going to be my priority. I'd actually never had an aching desire to be a mother, so it wouldn't be the end of my world if he was opposed to the idea.

He shook his head. "No, baby. Don't get me wrong. I like kids and I'd love to have a child with you, but you know it's painful, right?"

I snorted. "Maybe I haven't had one, but I'm pretty well aware of the process. I think I could handle it."

"It's not just the pain of having the kid. What about morning sickness and the hormones?" he asked, his expression a little less tense.

I let out an exasperated breath. "It's all part of the final product. A child. Our child."

"It's going to kill me to see you miserable, but I'd do everything possible to make it bearable. I'm also not about to promise that I won't be a concerned pain in your ass throughout the entire pregnancy," he said earnestly. "Otherwise, I'd love nothing more than to have our child."

I smiled because he didn't seem the least bit reluctant to have a baby. He just didn't appear to like some of the uncomfortable symptoms I'd have to endure in the process.

"You'd be an incredible father, Chase Durand. But we don't have to make a solid decision right now. We aren't even married yet," I murmured before I laid a soft kiss on his lips.

"A problem I'd really like to remedy as soon as possible," he reminded me.

Truthfully, I really wanted to be his wife, too, so I didn't mind speeding things up. Especially when I knew how important that was to him. "Give me a little time. I'll check out how soon we can arrange it without going to Vegas. How many people?"

"I know a lot of people, but not many that have to be at my wedding," he considered. "I can whittle the list down to a hundred or so. What about you?"

"Chase!" I exclaimed as I whacked him on the shoulder. "That's not exactly a *small* list. You know I don't have immediate family anymore, but I have a few from out of state I'd love to invite. And a few friends at the news station. My guest list won't be nearly as long."

My husband-to-be was a people person, so the size of his list didn't really surprise me.

"I can easily cut it down a lot more if it will speed things up," he said with an irresistible grin. "And most of that list will be family, close friends, and a few of the guys from Last Hope."

"It boggles my mind a little that you have that many friends," I said with a laugh. "And I'd definitely never want to cut out anyone from Last Hope."

He shook his head. "There's no way I can invite everyone, but I'm close to a few of the teams. Especially Wyatt's old crew. They live in Michigan."

"They all came to volunteer for Last Hope?" I asked curiously.

He nodded. "Many of them—as soon as they got out of the Army. Wyatt might be an asshole sometimes in the civilian world, but every guy who was part of his Delta Force team respected him."

"I'd love to meet them," I said honestly. "And Wyatt is not an asshole to people he knows or cares about."

Granted, he was surly sometimes to other people, but I'd never personally been on the receiving end of his sarcasm.

Chase let out a bark of laughter. "Believe me, he can be a major asshole."

He rolled me over to my back and covered my body with his. "Now that we've settled the fact that the wedding will happen soon, let's talk about this baby business. I don't want you to think I'm disinterested. I was just taken a little off-guard. The more I think about it, the more enthusiastic I am. I've never really thought about having a child, Vanna. Hell, I never imagined I'd fall in love like this. Maybe we don't have to make a firm decision right now, and I'd like some time alone with you before we start a family, but I'm always available to practice the getting you pregnant part in case we do."

A slow grin started to form on his face, and my heart tripped as I looked into his eyes.

"I don't think you really need any practice," I teased. "I think you're already a pro."

"Then maybe I need to keep my skills up," he said hopefully.

My heart completely melted.

What woman wouldn't want to be madly in love with a man like mine?

"I love you," I told him as I wound my arms around his neck.

"I'll love you until I take my last breath, Vanna," he vowed. "Sometimes I have to wonder if all of the debates we've ever had in the past were just bullshit. I always looked forward to seeing you. Maybe I just never believed you could really be mine."

"I had to keep you at a distance," I explained. "It was either that, or I'd be thinking about getting you naked."

His eyes lit up. "So you admit you had sexual fantasies about me?" he asked in a husky baritone that sent ripples of pleasure through my body.

"I'd never deny that," I said playfully.

He lifted a brow. "Would you like to tell me about them?"

God, I loved this man.

I pulled his head down until I could feel his heated breath on my lips. "I think I'd much rather show you," I whispered.

"I'm not about to argue with that," he said in a wicked tone right before he kissed me and made every one of my fantasies a reality.

Chapter 30

Wyatt

It was the middle of the damn night before my waterfront home in Del Mar was finally quiet.

I walked around my patio, breathing a sigh of relief that all of the guests for Chase and Savannah's reception were finally gone.

The two had gotten married in a nearby oceanfront venue earlier in the day.

Unfortunately, those wedding guests had all ended up *here* after the nuptials.

I hadn't been thrilled when Chase had talked me into hosting the reception at my place because I supposedly had exceptional indoor and outdoor space.

Number one…I wasn't exactly a people person.

Number two…I definitely wasn't a wedding person.

And number three…it had completely disrupted my fucking privacy, which was something I valued.

Nevertheless, I was glad Chase had managed to plan and execute this wedding and reception in less than two months after his proposal to Savannah.

Maybe now I'd finally get some peace.

I'd probably *never* understand why anyone actually *wanted* to get married, much less share space with another person for the rest of their lives.

I'd also never get the supposed happiness of falling in love.

At all.

Ever.

It seemed like a huge waste of energy to me.

Not that I didn't want my two siblings to wallow in wedded bliss if that's what it took to make them happy, but that particular way of living wasn't for me.

I hadn't and never would lose my mind over a female.

I was too damn rational to act like an idiot over a woman.

I'd thought that my younger brother was the same way until he'd suddenly decided that a woman he'd known and liked for most of his life was the only woman for him.

Okay, I liked Savannah, too. I supposed if Chase *had* to lose his shit over someone, he couldn't have picked a more exceptional female. Still, I had no idea why it had to happen at all.

What guy wanted to willingly put his balls in a wringer for the rest of his life?

I'd never met anyone who was worth that kind of torture.

Thankfully, Chase had kept the wedding guest list fairly small, but it had still been way more people than what I liked to see in my house all at one time.

I reminded myself that there had been a few positives during the evening as I stepped inside and locked the doors to the exterior.

The food had been good. Really good. None of those ridiculously tiny finger foods. All the sentimental bullshit that had taken place aside, it had been a classy and well-done event.

I'd also gotten to see and hang out with my old Delta Force team without having to make a trip to Michigan to see them.

Lastly, my house looked normal again. The cleanup crew had done a good job at giving me my home back.

My hope was, now that this wedding and reception was over, that Chase would get his head back into Durand Industries. If he did, sacrificing my privacy for a while would all be worth it.

Most of all, I really wanted to see Chase relax again, and not be so damn worried about how everything would work out.

Honestly, it was obvious that Savannah was just as happy as Chase with her wedded state. If being in love was really a thing, the woman loved my brother as much as he loved her.

I had no idea why there had ever been any need for Chase to drive himself nuts over Savannah's happiness when it was staring him right in the face.

I made my way to the kitchen, eager to see if there were any leftovers.

If I was still up at this hour, I might as well enjoy any food that still existed in the fridge since it was the best part of the reception.

I stopped to strip down to my tuxedo shirt and pour myself a drink from the bar.

Unlike my wine connoisseur younger brother, I preferred whiskey if I was going to have a drink, and I wasn't particular about what type as long as it went down smoothly.

I stopped short at the entrance to the kitchen when I realized I wasn't alone in the house.

Evidently, I still had an intruder, a statuesque redhead who was currently eating a plate of food with one shapely hip against the kitchen island.

What in the hell was she doing here?

Obviously, she wasn't a guest.

Her red hair was in a messy ponytail, the confined, fiery locks flowing over her back in fat curls. She also wasn't dressed like a guest. She was wearing a pair of black pants that hugged her curvy ass and hips, and a white and gray shirt that looked a lot like the server attire this evening.

"What in the hell are you doing here?" I growled.

Unfazed, she glanced up for a moment and said, "Getting a meal is in my contract. I fed over fifty guests the most expensive meal

I've ever prepared, and I've been here since late morning yesterday. I'm starving, even if I look like I don't need to eat another bite. I'll be out of your way in a minute."

She went back to consuming her dinner like I'd never shown up to interfere.

Okay, maybe I wasn't accustomed to being ignored, so it rankled. A little.

I was the boss.

When I spoke, everyone listened.

That was the way it generally worked, and I liked it that way.

It kept everything...uncomplicated.

Still, I grudgingly admitted to myself that the woman *did* need to eat if she'd really gone that long without sustenance.

I surveyed her, watching as she ate without a single inhibition, obviously enjoying every morsel.

No playing with her food.

No shyness about eating until she was full.

No bullshit about needing to count every calorie on her plate.

Maybe I was way too accustomed to female models who flipped out over a few extra calories, and damned if it wasn't attractive to watch a woman who could eat without apologies or guilt.

Did I think she didn't look like she needed that food she was eating?

Hell, no. I had no idea why she'd even said that, but I wasn't exactly an expert on the female psyche.

If that fare on her plate helped her maintain that nicely curved body of hers, she should just finish the entire lot. And then help herself to dessert.

Fuck! I probably shouldn't be ogling the wedding staff, but it was more her attitude than her gorgeous ass that had forced my cock to stand at attention.

She was...bold and unrepentant.

Maybe I wasn't used to being disregarded completely, and I was just intrigued by someone who didn't give a flying fuck what I thought.

For whatever reason, she amused me, and very few people did.

I folded my arms across my chest. "Why didn't you eat earlier?" I questioned.

She shot me an icy stare from those big green eyes of hers because I'd once again disturbed her dinner. "I was busy," she informed me coolly. "I was the head chef of a large crew. I don't eat until everyone else does. No offense, but food was a dominant factor at this reception, as I totally think it should be. But that also means I'm running for the entire reception. The prep was also long, and the cleanup was massive."

I moved close enough to see that she was dining on the filet mignon and lobster we'd had for the main dinner earlier.

Smart woman.

I put my drink on the island and headed for the refrigerator.

Evidently, she wasn't leaving before she finished, and for some damn reason, I didn't really want her to go before she was done.

Yeah, I'd send her packing after that, but I'd put up with her until the end of her meal.

"And you are?" I asked gruffly.

"Shelby Remington," she answered. "I needed a gig and my cousins know your brother, the groom. Actually, I think you're probably even better friends with them than Chase. Anyway, my cousins recommended me to Chase, and he took a chance, which will make me forever grateful to him. It will look good on my resumé."

Shelby Remington? Why does that name ring a bell for me?

Certainly, if I'd seen this woman before, I would have remembered her.

"How did you know who I am?" I questioned suspiciously.

"I've seen pictures of you with Kaleb," she replied right before she finished the last bite on her plate.

Obviously, she knew who I was, but she wasn't the least bit daunted by the fact that I was a Durand.

I paused in my pursuit of cutting a chunk of cake and putting it on a nearby paper plate. "Remington? Like in Kaleb Remington of KTD Remington?"

I automatically cut her a piece and grabbed another paper plate from the stack on the island. I dropped the second piece on a plate for her and pushed it toward her before I dug into my own.

She nodded as she chewed and swallowed. "Kaleb, Tanner, and Devon Remington are my cousins. We've been close since we were kids."

I nearly choked on my first forkful of cake.

Kaleb Remington and his two brothers were now self-made billionaires who lived in Montana. I'd known Kaleb since college. We kept in touch, and met up as often as we could. He was one of less than a handful of people I trusted.

That sort of explained why she didn't blink an eye when speaking to a guy with a boatload of money and power. She had three cousins who were in the same positions.

I suddenly remembered exactly why I'd recognized her name. Kaleb had tried to set me up on a blind date with Shelby about a year ago, when she'd relocated from Montana to San Diego.

I'd nixed the idea in a hurry.

I was way too big of an asshole to go out with a woman who was Kaleb's beloved cousin. He'd mentioned how sweet she was way too many times for me. Sweet and salty didn't always mix well, and I wasn't looking for a long-term relationship.

I watched as Shelby put her plate and utensils in the dishwasher.

She lifted an eyebrow when she turned to face me. "You do remember when Kaleb tried to set us up?" she asked in a frosty tone.

I nodded as I chewed my cake, my eyes never leaving her glacial expression.

Jesus! I almost felt guilty, even though I'd decided not to meet up with her for *her own good.*

"Just so you know," she shared. "I wasn't all that excited about going on that date with you, either. Did you see my picture and decide that tall, chubby, redheaded women weren't your thing?" She instantly held up a hand. "No, don't answer that. It doesn't matter. I don't care for men who are superficial assholes and stuck on themselves anyway. I'll never understand why Kaleb wanted me to meet a guy who lives in the world of luxury brands and high fashion. I'm not exactly your type."

I couldn't say a word as I watched her pick up my glass of whiskey, toss it back without flinching, and then sit the crystal tumbler carefully back onto the island. She picked up the cake I'd pushed toward her before she said calmly, "Sorry, it's been a really rough day. I'll take my cake to-go. Have a nice evening, Mr. Durand. It was really a beautiful reception and a lovely event."

She headed to the door so fast that I never got a chance to answer.

I tossed my cake onto the counter and followed her, but I saw the headlights of her vehicle leaving as I opened the front door.

What in the fuck had just happened?

I *hadn't* decided she wasn't my type. Hell, if I'd seen a recent picture of her, I probably would have been somewhat tempted to meet her.

And who in the hell would ever think she was too tall or... overweight?

"Son of a bitch!" I cursed as I slammed the door closed and locked it.

It irritated the shit out of me that she'd left with the last word, and without giving me a chance to say a goddamn thing.

That *never* happened to me.

I was tempted to call Kaleb even though it was the middle of the night.

Why hadn't he told me that she'd known about this attempted hookup? I'd assumed that he'd asked *me* first.

I stopped myself before I could call and ask him.

Would it have made a difference if I *had* known? Probably...not.

Her opinion of me was valid, if not quite accurate.

I was definitely better off leaving this situation alone, even though part of me wanted to correct her opinion of me for some odd reason I didn't understand.

Asshole? *Yes.*

Stuck on myself? *No.*

And what had happened to that sweet woman Kaleb had urged me to meet?

I forced myself to forget the whole incident as I walked back into the kitchen but didn't quite succeed as I eyed the empty glass on the island.

Shelby Remington was drop-dead gorgeous and obviously talented, but probably not quite as sweet as her cousin had always thought she was, after all.

Epilogue

Savannah

Paris, France

Two Weeks Later...

I took a sip of my morning coffee, completely enamored with the view from the balcony of Chase's luxurious home in Paris. It was a split-level apartment at the edge of Champ de Mars with nearly every convenience he had in his house in La Jolla.

I smiled as I surveyed the Eiffel Tower, which we'd just toured yesterday. It had been our first day here in Paris, and we still had over a week in France before we were going to return to San Diego.

We wouldn't hit everything that he wanted to show me in the country he referred to as his second home, but he'd assured me that we'd be back in the not-so-distant future.

Chase and I had been touring Europe for the last two weeks, and it was nothing like my hurried visits to those locations previously. Our accommodations had all been over the top, just like this Paris location. It seemed that my husband owned a ridiculously grand home in almost every major country in Europe.

Not that I was complaining.

After all, I'd gotten to stay in a few of them already, not to mention flying from place to place in his private jet.

The best part of this honeymoon, however, was the man sitting across from me at the small outdoor table.

I still couldn't quite believe that I was Chase Durand's wife.

If someone had told me that I'd be on my honeymoon with Chase Durand a year ago, I would have told them they were crazy.

But here I was, wedded to the guy I'd always wanted but had never in my wildest dreams imagined marrying.

And could the nuptials be anything else but dreamlike with my quality loving groom?

Of course they weren't, even if we'd only had a limited amount of time to make the arrangements.

As promised, Chase had helped with the wedding. For the most part, he'd let me plan most of the details with my preferences so everything was the way I wanted it. But he'd been responsible for the venues and food, which had made my responsibilities lighter.

We'd been married at an amazing location with glorious ocean views in Del Mar, which was followed by a beautiful reception at Wyatt's stunning waterfront home.

Torie had been my maid of honor, and Wyatt had stood up for Chase as his best man.

I'd gotten to know and adore Taylor and Harlow because they'd both insisted on helping with the wedding, a gesture I'd appreciated since both of them had recently married themselves.

I had no idea how Chase had convinced Wyatt to let us use his home for the reception, but I'd always be grateful since it had turned out to be the perfect setting.

My entire wedding day *had* been like a fairy tale, but small enough and intimate enough that I'd have memories of that day that I'd cherish forever.

I sighed as I picked up the chocolate croissant on my plate and took a large bite.

The last few months had been the happiest of my life, and I had no doubt that feeling was going to last a lifetime because I was married to the most amazing guy on the planet.

I savored the taste of the pastry as I chewed, reminding myself that I'd better watch just how many French pastries I consumed since I'd just taken off the last of my stress eating pounds shortly before the wedding.

Axel had slimmed down a little, too, since he'd stopped sympathy eating with me, but we'd taken long walks instead, so he hadn't really missed the extra cookies *all that much.*

"I hope that was a good sigh," Chase said as he poured himself another cup of coffee. "What are you thinking about?"

I nodded as I swallowed. "A very happy sigh. I was just thinking about the last few months. I had no idea it was even possible to be this happy. I've definitely found my *joie de vivre.*"

Chase shot me a wicked grin. "I think I've had mine back since the moment you decided to join me in the shower for the first time."

I smiled because I couldn't help myself. He was so outrageous with his naughty comments sometimes, and I heard a lot of them.

After our disagreement about the way he'd handled that horrible incident in the restaurant parking lot, Chase had relaxed significantly. Not that he wasn't constantly watching out for my safety, but he had regained his sense of humor and playfulness.

"You're insatiable," I said with a laugh.

"I warned you about what happens every time I look at you," he shot back with an even wider grin. "You weren't complaining about that earlier."

Nope. I certainly hadn't. I'd never thought of myself as a woman who loved morning sex. Then again, that was before I'd woken up beside a man like Chase Durand every morning.

For us, pretty much anytime we were together, and in almost *any* room, it seemed like the perfect time to get naked.

I really doubted that would change much after our honeymoon since it had pretty much been the same way since the beginning. My heart skittered as I reminded him, "You're looking at me right now."

He raised a brow like he was trying to figure out whether that was an invitation.

"Oh, no, you don't," I said with an actual giggle as I tossed my napkin at him. "I'm showered and ready to go to the Louvre. No funny stuff."

I'd gotten a shower while Chase had arranged our breakfast, much to my husband's dismay. Since we weren't showering together, he'd gotten ready himself in record time before we'd sat down to eat.

"Since I know how much you're looking forward to the museum, I guess I can be patient," he complained jokingly.

I swallowed hard, almost regretting my insistence as I watched him tear into another croissant.

He was dressed casually in jeans and a short-sleeved polo shirt, a sure sign that he was over being self-conscious about the small amount of scarring people could see when he didn't wear a long-sleeved shirt. *Thank God.*

It probably helped that no one stared. No one looked at those marks in horror and ran away.

He'd finally realized no one even noticed, or if they did, it wasn't a big deal.

My heart squeezed just seeing how at ease he seemed about those scars now, like he really didn't think much about them anymore.

I didn't let mine bother me, either. Chase thought I was beautiful, and he was the only man who would ever matter.

"I love you," I told him softly, unable to stop the words from coming out of my mouth.

There were times when the way I felt about him was overwhelming, and it made me want to cry.

Since I knew he'd much rather hear those words than see a tear on my face, the words just popped out without any real thought.

He swallowed the last of his croissant, rose from his seat and snagged me from the chair. He pulled me into his lap as he sat down again.

Wrapping his arms tightly around my waist, he said huskily, "I love you, too, Vanna."

I wrapped my arms around his neck and rested my cheek against the side of his head. We just sat there like that for a minute, savoring the intimacy, entwined together.

It wasn't the first time we'd done this and I knew it wouldn't be the last.

When words just weren't enough, or when we felt the vulnerability of such raw emotion, we took comfort in just being connected in some way.

It wasn't really sexual.

It was just our way of handling the intense emotions that sometimes flowed between the two of us.

I wondered how I'd never noticed quite how lonely I was before he'd come into my life after my kidnapping.

Even when I'd been with another man in the past, something had still been missing.

Maybe I'd never admitted it.

Maybe I'd never consciously thought about it.

But my heart must have known, even though I'd tried to tell myself that my life was just fine back then.

Being with Chase had given happiness a whole new meaning for me, and showed me firsthand how wonderful life could be when I had the *right* guy beside me.

He understood me and knew what I wanted and needed like no other man ever could or would.

He was my husband.

My partner.

My companion.

My friend.

And my lover.

Everything rolled into one rather spectacular body.

When I finally pulled back a little and looked into his eyes, I could see the way I was feeling mirrored right back at me, and it was beautiful.

"Everything okay?" he asked, his expression thoughtful.

"More than okay," I answered with a small nod. "I'm just wondering how I ever got lucky enough to not feel lonely when I'm in a crowd of people anymore. Even when you're not with me physically, you're still with me, Chase. Everywhere I go."

Keeping one arm tightly around my waist, he lifted my hand and kissed the beautiful wedding ring on my finger. He then entwined our fingers before resting them over his chest.

"You know I feel the same way," he replied, his expression deadly serious as he thumped our conjoined hands against his heart. "You're always right here, Vanna. No matter where I am. I'm the luckiest guy on Earth because you're mine. Don't think for a fucking second that I don't know that. There was never really anyone else for me except you."

I smiled because I felt that rightness, too, and I felt no compulsion to make sense out of that knowledge.

It was just…there.

All I'd really needed to do was open my heart to him. Since I'd done that, Chase Durand had rocked my entire world.

"Kiss me," he demanded hoarsely. "And then I'll introduce you to the Louvre. I think I can keep my horny ass in check long enough to show my woman the masterpieces."

"You've introduced me to so many wonderful things," I told him. "You might eventually get bored if we keep going to places you've been before."

He shook his head. "Never. I could never be bored when we're doing anything together. And we'll find some places to discover together someday. Right now, my main goal is to see you happy."

"I'm very happy as long as we're together, too," I assured him.

I leaned down and kissed him, my heart racing as our lips met.

The Louvre could wait another moment or two.

Chase was and always would be my number one priority.

We had a lifetime of experiences to share in our future, but none of them would ever be more important than what I was doing with the man that I loved *right this very second.*

~*The End*~

Please visit me at:
http://www.authorjsscott.com
http://www.facebook.com/authorjsscott

You can write to me at
jsscott_author@hotmail.com

You can also tweet
@AuthorJSScott

Please sign up for my Newsletter for updates,
new releases and exclusive excerpts.

❦━━━━━━━━━━━━━━━━━❧

Books by J. S. Scott:

Billionaire Obsession Series

The Billionaire's Obsession~Simon
Heart of the Billionaire
The Billionaire's Salvation
The Billionaire's Game
Billionaire Undone~Travis
Billionaire Unmasked~Jason
Billionaire Untamed~Tate
Billionaire Unbound~Chloe
Billionaire Undaunted~Zane
Billionaire Unknown~Blake
Billionaire Unveiled~Marcus
Billionaire Unloved~Jett
Billionaire Unwed~Zeke
Billionaire Unchallenged~Carter
Billionaire Unattainable~Mason

Billionaire Undercover~Hudson
Billionaire Unexpected~Jax
Billionaire Unnoticed~Cooper
Billionaire Unclaimed~Chase

British Billionaires Series

Tell Me You're Mine
Tell Me I'm Yours
Tell Me This Is Forever

Sinclair Series

The Billionaire's Christmas
No Ordinary Billionaire
The Forbidden Billionaire
The Billionaire's Touch
The Billionaire's Voice
The Billionaire Takes All
The Billionaire's Secret
Only A Millionaire

Accidental Billionaires

Ensnared
Entangled
Enamored
Enchanted
Endeared

Walker Brothers Series

Release
Player
Damaged

Just what the Doctor Ordered
Wicked Romance of a Vampire

The Curve Collection: Big Girls and Bad Boys Series
The Curve Collection: The Complete Collection
The Curve Ball
The Beast Loves Curves
Curves by Design

Writing as Lane Parker
Dearest Stalker: Part 1
Dearest Stalker: A Complete Collection
A Christmas Dream
A Valentine's Dream
Lost: A Mountain Man Rescue Romance

A Dark Horse Novel w/ Cali MacKay
Bound
Hacked

Taken By A Trillionaire Series
Virgin for the Trillionaire by Ruth Cardello
Virgin for the Prince by J.S. Scott
Virgin to Conquer by Melody Anne
Prince Bryan: Taken By A Trillionaire

Other Titles
Well Played w/Ruth Cardello

Printed in Great Britain
by Amazon

13930508R00145